J. Douglas White was born in Mississippi, USA and educated at George Washington University. He has worked for US Naval Intelligence in Washington DC, and designed electronic circuitry for California space programmes – including one which put man on the moon. He has restored period houses in Lincolnshire and Kent, and been imprisoned in Mozambique, charged with being an MI6 agent. He is now retired after this uniquely varied career and lives in Andalucia. He published *Siege!* with the Book Guild in 2002 and is co-author of *Scorpion Heart*, a novel set in World War II Gibraltar. He has also written on Mozambique for the *Sunday Telegraph*, and on England for various US newspapers and magazines.

EL CAMELOT

J. Douglas White

The Book Guild Ltd
Sussex, England

First published in Great Britain in 2004 by
The Book Guild Ltd
25 High Street
Lewes, East Sussex
BN7 2LU

Copyright © J. Douglas White 2004

The right of J. Douglas White to be identified as the author of this work has been asserted by him in accordance with the Copyright, Designs and Patents Act 1988.

All rights reserved. No part of this publication may be reproduced, transmitted, or stored in a retrieval system, in any form or by any means, without permission in writing from the publisher, nor be otherwise circulated in any form of binding or cover other than that in which it is published and without a similar condition being imposed on the subsequent purchaser.

All characters in this publication are fictitious and any resemblance to real people, alive or dead, is purely coincidental.

Typesetting in Baskerville by
Keyboard Services, Luton, Bedfordshire

Printed in Great Britain by
Athenaeum Press Ltd, Gateshead

A catalogue record for this book is available from
The British Library

ISBN 1 85776 808 6

AUTHOR'S NOTE

Alciguna, described in this book as a White Village in the Province of Malaga, Spain, does not appear on any map. All characters are fictitious, and bear no intended resemblance to any actual persons, living or elsewhere.

J. Douglas White
Spain, 2004

1

Fernando, my travel agent, sucked in his breath. 'Your company allows you a week to get to Malaga? *Fantastico!* Enough time to rent a car and explore Andalusia's super spectacular scenery on your way there.' From where I sat, his shop window framed a Boston grey with sooty snow, shoppers bundled and hunched like forlorn sheep against the icy wind. 'What's Andalusia weather like in February?' I asked, my knowledge of Spain limited to sunburst travel posters and nineteen-thirties Hemingway novels. 'Glorious sunshine in the mountains,' Fernando assured me airily, a Julie Andrews smile distending his mouth. 'Don't forget, "The rain in Spain –" and so on.' He took up his pen. 'I'll itinerary you through untrammelled country where mountaintops bristle with ancient castles; to isolated crags where Carmen shagged the bandits – *España!*' His Spanish accent fizzed the word like sparkling wine. 'It'll be an unforgettable experience. My guarantee, *amigo.*'

Sultry *señoritas* steam into view, dazzling black eyes invite. Yet ... yet the Black Forest would be a more appropriate retreat for my dark mood. Nothing like a marriage break-up to dampen your wick. Ellen is still my wife, I think, if she's not in Reno trashing our four-year hitch. Not my fault. I remained true blue despite my position in the hyper-charged advertising racket, spending nights on the road, abundant opportunities to avoid sleeping solo in cold hotel beds. Nor is Ellen to blame. Promoting *haute cuisine* for an up-market microwave oven company left her little time to play housewife. We simply declared 'Home' not crucial to either of our careers, 'Love and marriage' rhymed with 'Do we really need this?' The End. Except now I'm trying to minimize the claptrap relevance of that old song, 'Every time I say goodbye, I die a little'.

But wait. Mightn't a change of focus soften the blow and tune up my sluggish existence? New York to Madrid by air, drive from Seville to Malaga sounds loaded with rugged adventure. Follow smugglers' trails! Discover lost villages! Feast on midnight sherry and 'bull's blood' wine! Hey, why not? 'You're on,' I enthused, naively misreading Fernando's artful grin of barefaced audacity as he congratulated my decision to drive through Andalusia in February.

The flight to Europe was delayed four leaden hours by Atlantic snowstorms, adding urgency to my arrival in sunny Spain. *Olé!* – my rented Ford sloshed from Seville airport into a thundering cloudburst. Fernando, no doubt still laughing at my simple gullibility, would sober *pronto* if he heard the vengeance I swore against him. His promised 'scenery' consisted of highway seascapes and rainbows of oncoming headlights. Rain blotted out Seville, I skipped mist-obscured Jerez, hoping to find clear skies at Cadiz and the Mediterranean. No such luck. My windshield wipers didn't miss a flap as I tunnelled south under ever-blacker clouds.

On the N340 I glimpsed a small sign pointing, grudgingly it seemed, to Gibraltar. Daylight fading, my watch reading five o'clock, the name suggested insurance, suggesting security. I turned right. A dim seaside street led to the Spain–Gibraltar frontier, a phalanx of low customs buildings with high wire fences connecting guard shacks for controlling traffic across the border. I approached its single gate. A scowling border guard, bearded like a

Mexican revolutionary, hand-signalled from his sentry box for me to halt. He eyed my rented car, focused my face like a 'REWARD' poster and demanded, *'Pasaporte, Señor!'* He studied my pristine document as if it were contaminated, stamped it 'LA LINEA' with a thud and returned it with a sour grunt of disapproval.

I wonder: is his hostility a warning? Is Gibraltar struck by plague or civil disorder? Should I about-face and flee into Spain? Overriding dire apprehension, I inched forward. Only feet through the gate, a blue uniformed British guard sprang from his sentry box, snapped a salute and greeted, 'Welcome to Gibraltar, cradle of history!' Reassured, I asked about hotels, a place with good food and a good bar. He glanced at my passport, handed me a guidebook, and scurried for dry cover. Within minutes I found myself at the Cork Hotel.

The colonial-style edifice wedged high on a west-facing cliff would offer, in kinder weather, a panoramic view of the harbour far below. I abandoned my car to the doorman and dashed into the lobby. Bright décor, a white marble staircase and tropical greenery gleamed in welcome contrast to the storm outside. The desk clerk clicked his tongue at my damp clothing, his Spanish accent stronger than Fernando's. 'Welcome to The Rock. Good you come in this storm, otherwise you'd be delayed forever at the border.' Tired and gloomy, I handed him my passport, signed the register and asked if Spanish border guards were always this surly, or had the USA recently bombed Madrid?

The clerk's explosive response jolted my weariness. 'The Spanish are *hijos de putas!*' He waved a fist towards the border. 'We British have owned Gibraltar for three hundred years, yet the greedy Spanish still claim us. Across the border, leave your car on the street at night – *hey!* It will be stripped clean within seconds. No. We want no Spanish rule here, its crime and corruption.'

I backed away from the desk, muttering, 'Please send my bags to my room, I'll have a drink first,' and beelined for the bar. Across the broad reception hall of empty chairs, a cheery cocktail lounge beckoned, its barman engaged in the ritual of polishing glasses when there are no customers. He shook his head at my rumpled appearance. 'Evening, sir. Pity, arriving during our annual blow. But good whisky weather, if you ask me, sir. A little sunshine to brighten old February?' I answered, 'A good Spanish brandy sounds more warming.' He halted, eyeing me sharply. 'No Spanish brandy here, sir. Too raw. It's said they cut it with mule pee. We serve only legitimate French brands.' I have drunk Carlos III and found it smooth as almost anything French, but conceded, 'Right, then. Single malt.' Ready to chat, he served Glenfiddich with a small bowl of green olives. 'Here to see our famous Gibraltar apes?' I savoured a second swallow of the whisky's tart warmth before answering, 'No sightseeing in Gibraltar, I'm afraid. Off to Spain tomorrow. On business.'

'Spain!' he coughed, placed a bowl of cashew nuts before me. 'A suggestion, sir. If I were you, I'd leave early, before the queue starts. Wait for daylight, it could take hours to cross the border. The Spanish are having one of their periodic snits and cause endless delays by over-inspecting every car. They intimidate Gibraltar's visitors since we voted in a referendum ninety-eight per cent to remain British. So watch your step, sir, you'll find the Spanish a bunch of thieves.' He patted his very Latin moustache. 'Every one of them.'

Whoa! I thought. Thieves? Crime and corruption? Are there still *bandidos* in the mountains as Hemingway described? Fernando had dismissed these worries with a wave of the hand, which I now accepted as a guarantee that there would be outlaws waiting out there, licking their chops for this gringo. 'Another scotch whisky,' I called, holding back tomorrow.

Next morning, I heeded the bartender's advice and left the hotel long before daybreak. He proved right, for I got no hassle from the drowsy border guards. Back in Spain, I headed into the mountains as per Fernando's map guide. Roads awash with continuing downpour advanced my pessimism, black as the sinister clouds swirling above me.

Snaking through gale-swept mountains in pre-dawn darkness, eternity lurking behind every blind curve, my headlight beams stabbed a murky void. I stamped the brakes, spun out of control. A concrete barrier snagged my car on the brink of a gushing chasm. Metal scraped metal when I reversed a safe distance, I hoped, from the asphalt lip where a bridge had recently stood. The motor conked out. I yanked the handbrake, switched on the hazard flasher, collapsed over the steering wheel. Fernando's cactus-eating grin congealed in nasty shades of deceit before my eyes. Sue him! No, I'll castrate the bastard for selling me this preposterous joy ride.

Excited cries surrounding my car snapped me awake. *Bandidos!* I knew at once, and re-checked the door locks. The rain had eased off, the sky silvered with sunrise, allowing me to assess my surroundings. My car stood stranded on a precipitous hillside road; to my left, a jagged mountain chain bounded a valley of low trees and brushwood; to my right, a village of white buildings ranged up and over a hilltop. All pleasant enough, but the scene before me raised goose bumps. The stone bridge lying collapsed in the watery depths of the gorge was even more terrifying by daylight. More *bandidos* arrived. Three vehicles had pulled behind me, blocking my retreat. I was trapped.

On the road, natives chattered in a great state of

excitement. Soon they would wave amber bars of hashish for sale, a common occurrence during my vacation in Spain's offspring, Mexico. Or worse. I twisted to check the travellers cheques in my pocket, fondled my wristwatch, a gift from Ellen. An arbitrary move, for what value are worldly goods when your throat is about to be cut? And who would care? Certainly not Ellen.

Fingers drummed my window. Here we go, I thought, and looked out to gauge my assailant. A man with sharp blue eyes peered in; neat moustache, close clipped greying hair, average build, tweed jacket. He shouted, 'I say, are you British?' Astounding! A BBC accent in these wild hills?

His open smile emboldened me to lower my window, part way. 'No, American. Last night I damn near –'

'Yes, it was a near thing.' The man's sad gaze lingered on the flooded gulch. 'So the old bridge finally gave way,' he said glumly, then brightened and turned back to me. 'Are you here on a visit, or just passing through?'

'I had intended to pass through, until your bridge went missing.' I remained on guard, divulging little except my name. 'Robert Brooks.'

He offered his hand through the half-open window and rattled off the town's statistics as if he were selling it. 'I'm Henry Perry-Smith. You're now in Alciguna, Malaga, six-hundred and thirty metres above sea level, home to around three thousand souls, including some fifty expatriates, "expats" we call ourselves. The concrete kerb you connected with last night is a popular pavement café in summer. No harm to it, although I reckon a day or two to repair its revenge on your car. We'll ring Ronda for a towing truck. Alciguna's got a small hotel, more bars than patrons, but no repair garage. Besides, you might like it here. It's a place that – well, it takes over peoples' lives. Who knows, might even charm yours.'

Happy to banish Hemingway's macho Spain crawling with *bandidos*, I climbed from my car and stretched limbs to revive circulation. Townspeople were massed three deep on both sides of the abyss, delighted children squealed, pointing at water cascading over broken stone blocks from the stricken bridge and rivulets of mud spewing down the hillside. Henry turned sober. 'While their parents wonder how the bridge loss will affect their livelihoods, I imagine.' A man of quicksilver moods, he recovered his smile, took my arm, looked up at clouds breaking into bright patches and observed, 'Looks like a nice day, as you Americans say. Come. I'll take you to our Bar Suerte for something bracing after your road experience. No need to lock your car, there's no crime in Alciguna.' He halted, serious again. 'That is, no crime that concerns you, anyway.'

And what crime might that be, *bandidos*? I wondered. Climbing after him up a stony alleyway that rambled between time-roughened walls of whitewashed houses, we emerged on a triangular 'square' intersected by five narrow cobbled streets and encircled by buildings tinted a cool pink by the glow of sunrise. I stopped dead, mesmerized. Ahead, a stone tower topped by an arch supporting a single bell jutted skyward. Its surrounding ruins were the backdrop for the neat village nestled at its base, terracotta rooftops glistening within an arabesque of trees and granite boulders. Henry grinned, anticipating my question. 'The castle ruins? Originally a Moorish fortress. Tenth century.'

Pulling my eyes from the dawn-silhouetted tower to face south, another variegated diorama, painted in early spring hues, took my breath. A softly defined valley swept down before the village, a stream meandered between rolling hills, alternating dark forests with almond orchards in white blossom, radiant from the rain. At the distant end of this corrugated patchwork, a chocolate-drop Gibraltar stood sentinel over the Mediterranean. Henry pointed beyond it. 'That is Djebel Musa, in the Rif Mountains of Morocco. It and Gibraltar form the fabled Pillars of Hercules. As the crow flies, Gibraltar is less than thirty miles from here. The convoluted route you took this morning is twice that.'

'How well I know.' I rubbed my neck, continued to view the square. White plaster buildings of irregular sizes and shapes leaned at odd angles, lopsided windows spaced without symmetry, red and pink geraniums on wrought iron balconies all added vivid disarray. Unbidden, a primal surge activated my American genes. I couldn't control it. 'This view!' I blurted. 'It's worth a million dollars, you know that?' Allowing recovery from my lyric outburst, Henry urged, 'Let's get to Bar Suerte and grab a kerbside seat. With the bridge gone, all traffic will be diverted onto this ancient main street. Our villagers thrive on chaos, and I predict that today they'll have a glorious feast. Confusion galore.'

We found an empty table on the terrace before the bar's front door and joined the prosperous looking *hombres* growing noisy, animated by mounting tension. Henry bought two brandies. I sipped mine warily, happily concluding that, although not Courvoisier, neither was it cut with mule pee as the Gibraltar bartender had warned. Raising his glass, Henry pronounced, 'To 103, the workingman's breakfast.' He took a swallow, wiped his mouth, and blotted his eyes.

I ventured, 'I know that personal questions are taboo with the English, Henry, but do you work here? Do you live here full time?'

He shrugged. 'I'm retired, dear boy. Sold my plastics factory in Kent five years ago, my wife and I have lived here ever since. We've enjoyed every moment –'

A deep chested man in khaki work clothes shambled up, plonked down a tumbler of brandy on our table and addressed me in what I took to be formal Spanish. Flummoxed, I looked to Henry, who translated. 'May I present *Señor* Medrano. He wishes to thank you for saving his life this morning. Had it not been for your flashing warning lights, his car would have plunged into the ravine with his wife and six children.' Before I could respond, two men of man-mountain girth thrust more glasses of 103 at me and demanded to shake my hand. Henry overrode their raucous babble, 'They also wish to thank you, for your hazard light warning prevented certain death for both of them.' Eyes at every table on the pavement targeted me. Broad smiles beamed a galaxy of gold teeth. Swaying glasses soared to a chorus of '*Salud!*' Unsure how to respond, I raised my glass and smiled back, which satisfied them, but made me feel like a phoney.

Henry groaned. 'I'm dashed. I lived here for years before anyone bought me a drink, now you've accomplished it in one morning. If you lived here, you would be invited to weddings, first communion celebrations, and I'll wager that "Roberto" will now be the most popular name for boys. When a foreigner makes a favourable impression in Alciguna, he is doubly welcome.'

I remembered the business meeting that I had to attend in Malaga in four days time. Damn!

The air of expectancy intensified. Bar patrons cocked their heads towards the street, some climbed onto chairs for a better view. Farther along, stout housewives in flowered frocks moved chores into doorways, some sitting with pans in their laps, peeling apples or potatoes, keeping a watchful eye on the thoroughfare. Mothers held children back, dogs were roused and chased into alleyways. 'Since the bypass bridge was built during World War Two,' Henry explained, 'this narrow, cobbled street has borne no heavy traffic. The Romans constructed it for ox carts and chariots. Now we'll see how well they did their job, some twenty centuries on. Any moment, now.'

Taking my cue from Henry, I sat back, sipped my 103, and waited. The Alciguna bridge play was about to begin.

2

Bar Suerte occupied one corner of Alciguna's main square, shared by a bank, municipal market, barbershop and a general store called 'Fortnum and Mason' by foreigners. Heads poked out of every window on the square, alert for sounds from the bridge area. Henry told me that the main street, the Roman road transecting the square, until recent times served as a smugglers' route from Gibraltar to Ronda and beyond. As I was learning to expect, he threw in a note of intrigue. 'Germans built the bridge to divert traffic around the town. Hitler's idea.'

'Hitler!' I sputtered. Another of the day's fantastical revelations. 'Here?' Henry, listening for sounds of approaching traffic, shook his head. 'In 1943, Hitler launched "Operation Felix", a scheme to install big guns on the Spanish coast to blast Gibraltar to rubble. That would eliminate the only Allied airfield on continental Europe and open the Mediterranean for Axis ships to supply his German army in Africa. But Alciguna, this tiny mountain village, halted the mighty Wehrmacht in its tracks.'

Henry paused and swivelled to study three policemen striding onto the square. Impressively corpulent in dark blue trousers and short-sleeved white shirts boasting epaulettes and insignia, each wore a grommeted visor cap, firmly set. Handcuffs and a two-foot long wooden truncheon dangled from their wide leather belts, matched on the opposite hip by a holstered revolver. The policemen halted in the square, and then two of them marched with brisk purpose in opposite directions on the main street. The third man, of indomitable weight and command, remained at the intersection before us. Henry motioned with his head. 'That's Zorro, our police chief. He also sells health insurance, which we find, uh, convenient to buy.'

'But the Germans?' I insisted. 'Here in Alciguna?'

'Indeed. German engineers determined this to be the shortest route for transporting cannon southwards from France across Spain, and met no serious obstacles until they reached Alciguna, tantalizingly near their destination. Here, as you can see, the road reduces to one lane, too narrow for big guns. These buildings, with four-foot thick walls dating back to the time of Caesar, would have to be dynamited. But the Spanish government, fearing insurrection by the villagers, would not allow it.'

'End of story?'

After a swig of 103, Henry wagged his finger and wheezed, 'Nazi persistence, dear boy. They spanned the ravine on the town's north perimeter with the – late – stone-arched bridge, thus ingeniously bypassing this bottleneck.'

I feared for The Rock. 'Did the Germans reach Gibraltar with their big guns?'

A growing roar of motors distracted Henry, but he went on. 'By the time the bridge construction was completed, reverses in Russia forced Hitler to abandon plans to annihilate Gibraltar. Operation Felix became just another of his dream follies.'

I laughed. 'Must be one of the few times that anyone benefited from Hitler's attention.'

Henry agreed. 'Oh yes, the villagers loved their new bridge, especially smugglers, who could now avoid traps set within the town by the *Guardia Civil*. Unfortunately, the bridge foundations received scant attention for half a century. Everyone thought them as indestructible as the pyramids – until last night.'

'*Viva!*' '*Viva!*' Our fellow drinkers stood, waving their glasses. From the west, a policeman stalked into view, followed by a column of cars and trucks on the one-lane street. In step, the other policeman emerged, leading a like column from the east. The two men marched steadfastly onward, until they clashed belly to belly in the square's centre. Each stood bull firm, brandishing threats and bellowing rights of way for the vehicles following him. Henry chuckled. 'Now watch this. Zorro is joining Juan Luis and José María, his assistants. His word is law, but how will he solve their impasse?'

Zorro's solution proved simple. He ordered José María's westbound column to wait. Then, despite Juan Luis' shrill objections, those vehicles in his eastbound column that could not squeeze into lateral alleys were ordered to reverse to the main road. Fierce curses joined howls of protest as the drivers reluctantly complied. Fenders scraped the rough plaster walls of the narrow, curving street, gears ground, motors sizzled, yet, eventually, the mass back-up was achieved.

Zorro, puffed with success, directed ten cars in the westbound column to proceed. After they passed through town, he ordered ten cars from the west to move forward, which they did, in orderly succession. That is, until a youth in a Seat elected to change direction and head east with the flowing traffic. He became wedged between the walls, blocking the street. All movement ground to a standstill. '*Coño!*' '*Jode!*' The cacophony of profanity, Klaxons, whistles and tape decks would out-decibel all the headbanger rock music in greater Boston. Enraged, Zorro darted among the stalled cars towards the youth. He waved his truncheon and yelled, 'No! No! *Imbécil!* Straight ahead!' The driver, determined to complete his manoeuvre, countered with an explicit two-finger salute.

Henry caught his breath. 'Oh, oh. That unfortunate lad is obviously a stranger. Zorro's reputation for bashing Saturday-night disco rowdies is legendary.'

Zorro charged the Seat like an obsessed bull until suddenly, inexplicably, his determination evaporated. He halted, consulted his wristwatch, dropped his arms and sauntered with cool indifference from the field of battle. Juan Luis and José María met on the square, checked their watches and also departed. Bar patrons emptied their glasses and drifted away, leaving Henry and me on the terrace surrounded by empty tables and the angry noise of car horns. Henry grinned, answering my raised eyebrows. '*La hora de desayuno*. It is the breakfast hour, an ironclad tradition in Alciguna. At ten o'clock sharp every citizen drops whatever he is doing and has coffee, and bread spread with a paté much like lard flavoured with bits of fried pork. If not at home, the wife delivers it to her husband's workplace, field or building site. At this hour, I doubt if our *Guardia Civil*, our state police, would deal with rape or murder, although no such crimes have ever put this to a test.'

That statement again. 'No crime?' I asked. 'The mind boggles.'

Henry turned enigmatic. 'Well, hardly any. Into every Eden slithers the serpent. But come. Let's see the bridge. The flood must have receded by now.'

Serpent? I can't figure Henry. Do his asides contain substance, or are they merely attempts to sound profound? Well, what the hell. Doesn't affect me. I'm only passing through.

Having viewed the bridge disaster, we returned to Bar Suerte to find its clientele reoccupying kerbside tables, drinks in hand, eager for more live entertainment. The *Jefe*, Zorro, arrived on the square duly weighted with constabulary gravity: close shaved, shoes and belt polished to brilliance, formal blue uniform sharply pressed. He smiled lofty approval at seeing the errant Seat pushed aside, and began fluttering his truncheon in rhythm with the self-regulated traffic streaming across the intersection, ten vehicles from one direction, ten from the other. Blithely waving a six-wheeled fuel truck onto the square, his arms suddenly froze in mid-gesture. His face blanched. Open-mouthed with dread, he watched the large tanker marked INFLAMMABLE! rumble towards overhead power cables stretched unavoidably across its path.

'*Alto! Alto!*' The driver was deaf to commands. '*Alto! Alto!*' Zorro's frantic warning dance went unheeded. The tank truck shuddered ahead.

Defeated, Zoro clapped his hands over his ears and stared heavenward. We on the pavement cowered in our chairs. Disaster was imminent.

As if touched by heaven's hand, the truck's nose dropped, clearing the cables by inches. A geyser shot up higher than the surrounding rooftops. Henry leapt to his feet.

'The wheels have broken through a water main. Probably one built during Roman times.' Spectators, screeching with laughter, scurried for cover. Zoro, braving the deluge, ordered the tanker to reverse out of town. This inch-by-inch operation, involving the truck and nine cars behind it, would take hours. Enough time for lunch. And a *siesta*.

Henry and I ordered *tapas* and *tinto*. At four o'clock Zorro returned refreshed, immaculate, aloof as a matador. He took up his conductor's position, nodded approval that a village plumber had capped the water main and the town's supply no longer cascaded down the street. Finding the automotive flow resumed, Zorro swayed and waved his truncheon with its progress, displaying amazing grace for a man of his volume – until something clanged in his head. His eyes widened in panic. The normal ten

cars headed east passed through at a clipped speed – followed by an eleventh. Henry gasped.
'José María must have miscounted. This extra eastbound car will meet head-on the ten cars heading west!' Zorro brandished his truncheon, glared right then left at unsuspecting cars racing towards their collective doom. '*Peligro! Peligro!*' he commanded. Seeing all danger warnings ignored, he dived into a recessed doorway. Henry and I joined the bar patrons scrambling indoors.
The inevitable head-on collision preceded nine smaller crashes in quick succession. A moment of startled silence, then eleven shaken drivers emerged from their crumpled vehicles and stumbled towards Bar Suerte. The only real causality of the pile-up involved the bar itself. Without warning or hint of catastrophe, it suddenly ran out of 103.
Every man on the terrace relaxed into his seat, bemoaning empty glasses, yet enjoying the camaraderie of having survived an earthquake together. I felt moved by the happy scene shifting about me, immensely grateful to be absorbed in it.
'Does such a thing as a fax machine exist in this village?' I asked Henry, feeling compelled to send Fernando, my travel agent, an apology. It would be simple: 'Forget castration. I love you.'
And, in case Ellen still harbours any concern for my well being, I'll fax my sentiments to her as well: 'Paradise! Found!'

3

Don't even think about it, I warned myself repeatedly, on the two-hour drive to Malaga four days later in my repaired rental car. A place to put down roots? Alciguna? Impossible. Alciguna is fantasy. Does it really exist?

During my brief visit there I had found various nationalities living among the Spanish, free of any trace of nationalistic friction. I heard of a wealthy Scottish lady who lived in a cave, a defected Hungarian who lived in a mansion. Artists, ex-military and retired bankers were thick on the ground. A Dutch family, unable to afford electricity, dined elegantly by candlelight. Irish and English were good neighbours, even the French blended in. I had to laugh. *And not a bandido in sight!*

What would be the livelihood of a company man like myself in Alciguna? Doing odd jobs like other foreigners? Raising organic vegetables, or angora goats for weaving sweaters? Forget it. I'm lumbered with the philosophy that landlords and grocery bills must be paid. Like that old proverb, I'm activated only when a salary cheque is plugged into my system.

Driving east on the N340, I found the new buildings along Costa del Sol tacky and characterless, nothing approaching the charm of Alciguna's La Española, the cold-water hotel where I remained showerless for four days. An absence of cobbled streets and jumbled architecture left me resentful of order and straight lines. I entered my firm's Malaga office trying to remember what I had been sent to do.

The brisk activity in this branch of our Boston company amazed me. No *mañana* syndrome here, far from it. The manager, my old friend Jim McConnell, welcomed me Latin style, kisses on both cheeks, high pressure that alarmed me. 'Hey, *amigo!* Am I glad to see your ugly Yankee face. We're swamped. The Spanish have discovered kitsch, suddenly every can and box on the shelf must be updated. Greater reach. More grab. Miro slashes of basic colours. The chief honchos here called us in because we Americans have perfected hype, the new *sine qua non* of Spanish industry expanding like wildfire throughout the EEC.' Jim led me into the drafting room, where harried graphic artists were hunched over two drawing boards, the third one free. 'Grab an apron.' He patted me on the back, a besieged fortress welcoming the US Cavalry. I reeled from his reach. 'No way, José. I came to Spain to tackle an administrative problem. I advanced from the drawing-board scene some time ago, remember?' Jim smiled, eyes averted. 'I know that, *amigo*. I also remember your design smarts. Forgive me, but when I heard you were headed this way, I got on the horn to Boston headquarters. They offer your present salary, plus bonuses, if you agree to some board work here. Think about it. But in the next thirty seconds. OK, *amigo*?'

Glancing at papers stacked on tables, drawings thumbtacked askew on walls, floors littered with discarded sketches, I backed towards the door. 'In this mess? Even charitably I'd call it a pig pen.'

Jim dismissed the scene with a sweep of his hand. 'Baby, I don't care where you work, so long as your finished work reaches me by the end of the week. You can...'

'I heard you,' I said, disbelieving that I had. 'First, the administration problem I was sent to tackle. After that, I'll need all the artist gear you'll trust me with, plus a box to carry it in.' I shuffled through a job file, pulled out an order for new logos for a complete line of petroleum products, including service station signs. 'I'll return this oil company project in a week's time. Watch me create a riot at the gas pumps.'

Jim laughed. 'Hey, you caved in quicker than I dared hope. The Spanish scenery must have gotten to you on your drive through Andalusia. Let me guess. Blonde? Brunette? Love at first sight?'

My enthusiasm easily trumped his supercilious smirk. 'Have you seen those hamlets they call 'White Villages' that cling to Andalusia's mountainsides like lichen? There's a special one within commuting distance of Malaga where I can rent workspace. Its name is Alciguna.'

4

The diamond bright sunrise failed to clear my head, which remained unable to comprehend that since yesterday, I had been working in Spain. This was now my home.

Last night I returned to Alciguna and advised Henry of my revised future, and this morning he set about acquainting me with places deemed necessary for survival. He escorted me from my hotel through an archway connecting white buildings, down steps to a spacious, tiled patio. On one side, a lemon tree sagged with fruit, free for the taking. On the other, a sign said that the basement bar was open on Saturday nights for *flamenco* and *cante jondo*. Straight ahead, across the patio stood the Alciguna post office, doors open wide.

Henry pointed to it. 'The postman, Romero, is the no-nonsense father of eight. When he is ill, his children deliver the mail. But letters smeared with little fingerprints of chocolate or jam are not the reason foreigners prefer a post office box. The post is secondary. We come here to swap information. Oh, you'll find this site delightfully indispensable. It's a must for keeping tabs on anything of note: in short, every available rumour and scrap of gossip.'

As we talked, several people arrived, mostly expats giving me the once-over as they greeted Henry. He had said that tomorrow he was off to London for a few days, so would introduce me to those who could answer my questions about settling in. Already he had found temporary digs for me, with an Irish sculptor, Ryan, whose studio I could share. Grey-haired Maggie Potter, an elfin botanist

I had met on my earlier visit, was posting a box of dried grass to London. She rushed to greet me.

'There's a saying that once you visit Alciguna, you always return. Well, you see?' she tittered. 'But, my word, seldom the next day!' She offered to take me up among the crags and eagle nests to see wild plants she had named for the Royal Horticultural Society. Her enthusiasm wilted when I replied that I had little time for trekking, I must work for a living. That triggered a warning by a stout, round-faced woman posting a letter to Amsterdam, 'You're making a mistake. My artist husband tried to work in Ryan's studio, but found the constant tap-tap of hammer and chisel too distracting.'

'Yes, you must buy your own house!' Doreen Baker announced, over an armload of flyers for the real estate agency she owned. She brushed reddish, wind-blown hair from her face. 'You must buy now, to keep those dreaded barbarians, the developers, from getting a toehold. Have you seen those two weirdos snooping about our streets? Their Costa del Sol swagger means only one thing.' She paused for effect, then: 'Developers! They buy up a village, replace its old houses with cheap boxes, festoon them with "*rustico*" gingerbread, then sell them to foreigners as "authentic". The poor villagers wake up to find themselves in a new town totally stripped of its former character or native charm.'

A spiky lady affecting *Alice in Wonderland* straight hair and wearing flat heels, was listening. 'Developers!' She spat the word as profanity. 'Have you seen Mijas?'

I thought she was addressing me, until I saw people gathered behind. She went on. 'Mijas was once a charming village like ours, then – developers! Followed by tour buses, souvenir shops, and – oh, God, that ultimate surrender to the tourist classes, donkey rides!'

Paul Jones-Jones, a retired stock-broker, I later learned,

intervened. 'Ahem. You must admit, Olga, that house prices in Mijas quadrupled after the developers took over.'

'You would say that, wouldn't you,' Olga snapped. 'Bugger prices! Only quality of life is important in Alciguna. And now even that is threatened. Have you heard that our road to the coast is to be widened? Now, I have dynamite, if someone has the guts to help me blow up the river bridge.'

Doreen groaned. 'Oh, Olga, not again.'

Olga concentrated on me. 'Buy here, young man, and join my crusade to ban cameras on our streets, women in shorts, and shoot all bare-chested men on sight.' She removed from her mailbox several official letters and a Forbes magazine, stalked across the patio and up the steps to the street.

I turned to Doreen, whose dimpled smile urged tolerance. 'Olga Campbell,' she offered. 'Pesky, but harmless. Owns a farm near here. Her grandfather invented Campbell Cough Syrup and she still clutches the first penny of the millions she inherited from him.'

'Speaking of money,' I said, 'How friendly are house prices in Alciguna?'

Doreen patted her wayward hair and smiled even more prettily. 'Whatever suits you, my friend. From five thousand pounds sterling to five hundred thousand. The cheapy ones need renovation. The grand ones are white elephants. They all guarantee rewards to the venturesome; property prices are rising all over Spain.'

'*If* I were buying a house here,' I confided, 'I would have no time for renovating. My work is all deadlines.'

Sudden stillness. About ten post office patrons, foreigners of various ages, sizes and dress, snapped to attention, scrupulously disinterested, yet every ear cocked to listen. Doreen rolled her eyes. 'Come to my office. I have details there.'

Henry nudged me and spoke low. 'Now that all Alciguna knows that you are shopping for a house, you no longer need me for introductions.'

After he left, three dinner invitations were thrust upon me in quick succession. I accepted them all.

In no time I was enjoying coffee with new friends – Paul, Maggie, and two young expat couples – in Bar Seurte. It was quiet, since a makeshift bridge over the washed-out gorge now relieved the street of rumbling traffic. We also sat away from the 103 connoisseurs out front. We didn't need their raucous laughter, for the bar's acoustics, like all bars in Spain, were designed to amplify all sound by twenty. People I hadn't known an hour ago sat at my table, wishing me well, overflowing with suggestions on how to cope with mountain life in a cluster of whitewashed houses called a 'White Village'. Right away I learned that in Alciguna money is a commodity, you have it or you don't. Neither condition affects your social standing. Good.

I doubted that the switching on of my hazard lights at the collapsed bridge had triggered wholesale acceptance, and suspected that I was simply a new face that relieved social monotony. Yet, the openness of these people discouraged scepticism, and I appreciated their confusing medley of advice on prospective houses that I should buy, shouldn't buy, must buy.

Driving from Malaga that morning, the idea of buying a house in Alciguna would have struck me as ridiculous. I have never owned a house, considering maintenance too demanding in both time and cost. Nor have I lived in a village. Would Alciguna become claustrophobic? Would familiarity render its fantastic scenery commonplace? However, it sat conveniently between Seville, Cordoba, Grenada and Gibraltar, and for diversion there was the Costa del Sol, Los Vegas-by-the-Sea. How about living alone? Hell, I was getting used to that.

But before I could consider buying a house, there was the nagging question of Henry's 'asides'. He vaguely implied that something evil stalked Alciguna's streets. Was he serious, or playing me for laughs? Since he was leaving for London tomorrow, I would have to go to his house and confront him. I stood to leave.

An ear-splitting 'Whah-h-h-h!' blasted from the street and the bar echoed for a moment before falling silent. A pipe-thin old woman in a shapeless black dress and baggy grey sweater burst ass first through the beaded fly curtain at the front door. She shook her fist and screeched at a gang of hooting children that pursued her on the street. Laughing in high excitement, she brushed stringy black hair from her face and turned to survey the room. Her cackle didn't diminish until her black eyes doubled in size upon spotting me. She charged my table, making sounds I took to be peasant Spanish. Maggie snickered and translated the Andalusian demands being hurled at me: 'Who are you? What is your business here?'

'What's it to you?' I answered, none too gently The woman squinted at me, grinned and pointed at Maggie *'Tu rompey-pompey con esa?'* she croaked.

Maggie turned away, mumbling, 'You're on your own.' Seeing her face redden, and reading the old crone's lascivious smirk, I needed no translation.

'No!' I growled, rude enough to drive her away, I hoped.

'Ah!' she pointed accusingly. *'Eres gay?'*

I sat down. Everyone at my table laughed until Paul Jones-Jones finally intervened. 'That's Alejandra's favourite trick. Give her a hundred pesetas and she'll leave you alone.'

I dropped a coin into the outstretched claw. Alejandra winked at me, strode to the bar, stamped her muddy jogger's boot onto the brass rail and gestured to the barman. *'Camarero! Una cervesa! Pronto, guapo.'* He drew a glass of San Miguel beer and served it to her as if she were a queen.

I sputtered, 'Who – what – was that?'

Paul's tone was surprisingly gentle. 'That's Alejandra del Rio, the town pet. You'll get used to her. She roams the streets to nose into everyone's business, but she's harmless – if you've nothing to hide. She doesn't need money, we give her coins to prove that she's loved. We're all friends here.'

'Are there more pets like her in Alciguna?' I wanted to know.

Maggie answered, 'No, there's only one Alejandra, thank God. In Spain, instead of sending the elderly and – the quaint – to nursing homes, the government pays their families to care for them. It seems a sensible solution.'

Paul added, 'Evidently Alejandra has wealthy relatives, for they've set her up in a big house. Well-dressed men in a big car deliver food to her every Saturday. They're attentive too, always spend the night with her, poor old soul. They feed her well, she has enough energy to patrol the town without missing even the faintest rumour or hearsay.'

Maggie sighed. 'Too bad they can't force her to have a bath. The woman would never see soap and water if it weren't for Olympia forcing it on her.'

'Who?' I asked, admiring anyone who could face such a cringe-inducing task.

'Olympia Fairfield.' Maggie widened her eyes to stress importance. 'The town's undisputed social arbiter. You'll meet her soon enough.'

'Oh, that you will,' Paul assured me. 'Just remember to keep your eyes on heaven, and your hand on your zipper.'

'Paul Jones-Jones!' Maggie scolded. 'You dare give advice? You, with your congenital genital crisis?'

'I look forward to meeting the lady,' I laughed, and

again stood to say goodbye to Maggie and Paul, and to the young Danish and Dutch couples who hadn't been allowed space to insert their portion of grapevine. Intrigue seemed to form the staple of social life in Alciguna. Interesting, yes, but as a steady diet? Think about it.

I found Henry's house in a street near the foot of the castle ruins. Its plain front, two small iron balconies on the second floor, was the usual village design, except that his door featured a warning sign, SMOKE FREE ZONE.

Henry answered the bell, sleeves rolled up, eyes querying my visit, his greeting terse. 'Oh, hello, Robert. Serena and I are packing for our trip tomorrow. Have you got a problem?' He didn't invite me inside.

I glanced past him. His wife was not visible in the living room, yet a mental portrait materialized upon seeing Victorian chairs, ornate tables with tea caddies, potted plants and a biscuit-tufted sofa, all vying for floor space. Busy embellishments arranged in angles concealed much of the wall space; silver, crystal and brass glistened, wooden surfaces glowed with polished wax. Beyond doubt, I had discovered Henry's reason for spending most of his time on the streets of Alciguna.

I spoke hurriedly so as not to delay him. 'Sorry to bother you, Henry, but since I'm considering – might – buy a house here, some casual remarks you've made, bother me. You hint at some local crime...'

Henry flinched, stepped outside and closed the door. He scanned the street, spoke in a low, conspiratorial tone. 'Had I known you would return, I wouldn't have revealed my concern so recklessly. Do I have your solemn promise that you will keep secret what I tell you? You have met some of our denizens, I think you'll agree that "excitable" is a gross understatement. They must not hear of this.'

'How serious is "this" – whatever it is?'
Henry shrugged. 'I don't know.'
I felt qualms. Invest in a town with a closet secret? I needed more than a shrug for an answer and said so.

He pulled back his shoulders, took a deep breath and confided darkly, 'Lucy Prescott, a seasonal visitor, is a stenographer. During her last stay, she was called to do secretarial work for her boyfriend who works for the government in Malaga. Although warned about secrecy, she told me, only me, as many details as she dared divulge. She says that someone in Alciguna is engaged in something enormously illegal, internationally so. Those two men that Doreen Baker thinks are developers snooping about, are actually undercover lawmen.'

'Aha! Secret police. My belief in Hemingway is justified.'

'Dear boy, if I went to America, would my wagon train be attacked by Red Indians? You need lessons in current Spanish history. Secret police disappeared when Franco died, when Spain became a constitutional monarchy.' Henry's voice darkened. 'No, Lucy says these men are from Interpol.'

'Interpol!' I scoffed. 'In this town? Are you sure your friend Lucy wasn't feeding you a line? If not, I'd better think twice about buying a house here.'

Henry shrugged again. 'You'll note that I'm not rushing to sell *my* house. Not yet, anyway. Now if you'll excuse me, I must return to my packing, or Serena will beat me.' He paused at the door. 'If what I told you became public, Lucy could be prosecuted. Therefore, I trust your American honour to keep a secret.'

American honour? I pondered that little nugget as I left, deciding that American horse sense would be more appropriate for this ridiculous prospect of my buying a house in Spain. Should I ignore Henry's flaky exposé? Or maybe chew this over some more?

I have always believed that emotions imperil wise decisions. Give up my Boston apartment, have the company store my furniture? Invest in Spain about which I knew absolutely zilch? *Ergo*, don't buy now. Then why was I headed for Doreen Baker's real estate agency with one implacable purpose in mind? Logic, why hast thou forsaken me?

Those women yapping about 'developers'? Nonsense. There's absolutely not a more congenial spot, than Alciguna. Developers wouldn't dare mar its perfection.

5

Without my asking, Doreen Baker volunteered that her Serbian husband's original name had been Ernst Pastrivic, and that she had met him at a hippy love-in in exotic Margate. Ernst was tall, bearded, dull eyed and taciturn, limited to grunts and shrugs when conversation proved unavoidable. The Bakers owned La Casa Vic, a bar-restaurant combining the adjacent estate agency, a cubbyhole where I now sat before a desk strewn with mimeographed descriptions of properties for sale. I explained again that I couldn't spare time to renovate a derelict building, even those on the market at give-away prices. If I forewent plans to buy a new Porsche, I would have enough dollars to avoid the delay of a mortgage on a 'better' house. Doreen was delighted.

She spread out fact sheets describing houses that matched my space and price requirements, photographs showing near identical exteriors. Doreen explained, 'By town law, all houses must be painted white and must have terracotta tiled roofs. House taxes were once levied on appearance of wealth, thus all the plain fronts. It's on the inside that houses differ; modernized antique olive oil mills, old *bodegas*, pork curing smokehouses, sausage mills, some now converted into *House and Garden* show places. Many buildings are Moorish, some were second-century dwellings for Roman soldiers. All have thick stone walls, which keep them cool in summer.'

Cleverly, I found later, she omitted mentioning that the same applies for winter.

I pointed to a snapshot of a three-bedroom house with

a light, airy interior, large patio and a roof terrace view that one would kill for. 'This house stands out above the others,' I said, 'What's the catch? Why hasn't someone bought it?'

Doreen hesitated before answering. 'Yes, it is very attractive. Renovated by a television set designer who lives in London.' She stood, insinuating that the moment of truth was at hand, and thrust her selection of description sheets into Ernst's hands. With barely a nod, he led me to the houses Doreen had designated. To my dismay, I found those in my price range had been renovated by foreigners with peculiar ideas of what a Spanish dwelling should be; over-abundance of decorative tiles, everything artsy *rústico*. I began to suspect that non-renovated houses were a better buy, but I hadn't the time to tackle them. Back to square one. Forget that I asked.

Ernst accepted my rejections with stoical disinterest and motioned me to follow him down another street, past a lean-to public washhouse loud with chattering housewives scrubbing clothes, sheets and rugs in square cement tubs attached to the wall. The women interrupted cold-water laundering to wave to us, then resumed their full-throated gabble. Returning their greeting, I noticed that we were treading on soft brown pellets that littered the cobbles. I paused. Ernst shrugged and uttered his first words, 'Goat turds'. We trudged on. A grey-bearded man astride a *burro* greeted us by raising a goatskin bottle to squirt a draught of wine into his mouth. His work clothes were patched but clean, a garland of lettuces hung from his shoulder. He wiped his chin, plucked a lettuce from the string, tossed it to me and laughed, '*Somos toda amigos aqui.*' He spurred the *burro* with his sandalled feet and squeezed past us on the narrow street. 'We are all friends here' was easy to translate. That's what they said about Alejandra, I recalled with a shudder.

The last house on Doreen's list, the one renovated by the TV set decorator, looked identical to all the others: plain white front, terracotta tile roof, barred windows on the ground floor, two wrought-iron balconies above. By now I felt discouraged and ready to call it quits. But a shock awaited me when I pushed open the weathered oak front door. Inside were clean white rooms with uncluttered walls, only the kitchen bordered on the kitschy, but I don't cook. Three bedrooms, three ample bathrooms, three fireplaces, the one in the living room supporting a magnificent axe-hewn, oak-beam mantelpiece. The house surrounded a patio, and in it was a flower-bordered circle of granite, where a large conical stone, once used to crush olives, I later learned, rested picturesquely on its side. I saw it as a base for a table, if upended in the centre of the circle and supplied with a glass top. A great patio for summer dining. The renovator had done a beautiful job of converting an old olive mill into a tasteful dwelling. Its walls gleamed, as if all the surfaces had recently been gone over with a wet cleaning cloth. Its casual perfection was as handsome as any Spanish film set. I almost ran to tell Doreen that I would gladly pay the rather steep asking price.

I felt slighted that she did not congratulate me on buying such a treasure of a house. She didn't smile, merely produced contracts for me to sign. I wrote a cheque on my American bank. Simple. Next day I moved in.

Even before inspecting all the rooms, I set up a makeshift drawing table in the entrance hall and began work on my design assignment with inspired creativity. Nothing like working in your own home, I congratulated myself. Except, when evening approached, I found myself in the dark. All the light bulbs had been removed, and Doreen had been instructed to collect a thousand pesetas for their return. When I complained, Doreen shrugged. 'Wait till you meet the previous owner of your house, Benedict Beardsley. Scrooge incarnate.' Enraptured by the house at that time, I failed to grasp the dire reality of what dear Doreen was telling me.

During the following week I bought the basic requirements for living alone: a single bed, table and chair. But no kitchen utensils, because I planned to eat most of my meals at a local *venta*. Then I learned, with gourmand delight, that dinner parties were the favoured entertainment of the expat community. Being new kid on the block had its advantages, and in no time I was gaining weight alarmingly.

'What is the name of your house?' was the opening gambit at every dinner table.

'No name,' I had to answer. 'My street number is my address.'

Always came the disparaging reply, 'Houses such as yours must have a name. Our street numbers are not in sequence and are maddeningly confusing to visitors.' I recalled that my house had been an old olive oil mill and ventured a name I thought appropriate, perhaps even a little *rústico* romantical. 'El Molino?' I waited for applause. My hostess, formally of East Grinstead, clicked her tongue. 'Oh, Robert! Really! There are legions of El Molinos in every mountain village. So *déclassé*.'

OK, I tell myself, on the way home. Quit stalling. Your house has got to be labelled. Something classy, yet functional. Not banal, but not too damn clever, either. Think about it.

The next morning I met a neighbour, Polita, on the street. A local resident of long standing, she might know if my house had ever had a name. My English and, in return, her Spanish, got us nowhere. Using a language of semaphore we invented on the spot, she suggested that I consult the mayor's secretary, Josefa. I left for the *ayuntamiento* at once.

I found the town hall to be a two-storeyed white building with decorative iron balconies on its plain front, a national flag on an angled staff over its front door. An arch atop the front gable supported a silver bell that tolled the hours like a thump on crystal, a delicate tone almost too ethereal to be functional.

I had heard that Josefa held the town hall together; mayors come and go, it is Josefa who keeps the keys to everything, including the vaults containing the town's records. She seemed to be arguing with a reluctant photocopy machine when I climbed the stairs to the office she shared with other municipal employees. The large room, deep in paper, was orderly; the clutter of controlled action. On each desk, wedged between stacks of files and government forms and brown envelopes, stood a small vase of fresh flowers. Josefa listened with spent patience when I described my far out request.

She raised her sad, black eyes, her voluptuous body broken with regret, a Violetta as touching as Montserrat Caballé's final moments in *La Traviata*. 'Oh, *señor*, I am so sorry,' she moaned, 'I am too busy to help you. We are preparing new tax bills for people who have installed swimming pools.'

I raised my sad, blue eyes in silent plea, my soul racked with disappointment.

'However,' she added, smiling at my act, 'if you come back day after tomorrow, I will examine the archives in the cellar to find the names your house has possessed in the last three hundred years of its history. After *siesta*.'

Impatience must have shown on my face as I left the building, for Carlos Méndez, a Bar Suerte acquaintance, stopped me on the street. I had heard that he was a self-styled communist, yet worked with a solid devotion to profits. He clasped my shoulder with vice-like fingers, proving his Latino wrestler physique to be genuine. He frowned mock concern. 'Ah, *Señor* Roberto, look at you. You are having trouble with our conservative mayor?'

On guard, I answered, 'Nothing legal. Why?'

He released my shoulder. 'Because you come out of the town hall looking like an American politician who has lost an election.'

'I am told that using a number as a house name is too common.' I rubbed my shoulder and checked for blood. 'I need a better address.'

'Oh, that's not necessary, Roberto,' he assured me. 'Romero, our postman, knows your name. You receive your mail even when you are in prison, OK? And do not worry about a common name. Nor being a common man. Look at me.' He flaunted a gold-studded grin.

'I am looking, and I see money. I'm told that for electrical work you are the best in town – unless you go overboard with your Marxist crap.'

'Of course, I am the best electrician in all Andalusia,' he agreed. 'Naturally I make money. "Each according to his abilities" pays dividends.' He jabbed my shoulder with a light touch, fortunately, and strode away.

Two days later, I again met Carlos outside the town hall, but before his fingers could mangle my shoulder, I dashed into Josefa's office. The odour of ancient dust and mould suggested several hours spent in the catacomb archives. Her desk had been cleared, except for a tray of rolled documents blotched with age, perforated by silverfish and brown-edged with decay.

She addressed me officially. '*Señor* Roberto, I have found three ancient names of your house. Shall I tell you the oldest first?' Demure with inner knowledge, she crossed her dimpled arms and waited.

'Yes, yes, please go on. Whatever order. Please go on.'

She plucked from the tray a brittle roll of parchment. To avoid damage, she unrolled it partially and held the curled ends apart so she could translate its faded script. 'In 1747 your house was called *El Molino del Mulo Ciego*.' She sighed, eyes downcast. 'Not a pretty name I'm afraid. "The Mill of the Blind Mule".'

Carlos had been listening, and bounded into the office, fortified with indignation. 'Exploitation of a poor, blind animal!' he raged. 'The fascist owner must be prosecuted!'

'The mule wasn't blind,' Josefa sniffed, 'but blindfolded so he wouldn't become drunk from pulling the olive crushing stone round and round in *Señor* Roberto's patio.'

'Yes, the crushing stone is still there,' I confirmed. 'Also the stone circle for crushing olives. But I do feel sorry for the poor animal, rotating that heavy weight all day long.'

'Donkeys worked the same hours as their owners, including donkey *siesta* time.' Josefa selected a second scroll and pulled it open. 'Now, the name of your mill in 1860 was "Mill of the Exploding Boiler". Did you know that the second pressing of olives is done with steaming water?'

'Any note as to why the boiler exploded?' I wanted to know.

'Why does an American atomic bomb explode?' Carlos put in. 'Don't your capitalist schools teach basic physics?'

I refused to quibble, my house name taking precedence over communist dogma. 'The last name, please, Josefa,' I insisted.

'In 1918 it was renamed *El Molino del Muladar*.' She sat back with infuriating smugness and translated, 'The Mill of the Dungheap'.

Carlos patted my bruised shoulder. 'Ah, Roberto, you look like you have lost another election.'

'Gross!' I howled. 'What an impressive letterhead that would make!'

Carlos abandoned my shoulder and snatched the delicate document from Josefa. He studied it for a moment, wagged his forefinger and shouted, 'No! It is not *muladar*, it is *mulada*, which means a team of mules.' He puffed his chest in triumph, as if expecting the Order of Lenin.

'No, *Señor* Carlos!' She shook her finger in return. 'I see an "R". It is *muladar*!'

Gloria, an Australian embroiderer, rushed in. 'I heard noises and wondered if I could help...'

Carlos stomped his feet and trumpeted like a Siberian crane. '*Mulada!* That "R" is an age spot. *Mulada!* Maybe six mules.'

Despite my distaste for her argument, I had to side with Josefa. 'Six mules to pull that crushing stone around in my small patio? Not a chance.'

'I agree,' Gloria volunteered. 'My Citroen gets by quite nicely on only two mulepower.'

'*Muladar!*' Josefa insisted, stressing her authority.

'*Mulada!*'

Zorro, the police chief, stalked in, eyebrows raised, his two hundred and fifty pounds exuding suave superiority.

'Has there been an accident?' he boomed.

'It's all right,' I assured him. 'Carlos and Josefa can't agree on the name of my house.'

He placed his hand on my tender shoulder. 'Why didn't you ask me, *Señor* Roberto? Older people call your house *El Molino de la Ciruela*, The Mill of the Plum Orchard.'

I remained sceptical. 'But there's not a plum tree in sight.'

Zorro seemed to shrink, in bulk and in voice. 'I know. Last year I cut the last one down. Its leaves clogged my gutters.'

Overcome with brotherly love, Carlos wailed, 'The fruit from that tree could have fed the poor!'

Gloria nodded to me. '*El Molino de la Ciruela* does have a nice ring to it. I could embroider it on all your towels.'

'Better than "Dungheap",' Josefa agreed, gathering up her dusty records.

'Case dismissed,' I pronounced, after considering all that I had learned. 'I'm afraid that those names would confuse the hell out of my American friends. I'll just settle for its street name, *Calle de las Sagrados Martires de la Revolución de Julio 1932, Número 75*, until something better comes along.'

How could I know that there indeed existed a perfect name for my house? One that described it with such ruthless accuracy as to make me want to commit murder.

6

During the night, heavy pounding on my door awakened me.

'Robert? Are you there?' Henry's highly charged voice clanged from the dark, otherwise silent, street outside my house, now simply named '75'.

I staggered towards the noise, released the rusty *rústico* latch. Henry sprang inside and closed the door after him even while I complained, 'For God's sake, Henry, it's after midnight. I'd gone to sleep. Glad to see you back from London, but couldn't you wait until morning?'

He stepped over wads of crumpled sketches littering the floor and glanced disapprovingly at my untidy entrance hall used as a studio. 'Well!' he snapped, 'If it's an imposition, I'll call back tomorrow. I thought, obviously incorrectly, that it's extremely important that you be informed...' He strode towards the door.

I stifled a yawn. 'Henry, you know damn well I couldn't sleep after that razzle-dazzle. Now what news from London that's so all-fired important?'

'Not London!' Henry surveyed the room for security before confiding, 'When I landed at Malaga airport this afternoon, I went to the *Guardia Nacional* and spoke directly to the *comandante*. I told him point blank that we suspected the two men wandering our streets were from Interpol, and asked if something nefarious was transpiring in our fair village. Well! He gave me the grim facts without hesitation. He ... are you ready for this?' Henry paused.

I have noticed that some English people like to build suspense, and obliged, 'So tell me, what did he say?'

Henry puckered his lips as if to spit. 'Child pornography!' he spat.

'*What?*' I was awake now. 'This town is too small for producing something that dangerous. Everyone would know.'

'Not producing. Distribution.' Henry lowered his voice to a whisper. 'It is suspected that Alciguna is the distribution point for all southern Spain. Probably a spin-off from Castellar.'

'Castellar? You're confusing me. You mean that decaying mountaintop village on the way to Gibraltar?'

Henry volunteered, 'A few years ago the state-owned Paradores hotel chain drew up plans to make that historic walled town into a hotel complex. In compliance, the government built a modern village down the hill and moved all Castellar inhabitants into it. When the *paradores* scheme was deemed too expensive, the project collapsed and was closed down. Hippies at once took over abandoned Castellar, turning it into a drugs haven, a depository for stolen cars and headquarters for numerous other illegal enterprises.' Henry no longer whispered. 'This influx of crime overwhelmed our local lawmen. Since a majority of the hippies were German, the *polizei* were called in, who bused them back to the Fatherland. That is, most of them.'

The picture cleared. 'But some escaped to continue this trade?'

Henry nodded affirmative. 'Some escaped, some returned. But not to Castellar. Now they are more professional, and have joined forces with the Russian Mafia. It is rumoured that the drug trade re-emerged in Hernando, a village west of here. And it would appear that the new child pornography centre is – Alciguna!'

'Oh, no!' I moaned. 'Why here? Why this remote little village?'

Henry gave a wry smile. 'As I've told you, we sit on a centuries-old smugglers' trail. Some of our leading citizens, now paragons of respectability, were smugglers until Franco died. Cigarettes from Gibraltar, as well as Maidenform bras, nylon stockings and condoms were fashionable moneymakers. Oh yes, contraband figures prominently in Alciguna's chequered history.'

'It seems to have reverted to form,' – my hand automatically struck my temple – 'just when I've bought my dream house in "paradise".'

Henry stood erect, shoulders back, voice steadied with resolve. 'Since the officials are stymied, we must tackle this crisis ourselves. At once, dear boy, at once.'

'Hold on,' I protested. ' "We?" Why not someone who has lived here longer?'

'Mustn't tip our hand too early in the game, we mustn't.' Henry swept his hand towards the door. 'You see, the whole town is suspect. Should I approach the culprit himself for help, our purpose would be compromised. Or, if innocent, he might panic and tell all, which would no doubt create mass hysteria. You saw what happened when the bridge fell into the gorge. We don't need a repeat of that excitement.'

Shivering in my pyjamas, a sneeze erupted. 'Henry,' I snivelled, 'until my clothes arrive from the States, I don't have a robe. I am cold. I have a deadline to meet tomorrow. I don't have time for your crusade, however noble. Find someone else.'

He resumed his plan as if I hadn't spoken. 'We have perfect cover, dear boy. As a recent arrival, you need to be properly introduced to your new neighbours. I, the town's "do-gooder", will see to that. Once in their houses, we can check cellars, attics, locked doors, extra telephones, suspicious wiring. And of course, note if our host shows nervousness or undue annoyance. Everything discreet, mind you. We'll eliminate each house, one by one, or list it for further investigation as needs be, until we find the evil distribution centre that afflicts our town.'

'You're out of your mind, Henry,' I told him, knowing that he wasn't listening.

'Remember Agatha Christie. We follow her canon; the least suspected character is the most likely culprit.'

I felt my annoyance growing. 'Henry, you have every right to express righteous revulsion, which is understandable and admirable. But shouldn't you wait for something more concrete than suspicions before attacking windmills head-on?'

He stiffened, his tone brittle as steel. 'Suspicions? Suspicions!' Spray flew from his mouth. 'On my way to Malaga, about ten miles from the coast, I saw patrol cars lining the road and groups of policemen combing a nearby hillock. Naturally I stopped to enquire, and eventually pieced their guarded remarks into a coherent whole.' He eyed me like a triumphant chess player. 'Not suspicions, dear boy, cold facts. A goatherd had discovered three shallow graves on the hill. The bodies were identified as Russian Mafia, members of a gang that operates on the Costa del Sol. They were victims of gang warfare, police said. Scattered in their abandoned car were photographs and videos, every conceivable type of child pornography. Now hear this: the car is reported to have been seen in Alciguna on the night of the murders. Need I say more?'

I had barely started work the next morning when Henry arrived at what I called my studio, brandishing a list of names with addresses. That bothered me. 'You know this is a sneaky thing you're suggesting,' I told him. 'Should anyone suspect what you're proposing, this town would explode. Considered that, have you?'

'Deadly ills require drastic remedies,' he stated. 'We will start at the top of the town and work our way down, until we've checked out every expatriate's house.'

Returning to my work, I touched up a brown and gold label I was designing for a Spanish liqueur bottle. But my artistic muse had deserted me. I cleaned my brushes and stored them. 'Has it occurred to you that the Mafia's contact in Alciguna might be Spanish?'

'Out of the question,' Henry huffed. 'Magazines, videos, every label in the murder car; everything was in English. Against that, I imagine few of our villagers speak gutter English, even fewer would read or write it. No, I assure you, we are on the right track. Our Russian Mafia contact is unquestionably one of us expats. We start our search tonight.'

7

I didn't agree to join Henry's war on evil. Neither did I disagree. I would see what developed, I decided, frankly intrigued. If he goes over the top, which I thought probable, there was always the option of dropping out. Disengage from Henry's civilization-at-stake rescue mission? Any time, I told myself. Any time.

He arrived at my house at dusk, grave and resolute, steeled to purge Alciguna of its heinous crime, by whatever means.

'Have you studied the list I gave you?' He pointed to his own copy. 'We'll work down the hill from the castle. The topmost house belongs to Grace Pennington, we start with her. But be careful, her famous charms could be a front. We must catch her off guard. Evaluate her reaction. I've got a torch, screwdriver and wire detector concealed in my coat, anything more sophisticated might alert a professional criminal, you see. Smooth expertise must be our watchword.' He thrust his fist forward. 'Ready? Steady. We're off!'

I trotted after Henry, the obedient hound dog headed towards the castle at twilight, wondering what next. Despite his chin out-thrust with noble purpose, my doubts of his mission increased with every yard of our ascent. We tramped onto a well-tended private road at the base of the castle cliff and stopped at an ornate iron gate supported by two heavy brick columns. Henry stabbed a button near a small circular wire mesh lamina on one of the columns and stood back, arms folded. The intercom rattled, static became a female voice. 'Yes?'

He shouted at the column, 'Henry Perry-Smith, here. We were passing, and I thought you might like to meet your new neighbour, Robert Brooks.'

The column answered, 'Oh, do come in.' The gate buzzed, we pushed it open. Inside, an incongruous scene struck us head-on. As if transplanted by magic, we found ourselves in a formal English garden. Gravelled paths traversed geometric plots of clipped grass and flowering plants in bright, formal patterns. At the far end of a pebbled driveway stood a stately home, basically Georgian, with touches of tile and wrought iron in respect of its Spanish locale. Grace Pennington waited at the front door, smiling a warm welcome. After introductions, she ushered Henry and me into the house, where again we found upper-class England. The living room, with soft green walls, period furniture and oriental rugs, appeared under stern surveillance by ancestors, gold-framed paintings of military and civil authorities and courtly ladies flaunting splendid styles of past centuries. In the refracted crystallized light from chandeliers, Grace stood slim and handsome in a semi-formal forest green dress with an emerald brooch at her collar. Only crowfeet at her eyes betrayed her age of middle sixties. Despite an easy greeting, she seemed a little flustered. Henry noticed it too.

'I must apologize,' she explained. 'I have guests arriving for dinner, hence the party dress. But there's time for you to have a neighbourly drink. Oh, you must. Sherry? Gin and tonic? Whisky?'

'Thank you, we won't,' Henry answered. 'We thought we would just drop by to –'

'Yes, I'd love a drink,' I corrected Henry. 'Would a scotch and soda be too much trouble? I promise we won't stay long.'

I followed Grace into her blue and white tiled kitchen, helped dislodge ice from a frozen tray, and thanked her for the large lacing of scotch whisky she poured. 'Your garden is beautiful,' I told her. 'A pleasant contrast to Alciguna's stone and plaster.'

She smiled to cover a pause, and then spoke softly. 'It was my husband's dream to have an English garden. Since he died a year ago, I've tried to maintain it – impossible! Wrong soil, wrong climate, scarcity of water this high in the village. Yet, it's what he wanted, so I make an effort.'

She and I returned to the living room to find Henry peering behind a window curtain. He spun round, the kid caught with his mit in the cookie jar, but with a ready explanation. 'I was wondering if your windows leak the way mine do.'

'No,' Grace answered without a hint of annoyance. 'My husband Albert used all the latest technology when he built this house.'

'Your husband *built* this beautiful place?' I was genuinely impressed. 'It's a work of art.'

Grace answered the question she saw I was reluctant to approach. 'Albert served as New Zealand Commercial Attaché in Rotterdam until he retired seven years ago. We bought a caravan, took the cat and toured all Europe, seeking the perfect spot for retirement. Eventually we arrived in Alciguna, and without further ado, knew that the search was over. We found this acreage for sale, Albert designed and supervised every inch of the house construction. Then, as the last nail was driven – heart attack. I've tried to carry on without him, but, dear oh dear, the maintenance.'

Henry gestured. 'The two sheds behind the house; he built those also? Do you use them?'

'What an odd question.' Grace again avoided annoyance. 'The sheds were built to store building material. They are to be pulled down. Why on earth do you ask?'

'Alciguna is running short of garages,' Henry answered, showing not a hint of embarrassment.

Grace flashed resentment. 'A garage entrance across my rose garden! Henry, are you on crack?'

I thanked her for the drink, accepted a future dinner invitation with grateful anticipation, and shoved Henry out of the door. Beyond the iron gate, I let loose. 'Henry, don't you feel like a jackass for even suspecting Grace Pennington of anything nefarious? Wow, what class, what taste.'

Henry stopped, offended. I walked on. He caught up. 'I can't believe you're from the land of Sam Spade and Mickey Spillane. Clues abound, while you concentrate on whisky and soda.'

Now I was annoyed. 'Henry, you can't be serious. This witch hunt has addled your brain.'

'Charming, I'll admit, but too many smiles. The usual cover for nervousness. And did you notice how anxious she was to get rid of us?'

'We're lucky she invited us in at all. I saw the dinner table, set for five. Two giant silver candelabras, crystal and flowers, what a picture.'

Henry was mumbling, 'Hidden wires around the windows. They might belong to a burglar alarm system, then again ... clandestine antenna in the attic? Communications with God knows who?'

'You're puffing wind,' I told him.

'Oh, probably not Grace Pennington,' he admitted, 'but somebody might be using her. Or her house.'

This really was enough. 'Henry, include me out. I don't want to antagonize the people I've chosen to live with. As of now, find yourself another Sancho Panza.'

Henry halted again, demanding attention. 'Robert! I credited you with more gumption. Picture your daughter! Your sister! Kidnapped, raped on camera –'

I balked. 'I have no children, I'm an only child.'
'Your wife –'
'Much too old for child pornography.'
'Incredible!' Henry walked faster. 'A red-blooded American like you, yet you leave me to fight alone for common decency, to protect the reputation of Alciguna, our property prices –'
'Ah, now we're getting somewhere. But not even dollars could tempt me, Henry. You're barking up the wrong tree.'
Rhinoceros-hided Henry went on as if I hadn't spoken. 'Before we return downhill, there's another house up here that warrants attention. Locals call it "Colditz". It's the summer home of the Scottish owner of Beaks whisky. It's just ahead.'
'Beaks? My favourite blend. But no lights, nobody holed up in Colditz tonight. Let's go home.'
'As long as we're here...' Henry pointed to nearby steps hewn into the cliff leading up to the castle ruins. 'The moon is full tonight,' he observed with expert satisfaction, 'bright enough for us to survey the whisky house from the cliff. You just might find it – interesting – from that angle.' We turned onto a steep, rocky path and climbed between dark dwellings towards the castle. Low trees and brush kept us stumbling in darkness until we reached the steps, which we mounted mainly by sense of touch. It was not a pleasant climb, for at each house, dogs, behind fences, I hoped, started to bark, challenging our presence. Lights flashed on in windows, harsh voices questioned the disturbance. 'Just a few more steps,' Henry urged, resolve intact. We reached a flat ridge above the houses and halted. Ignoring the dog furore, he puffed, 'Now look down there. Colditz.'
The grim, windowless walls of the square fortress did indeed look built to support turrets, its tall profile out

of keeping with neighbouring architecture. Henry pointed. 'You see the house is built around an open court, ample for loading and unloading contraband into its veritable warehouse proportions.'

'Come on, now,' I objected. 'Even in the dark, I can see that the house surrounds a swimming pool. Besides, the owner of a major whisky company is highly unlikely to be engaged in something unlawful.'

Henry shook his head at my lack of perception. 'Swimming pools can easily be boarded over and used for storage. And there's something else you Americans can't comprehend. The Scots are a rascally breed, they love to cock a snook at the law. It's inbred.'

'We can discuss endearing racial traits later,' I countered. 'Those barking dogs are going berserk. What if they get loose? We're obviously not sightseers at this hour, someone could suspect us of reconnoitring for a burglary.'

Henry shook his head. Don't worry. It's against the law for dogs to run free. What we...'

Despite its illegality, the dogs were suddenly charging full fury in our direction. Henry, displaying unimagined agility, leapt down the steps three at a time, with me hard behind him. We raced like thieves, hoping that the dogs would soon reach the bounds of their watchdog responsibility. But distance didn't deter their speed one whit and each yard brought snapping teeth closer to our rears. Desperate, I tried to remember if my insurance policy covered dog assault. An approaching car crunched to a halt in front of us, catching us in its headlights. The dogs cringed and ceased their attack. I could feel their disappointment as they retreated up the hill, spirits frustrated, the thrill of the chase thwarted. Screw them. Two couples peered at us from the car, men in coats and ties, women dressed for dinner. 'Are you all right?' the driver asked, meaning, *'What the hell are you two up to?'*

Henry answered between gasps for breath. 'We – we've just come from Grace Pennington's...'

One of the women looked aghast. 'You must have done something dreadful, to have her set her dogs on you.'

Henry bristled. 'Grace hasn't any dogs, that I know of. She was in good spirits when we left her.'

'Good,' the driver scoffed. 'We're on our way there for dinner. If she doesn't corroborate your story, we'll assume that you're up to no good. In which case, I intend to call the police to check you out.' The car drove on.

'What did I tell you!' Henry boasted, as we walked homeward. 'A brazen attempt to frighten us away from Grace's house. Those people are from the coast, I'll wager, where the Russian Mafia flourishes. I would give a king's ransom to know what they're carrying in their boot.'

'You never give up, do you,' I groaned.

'The word is tenacity. At school I was called Bulldog Drummond.'

I turned onto my street. 'Thanks, Henry, for clueing me in. That explains everything. Now don't bother me tomorrow, will you? I've got another work deadline to meet. It's important.' He continued towards his house. I am sure that he heard me, but he gave no sign of it.

8

New York, NY
April Fool's Day

Dear Mr Brooks,

So you've discovered paradise in the unspoiled underbelly of Spain. Why waste golden moments faxing me, a money fundamentalist in greenback Mecca?

I have also found La Dolce Vita since our marriage ended. Call me Sales Manager for Gourmet Microwave Ovens, Inc. I have promoted some of my recipes on national TV. Hey, I'm famous.

Sorry, but your second message, your suggestion that I visit you to sample 'Spanish tranquillity', registers zero on my scale of Must Dos. I followed you to Mexico, remember? Spain, being the mother country, must be even more crime-ridden. No thanks.

Oh, yes, I do miss you, when the sink is plugged or a fuse needs replacing. Fortunately, we wasted only four years of each other's lives before admitting that domestic bliss was not our bag. Now I'm making up for lost time, loads of new friends in the Big Apple, the sky's the limit.

It was sweet of you to remember me, but if you write again, my love, schedules might prevent me from answering.

Thanks for the memory,
Your Ex.

I read Ellen's letter over a glass of *tinto* on the terrace of Bar Suerte. Well, if she isn't impressed by my discovery of contentment, it's her loss, not mine. Just thought my total switch of menu might amuse her.

Meanwhile, the fresh April day was perfection, as were the two *tapas* I had for lunch. New friends waved greetings or paused at my table for a few words of chat, and I thought how pleasant it is to be here. Despite Henry's utterly wacky 'investigation', he had introduced me to people that might otherwise have taken months to meet. Not unexpectedly, he ambled onto the terrace, face flushed from the day's heat. He collapsed into a chair at my table, dabbed his sweating brow with a limp handkerchief and wheezed, 'Are you free tonight?'

I was ready for him. 'I'm afraid it's early beddy-byes for me. Must get an early start for Malaga tomorrow.'

He leaned closer. 'But we must visit the Bangs before Gus returns to Copenhagen. He's an airline pilot, spends his off hours here. Recently bought a big house, far too grand for a pilot's income. Get the picture?'

I played for time. 'Maybe his wife has money. He is married?'

Henry was ready for me. 'Karen is her name. A real charmer. Too bad Spanish women avoid her...'

I bit like a hungry herring. 'OK, why do they avoid her?'

He drew himself up, reproof in his voice. 'I'm not a gossip. If she wishes you to know, she will tell you herself. Ah, quite a story...' Henry's lures are as obvious as they are successful. I flagged down the waiter. My bill for lunch was half the price of a cup of pallid coffee back in Boston. And entertainment here, provided by Henry, is gratis.

As planned, we climbed the murky street in a cool wind to reach our target for the night, the Bang house, large, smug and imposing on a cliff overlooking the moon-drenched valley. Algeciras, some thirty-five miles away, was a twinkling ribbon of lights stretching along the Mediterranean coast. The harbour of Cueta in Africa, twice that distance, was almost as bright. We arrived unannounced, Henry's 'surprise' strategy. Pausing to study the angled planes of the ancient stone house, he pressed the brass doorbell button beside an oak door studded with iron bolts. He pointed with professional suspicion and spoke low. 'Notice four doors opening onto the street? Superfluous, don't you think, for a private house? Most unusual.'

On the second ring, Karen Bang opened the front door. She was a large, blonde-haired woman, hair reaching her shoulders, and a refined face with high, Scandinavian cheekbones. Her blue eyes narrowed on seeing Henry, her smile was tentative. 'Oh, it's you, Henry. Do come in. Gus is watching TV.' She led us into the spacious living room where Gus lolled in a deep upholstered chair, light hair tousled, drink in hand, long legs stretched on an ottoman before a blazing fireplace.

He gestured his glass in my direction when Henry introduced us. 'Oh yes, Henry's new sidekick. What would you like to drink? I'm pushing whisky, stocked from the duty free on my last flight from Oslo.'

I cringed at being called Henry's sidekick, but swallowed it for the moment. 'Whisky,' I answered. 'I don't know if Henry is drinking tonight. Are you, Henry?'

'What?' He was concentrating on the book-lined gallery at the top of the stairs. 'Oh, no, no thank you. This is just a quick call to acquaint you with your new neighbour.'

'Really?' Gus turned to me, blue eyes serious, something like compassion in his tone. 'We hear you've bought the Ben Beardsley house. Before or after the big rain?'

For some reason, I found his question disturbing. 'Why do you ask?'

Gus paused, started to answer, then turned away. 'So, on another holy crusade, are we, Henry? Who are we this time? Henry II? Henry IV?'

Henry pulled his eyes from the wires connecting the hi-fi equipment. 'Crusade? I don't know what you mean.'

'Your penultimate crusade was my favourite,' Gus chuckled. 'Which was it, your third, or fourth? You know, the time you tinted Alciguna virgin blue.'

Henry shrugged in an airy attempt to conceal his embarrassment. 'Simply lost my grip on the bottle. No harm done.'

I jumped to his aid. 'Henry! You went on a binge? That's no mortal sin. We're all allowed an occasional lapse.'

He remained on the defensive. 'It wasn't poison, it didn't harm anyone.'

Karen attempted to help. 'Henry is too modest. Gus is referring to a few years ago when a nearby village, Gatocia, ran short of water. Alciguna enjoys an unlimited supply from mountain wells, and Henry was convinced that our Mayor Luna was selling it to Gatocia and pocketing the proceeds.'

Henry agreed. 'I had proof.'

Gus added a punishing chuckle. 'Government officials were not so convinced...'

Staring into the fireplace, Henry explained, 'I could find bluing only in bulk form, at a supermarket on the coast. Blue dye is the old-fashioned way of making clothes whiter when laundered.'

'Or bluer!' Gus snorted into his glass.

Henry reached for the high ground. 'I poured the bluing into one of Alciguna's water storage tanks, summoned our police and the *Guardia Civil,* along with magistrates from Malaga, even from Madrid. When

Gatocia's water showed streaks of blue, there it was. Proof that our Mayor Luna had sold it to them.'

I clapped my hands. 'Bravo!'

'Bravo, with conditions,' Gus corrected. 'Henry, aren't we deliberately omitting a few colourful details?'

Anger flickered in Henry's eyes. 'Regrettably, the bottle slipped from my hand and a little of the blue dye got into Alciguna's water supply.'

'A little!' Gus spread his arms to stress the opposite. 'For days everything in Alciguna was blue. Blue bread, blue tea, blue teeth, all our grey haired ladies were suddenly blue rinse Americans.'

Karen came to Henry's aid. 'He was a bit of a hero, catching Mayor Luna red-handed.'

'Blue-handed,' Gus corrected.

'Good ol' Henry!' I whooped. 'The mayor got the book thrown at him, I assume?'

Karen shook her head. 'Political cronies came to his aid, he got only a fine. Ah, but Henry's next crusade was more effective, wasn't it, Henry?'

'It was vital. It had to be done.'

Before I could request details, Karen explained, 'With much hoop-la the Madrid government allotted funds for a bridge over the Rio Guadal on our road to the coast. When no bridge was forthcoming, Henry pestered local banks until he found that Mayor Luna's personal account had gone astronomical on the day of the allocation.'

'Was the mayor convicted this time?' I asked.

Karen laughed. 'Are you kidding? Not Luna. He absconded with the funds. When the furore died down, he returned as a most respectable, and wealthy, law-abiding citizen, patron of the town's saint.'

'After all of Henry's efforts,' I lamented. 'What a waste.'

Henry clenched his jaw. 'But he was never elected mayor again.'

Gus poured another whisky for me and one for himself, which he raised to Henry. 'So when Henry is on his high horse, everyone cooperates, such as now. I know this is not a social call, Henry, so what wild-assed crusade are we on this time?'

Henry's eyes glinted like a trapped animal's until a sudden wiliness softened them. 'Saw your son today, Gus. Handsome little scamp.'

Gus set his glass down hard. 'Damn you, Henry, that mistake was rectified years ago. Everyone has forgotten it. You've no right to bring it up.'

This was not a new subject in the family, I realized, when Karen reacted sharply. 'Local women still don't speak to me because of your "mistake", Augustin Bang.'

Gus stoked the fire and added a eucalyptus log. 'You know I was younger then, and you were away. On top of that, the bitch swore she was on the pill.'

Henry could not let go of what he had created, and turned to me. 'In case you didn't know, your neighbour across the street, Limosna, makes her living on the docks of Algeciras on weekends. But I understand she gives a discount to local clients, eh, Gus?'

'You're a shit, Henry,' Gus muttered, and offered me an oblique apology. 'I paid for my lapse into tomcat morals, never fear. Two thousand pounds sterling, even though she couldn't prove I was the father. Quite generous, everyone said at the time.'

'My neighbour?' I thought back. 'The bleached blonde that goes to market in mini-skirt, high-heels and fishnet stockings? Yes, I admit, I had wondered.'

Gus grinned. 'Don't get excited. She won't touch Americans. Says they invented AIDS.'

Karen, unable to conceal her annoyance, stood, a signal that it was time for Henry and me to leave. But, being Danish, she offered us dinner.

'Oh, no thank you,' Henry said, ignoring my longing glance at the kitchen. 'Serena is cooking dinner for me, and Robert has an early trip tomorrow. Now tell me, Gus, why do you need four doors on the front of your house?'

Gus almost dropped his glass. 'Henry, anyone else, I'd tell them to get stuffed. But since you're obviously on one of your crusades, I'll volunteer in self-defence: front door, fuel supply room, kitchen, and entrance to garden. OK? Do you suspect me of harbouring weapons of mass destruction, or simply biological warfare chemicals?'

'You're wrong,' Henry shot back. 'I came only to introduce you to your new fellow townsman.'

'Sure, Henry,' Gus laughed, 'and my airline hostesses quote Einstein. Keep me informed of your progress, will you? So I'll know whether to dance in the streets or to commit suicide.'

As we left, I thought Gus slammed the door after us a little harder than necessary. We walked down the hill in prickly silence. Gus Bang calling me Henry's sidekick still rankled. I didn't want to hurt Henry's feelings, for all his actions, I knew, were well intentioned. Yet, being a newcomer, I felt it best to cease acting as battering ram for his invasions into peoples' homes. I softened my words, hoping not to sound brash or unappreciative, yet determined. 'Henry, old friend,' I confided, 'I'm sorry, but my work schedule no longer allows me time to help with your investigation. I'm afraid you'll have to carry on without me. I'm sorry.'

My speech rallied him from deep concentration. 'Yes, yes, dear boy. We're making inroads, aren't we? Notice how Gus kept trying to put me on the defensive? A common ploy. Could Limosna, your neighbour, be his conduit to the port of Algeciras, entry route for every conceivable contraband? And his frequent trips to drug saturated Copenhagen, what ho! You notice he didn't offer to reveal what lies behind the door of his so-called fuel supply. Child pornography, fuel for warped minds? Yes, when we spring our trap you will be proud that you donated your talent to do war on the evil that threatens family, democracy, yea, civilization itself.' We had reached the turn-off from the main street to Henry's house. 'See you the day after tomorrow at Bar Suerte. Around one o'clock,' he sang over his shoulder as he strode into the dark, his steps sure and purposeful. And I would be there. Never before had I understood drug addicts; now, they had my full sympathy.

9

It was easy to fall into the pleasant habit of lunch at the Bar Suerte, enjoying one of Spain's great contributions to mankind, *tapas*. Add to that *tinto de casa*, simple table wine that would do The Four Seasons proud, at one-one-hundredth the price. The only shadow on the horizon was Henry, sitting at my table, taking mental notes as he surveyed other expats on the terrace: chatting, laughing, each one a suspected child molester. I had just ordered a second glass of *tinto* when all restaurant talk turned silent, as by a volume control knob. Heads turned to see a brilliant white limousine gliding onto the square, flouting quiet swank. Its driver, a short man of about forty, peered over the steering wheel, a statuesque woman sitting beside him stared ahead, aloof as Buddha. Two small children shared the back seat with packing cases and bulging luggage.

'So the Baldocks have arrived,' Henry confided with sudden interest. 'They're Irish, and until the Middle East turned sour recently, Baldock was court musician to the royal family of Sandistan, tutor to some thirty sons and daughters of its ruler. Now the Baldocks have bought a house here for retirement. My only hope is that they haven't arrived with any of those disgusting oriental customs so in vogue in today's permissive society. What we –'

The car lurched forward like a bucking bronco. It backfired a thunderclap, exhaled a series of laboured coughs and, in front of the terrace of spellbound observers, expired ignominiously. The driver sprang from the car, yanked up its hood and threw up his hands in dismay. Sparks hissed. He gasped audibly when black smoke roiled from the engine. Flames shot out, shattering Mrs Baldock's composure into a shriek of panic. She scrambled from the stricken car to lead her children, screaming with terror, to the security of the corner bank.

Bar Suerte's customers scrambled inside for safety, then crowded the windows to witness and lament the unscheduled drama. I remembered Henry saying that since all buildings in Alciguna are made of stone, cement or tile, the town has no firefighting equipment. To be on the safe side, the bartender telephoned Gatocia, eight miles away, to send its fire engine.

Baldock rushed to extract baggage from the back seat of the burning car. Henry, bravely disregarding the possibility of explosion, flew to his aid. To keep from looking like a cowardy shirker, I joined them and started emptying the trunk, until one glance explained Henry's uncharacteristic courage. He was tearing into each packing case and rifling through its contents.

'For God's sake!' I groaned. Baldock, also spotting Henry's none too subtle rummaging, furrowed his eyebrows, demanding explanation.

'Checking for sparks that might have fallen into the cases.' Henry closed the last case and patted it. 'All safe,' he assured with official aplomb, and strode back to the terrace, face bland with satisfaction.

Customers relayed buckets of water from the bar to quench the blaze, creating whirls of acrid smoke. A siren echoed in the mountains, announcing the Gatocia fire engine that eventually lumbered onto the square, red and ponderous, adding more smoke and fumes to the scene. Three firemen leapt from the ancient truck, wielding axes with expert abandon and unfurling heavy water hoses. Poised for action, they faced the pyre with grim courage.

Then, observing that the car had burned beyond rescue, they dropped their equipment and ambled into Bar Suerte. After three free glasses of 103 brandy each, they reloaded their firefighting equipment onto the formidable vehicle and roared off back to Gatocia, siren wailing.

Sombre patrons refilled the sidewalk tables to watch the local junkyard truck clear away the carbonized automobile carcass. The Baldocks stood on the curb beside their stack of worldly goods, forlorn and bewildered, probably trying to figure out how to contact their insurance company. But not for long. Fellow expats approached them, women offered solace and encouragement, men ferried the baggage to the empty Baldock house three streets away. By evening, neighbours had donated enough bedding to see the family through the night.

The kindness of these foreigners highlighted Henry's rudeness, I felt, and told him so. 'Breaking into those cases was despicable. They contained personal things.'

He sniffed, 'Robert, the Baldocks have just returned from the profane East. One can only imagine what exotic paraphernalia they may have brought with them. Enough to corrupt every child in Andalusia.'

'Well, you didn't find anything. Now you can eliminate the Baldocks from your investigation.'

Henry winced, pained by my shallow observation. 'Good Lord, no. When their household shipments arrive, then the real search begins.'

During the limousine conflagration, I noticed a plumpish woman in her fifties (or sixties?) sitting alone at a table on the terrace, brown hair swept up into a loose bun, hand clutching a frequently raised tumbler of clear liquid, no ice. Her short, denim skirt revealed thin legs below medium-broad hips, her plain blouse sagged under the weight of an oversize purple stone set in a silver brooch. Brighter stones flashed on her fingers. Her metallic red nails glistened as she raised a cigarette to lips set as non-committal as a Venice carnival mask. Her ice blue eyes *could* have been observing Henry and me; they watched the whole scene, focused on nothing in particular.

'That lady with all the costume jewellery...' I enquired.

Henry leaned close, voice low. 'No costume jewellery, dear boy. Everything about Olympia Fairfield is absolutely genuine. Except, that is, sincerity. You should know that before I introduce you.'

From Henry I learned that Olympia descended from a notable Scottish clan, but pooh-poohed her title, preferring first name give and take. At the age of sixteen she eloped to Aden with her mother's lover, who happened to own a Middle-East airline and had faked Mohammedanism in order to transport pilgrims to Mecca, which made him hugely wealthy. After the honeymoon, Olympia was assigned a staff of twenty to entertain sultans and oil magnates with extravagant dinners and banquets. These unromantic responsibilities prompted her to plan escape back to England, just as the hand of Allah intervened. Her impostor husband's plane crashed and he left her just under three and a half million pounds sterling.

I stole another glance at Olympia gazing over her drink at Henry, no doubt assuming she was his topic. She tapped ash from her cigarette, impatiently awaiting an introduction.

'Wow. All that loot at sixteen. A teenager's technicolor dream.'

'Oh, there's much more to her history,' Henry informed. 'I've seen pictures of her at that age: kitten eyes, Cupid's bow lips, shapely body. In no time she was married again. Dear me, another tragedy.'

Impressed by Henry's command of true romances, I

guessed, 'She was swept off her feet by a handsome gigolo who took her for all she was worth?'

Henry laughed at my naivety. 'Our Olympia? Hardly. Her second husband was even wealthier than the first. After one child he went mad; there was an enormous settlement, of course. Then she married Pete Fairfield, one of Europe's biggest paint manufacturers. When lead-poisoning killed him, she was left more millions.'

Henry paused for me to digest that success story and then stood, flurried as if urging me onto a roller-coaster. 'Come. It's time you were initiated.'

I followed him to Olympia's table, he introduced us, she raised nicotine-stained fingers. I recalled what I could of continental etiquette, located a space between diamonds, and kissed her hand.

'Welcome to Alciguna,' she lisped, faking vulnerability. 'We don't greet every new arrival with a fireworks display such as you've just been given, hneh, hneh, hneh.' Her nasal chortle brought on a tobacco cough.

When she had finished, I agreed. 'I should hope not.'

Without pause she gushed, 'Come to my house for drinks at seven, darling,' and added a dash of intrigue, 'there are things about this town that you should know.' She pointed her cigarette at Henry to emphasize, 'But don't bring *him*. Rumour has it that he's on another of his crusades. I'm presently building a house, and I don't need the distraction of his famous crisis build-ups. One erection at a time, if you please.'

I thought of my work, and the deadline I had to meet. I had been told that Olympia's style had set a certain tone for the town; she alone had established its prestige over all the other White Villages in the area. In short, she was a person whom I should know. Also, frankly, I had the gut feeling that one ignored a Fairfield command at great social peril.

10

At seven o'clock I located Olympia's house on a side street, the usual white stucco front with barred windows on the ground floor, and two iron balconies above. It differed from its neighbours by having a hand-painted sign, FAIRFIELD'S FOLLY, nailed above its door, and beside it a bulky cluster of small bells. From them dangled a rope. I yanked it, raising a clangour like a goat stampede.

'The door's unlocked,' came a response from the depths of the house. I stepped onto rough stone cobbles in a dark room and knew at once that the afternoon sun had bedevilled my eyes. The scene was staggering. Leaning stacks of cobwebbed boxes were jammed floor to ceiling, with only a jagged tunnel leading towards her voice.

'I'm slaving in the kitchen,' Olympia trilled. 'Turn right, through the sitting room.' Darkness forced me to grope my way towards the cramped cubicle that featured a gutted fireplace between stone benches holding rotting straw cushions. A cigarette-butt strewn table fashioned from a wagon wheel completed the room's appearance of an untidy druid's cave. Through this chaotic disorder, the kitchen further jolted me. Its ceiling was a hanging gallery of dried vegetables, dead flowers, an old straw hat and worn tennis shoes, a rattan rake, a broken toilet seat, bicycle wheels; in sum, it included about everything that could be swung from heavy oak beams by a zealous collector of otiose *objets d'art*.

Below stood an enormous table heaped with newspapers, Christmas cards, flowerpots, saucepans, mixed china and glassware, and rusty tins of food for human and dog consumption. Behind that soared a pyramid of bottles: alcohol of numerous origins and potency. And behind *that* stood Olympia. She offered both cheeks, which I kissed to her obligatory 'Um-wah, um-wah.' Whether to put me at ease, or more probably, to mock my American accent, she drawled, 'Name yer poison, podner. We're having vodka-tonics.' She drew on a cigarette, directing her smoke towards the back door. Talk and low laughter drifted in from an overgrown garden.

'Right kindly of you, ma'am,' I drawled back. 'A doggone ol' vodka-tonic does sound mighty fine.' She poured my tumbler full of vodka and gestured a stingy drop of tonic water towards it, reminiscent of old martini jokes. I sipped my brimming glass and headed for the garden, but found the narrow passageway blocked by an enormously fat dog, rheumy and blind with age, squatting over a spreading puddle on the stone floor.

Olympia eliminated the problem by throwing a newspaper over the yellow pool. She scolded lightly, 'Oh, Tulipan! How gauche, in front of guests!' and returned to mixing a dip for potato chips. 'Have you met the Bangs? It's Gus' birthday. Go out to the garden. I'll join you as soon as –'

We heard the front door crash open. 'Whah-h-h-h!' vibrated the room. Alejandra, the old Spanish woman I had last seen at Bar Suerte, stamped into the room, as agitated as I had last seen her. She stopped short when I came into view and her bushy eyebrows rose like a tripped window shade. She grinned, rushed to shake my hand and cackled delight, '*Tu rompy-pompy Olympia?*'

Olympia overrode the happy giggles with three sharp commands: 'Vodka! Harrods! *Pronto!*' She counted out several coins for Alejandra, who squeezed them protectively and ambled from the room. We heard another 'Whah-h-h-h!' as she closed the front door after her. An encounter with Alejandra, I concluded, emphasized Spain's uniqueness, not its charm.

'Some people find Alejandra a pest,' Olympia confided as she chopped an avocado. 'But she runs errands for a pittance. Besides which, she's an absolute goldmine of gossip.'

'I don't think I'll need her,' I mumbled.

Olympia sloshed Pernod into the avocado dip. 'Have you tried our Harrods that's next to the Roman fountain? It's fundamental for life in Alciguna, darling. Unlimited stocks of Larios gin and Smirnoffs. They deliver, too, unlike Fortnum and Mason, who don't have a wheelbarrow.'

'I'll make a note of it.'

She handed me an oil-browned wooden bowl of aromatic green mush. 'Now go and join the Bangs. I'll bring the crisps when I've enlivened my drink.'

Gus and Karen sat relaxing on log benches in a patch of vines and weeds, chatting over a wormy old door resting on sawhorses: the cocktail table. They looked up when I exclaimed, 'Wow!' I was facing an open privy at the end of the garden. 'Some establishment.'

I located a level place on the table for the bowl and Gus stood to shake my hand. Karen offered both cheeks, explaining as I sat, 'Don't be put off by Olympia's lifestyle. Temporary, or so she has claimed for the past seven years. By contrast, have you noticed that baronial structure on the hill that rivals the castle for prominence? That's Olympia's dream house. She's gone through three architects, three complete redesigns, two rebuilds, and it's still nowhere near completion.'

Gus shrugged. 'It's her Neuschwanstein, costing her a bomb, I imagine. I doubt if it will ever be finished.'

Olympia swept from the kitchen, balancing her dripping glass, an open bag of Doritos and a gift-wrapped box, which she dropped onto the table. Settled on one of the benches, she placed the box before Gus. 'Happy birthday, Gus, many happy pursuits. Hneh, hneh, hneh.'

'Ah, Olympia, you shouldn't have!' Gus threw up his hands in mock surprise, then tried to stuff the box under the table.

'Oh, do let me!' Olympia snatched the box from him, impatiently ripped away its cover and pulled from it an elongated object which she wound like a clock and set on the table. We sat utterly dumbstruck, watching this titled lady release a lurid pink penis with purple balls and green feather pubic hair to hop about with sparrow legs on the tabletop. She ridiculed our shocked silence with a high giggle. 'Oh, there are more little Gusses,' she promised merrily, and reached again into the box. Shortly the tabletop was a playground of crouching, leaping penises, threatening to upset our drinks and invade the bowl of avocado dip.

I don't believe in omens, yet I froze when a breeze prickled the back of my neck. 'Oh, no!' I breathed, as Henry appeared. He viewed the phallic frenzy with slant-eyed revulsion, his jaw locked in a curious smile. He was certain, I could tell, that he had struck pay dirt. The mind that invented this show would be the mind responsible for child pornography in Alciguna. Not for money, in this case, but for sheer fascination with a perverted subject. What will Henry do? I wondered. Call in the *Guardia Nacional*? The Royal Marines?

Olympia stopped re-winding the gadgets of Henry's glaring disgust and drew sharply on her cigarette. 'Henry! What are you doing here?'

He answered coolly, 'My ringing your goat bells at the front door brought no response – for obvious reasons. The door was unlocked, so I took the liberty...'

She continued her winding. 'You know my door is always open to friends, Henry. Why don't you climb down from your holy steed and have a drink with us? We're celebrating Gus' birthday, hneh, hneh, hneh.'

'Yes, join the fun,' Gus grimaced.

Henry chose to hear neither of them. 'I intended to inform Robert that there's a message addressed to him on the Fortnum and Mason fax machine. But I see that I've rudely interrupted an obscene sex orgy.'

A fax for me? I wondered. A missed deadline? I asked, 'From Malaga?'

'I didn't read the message,' Henry informed me, 'But I saw that it's from Madrid.'

'Madrid?' I thought for a moment. 'Must be some mistake. I know no one in Madrid.'

'Of course I didn't read the message,' Henry repeated, but it's signed, 'Your Ex,' whatever that means. 'She's coming here.'

11

Robert Brooks
Calle de las Sugrados Martires de la Revelucion de Julio 1932
Numero 75
Alceguna, Malaga

Dear Mr. Brooks,
 This is not a peace offering. I'm in Madrid on a promotional tour for my microwave cuisine and can spare a day to check if your El Dorado is for real or just more of your bull baloney. Malaga Airport, Tuesday, 4:15 PM, Flight 203. If you can't make it, forget it.

Your Ex.

'Tomorrow night?' Henry's brow wrinkled in doubt the next morning at my house. 'A welcoming party for ten? You'd best see Olympia. That is, if you can pull her away from her playthings. She's got some serious explaining to do. Those "things"...'
 'Good Lord, not now, Henry!' I barked, forgetting politeness. Slightly miffed, he left to attend more pressing matters. I rushed to see Olympia. Black clouds scudding up from the Atlantic coast thundered a threat that April was still the wet season, and the first drops of rain struck my hand as I yanked on Olympia's goat bells. Within seconds I found myself sitting at her kitchen table, gripping

a huge glass of vodka, explaining my domestic emergency in terms of panic.

'Darling, I'm intrigued!' Olympia rattled the ice in her glass, eager to assist. 'Our roving chef, Guisante de Olor, can cater your party. Nine guests, you say, plus you and your wife? He will set up a bar, furnish chairs, glasses, even cook a *paella* in your kitchen. His wife will serve drinks and wash up afterwards. We expats have trained him for every emergency. He is absolutely essential.'

Sceptical of miracles, I asked, 'What cash does this Guisante guy expect?'

Olympia fortified her vodka glass. 'Depends on how much booze your guests consume. But count on at least five-hundred pesetas per head.'

'Three dollars fifty?' I calculated. 'Incredible. How do I contact this magic chef, Guisante?'

'Dear Robert, leave everything to me. Go tidy up your little nest for your spouse. I'm looking forward to meeting her, Henry says she has her own television show. Oh, she'll fit right into our Alciguna society of creative movers and shakers; writers, artists, sculptors, me and my house...'

'Sure, sure,' I coughed. 'Like a gryphon at a tea party.'

Another worry was the worsening weather forecast for tomorrow: rain and wind. How would Ellen react to a deluge such as had welcomed me to Andalusia? Oh, God! Why did she have to come now?

Earlier on, I had choked down memories of my Porsche stored in Boston while purchasing a set of Japanese wheels, the cheapest on the used-car lot. It was adequate for runs between Alciguna and my office, despite its rust and surfeit of gauges, buttons, toggles and warning lights, none of which worked. Besides, I never intended for Ellen to see it. Yet, here I was, rattling into a parking slot at

Malaga airport, an hour before her scheduled arrival. Unheard of, I know, but her flight arrived on time. The cavernous main hall at the airport terminal was milling with people waiting for friends and loved ones to emerge from the customs area. Strong misgivings kept me from joining in the expectant smiles. At last the arrivals started streaming into the hall, and finally, my wife. The trim khaki suit with epaulettes and a cartridge belt distinguished her from the other passengers hurrying past in 'ready for the beach' holiday attire. Large sunglasses protected her brown eyes and her blonde hair was hidden by a straw hat more appropriate for arriving in Nairobi. When we met she gave me a peck on the cheek, as good friends do, and handed me her canvas safari bag.

'Where's your elephant gun?' I asked, considering it a quite natural question.

'I'm glad to see you, too,' she shot back. 'Well, am I not dressed appropriately for the Spanish outback? You have a four-wheel-drive, I presume?'

The sight of my car in the parking lot clearly jolted her. She approached it warily, making an elaborate attempt to avoid its blotches of rust as she squeezed inside with a derisive grunt. 'Uh, I see you're doing all right, Irving.' Nor was she impressed with the Costa del Sol. A monsoon struck us head-on when we joined the coastal highway, yet it was not dense enough to obscure the gaudy architecture, the scaffolding and the unfinished shopping complexes. Traffic was coagulating in the evening rush hour as cars tail-backed and heavy trucks stalled at every traffic light. I attempted to lift the air of grimness within the car. 'I hear the government is planning a superhighway that will bypass these coastal towns. But never mind, the scenery improves enormously when we reach the mountains, you ain't seen nothin' yet.'

During the two-hour drive Ellen remained politely

indifferent, leaving me to guess: is she being sullen, or simply wishing she hadn't made this trip? At last I turned off the highway and headed into the dark mountains towards Alciguna. Until tonight, I hadn't noticed how pot-holed the narrow road had become; paved in summer, now washed out in stretches, deeply incised with craters and cauterized with detours. Ellen appeared thoroughly shaken when we finally reached the flooded streets of Alciguna, our seasonal Spanish version of Venice.

I pulled into my usual parking space by the washhouse, as close as I could get to my front door. 'We're on our own the rest of the way,' I apologized. Thunder rolled as I handed her a newspaper to cover her hat. I took up the safari bag and led her in a twenty-yard dash to my house. Lightning stressed the front door, which stood ajar. Puzzled, I pushed it open. I found Guisante in his tuxedo, hunched like a fat Picasso bull over a bucket; his wife, petite and pretty in a maid's starched uniform, was scooping up water from the floor. Candles on tables and shelves reflected gaily in the floodwaters of my entrance hall, living room and kitchen. I stood petrified, trying to comprehend the waterworld scene. Ellen, drenched and dishevelled, remained cool, collected, and, I was certain, delighted. In a flash, I deemed it more urgent to dam the water gushing under the patio doors than try to explain something I had no explanation for, and turned to Guisante for help. He bellowed, 'The patio no have drains!'

I snatched up a pile of strange rags from the floor and rushed outside to sandbag the doors. Although the patio made a most impressive swimming pool, I was able to plug the flow to prevent it from including the living room and kitchen. That accomplished, I yelled, 'Lights! Turn on the lights!'

Guisante sat back on his heels, rebellion keening his

voice. 'I already turned on lights. Everything explode. *Señora* Olympia say we must not use the *electricidad*. It is not earthed, we could all be electrocuted to death.'

Now I rocked on my heels. 'How does she know that?'

Instead of answering, Guisante pointed upstairs. 'She and Alejandra brought candles and rags, and buckets to catch all the water up there.'

'Upstairs?' I gasped, rushed up the steps and found a landscape of buckets spread to catch water flying through the porous ceiling. Olympia had done a good job of covering the floor with them, I admitted, for little water was escaping their plink-plonk spread. Bless her, I breathed, but – how did she know...? I returned to the living room to start a fire, anything to generate a little warmth in the damp, candle-lit gloom. By dismantling the original owner's artistic *rústico* log display arranged beside the fireplace, I found dry wood, easily lighted on the grate, and it quickly crackled into leaping flame. At once smoke billowed over the room in choking clouds. Equally alarming, smoke spiralled down the stairwell. Again I ran upstairs, and discovered with one glance that the chimney had been built over a ceiling beam, which not only blocked the chimney, but was spewing flames from both sides like a fire-snorting Janus. I threw ready rainwater onto the blaze and dashed downstairs to douse the fireplace. Although copiously drenched, smoke continued to swirl. I saw that it was not coming from the fireplace, but from the oak mantelpiece, which was a block of smouldering coals ready to erupt into full blaze. Guisante and I tossed more rainwater, the mantelpiece hissed scalding steam. A booming rap sounded on the front door. Ellen, now recovered and thoroughly intrigued, rushed to open it. A blast of wind drove in an avalanche of clamouring guests with rainslicks, umbrellas and dripping hats. They stopped dead, blinked, fell into silence, eyebrows raised at the candles and the mantelpiece spitting sparks.

'Welcome! We're experiencing a little technical difficulty tonight,' I greeted, trying to invent as much cheer as I could. Olympia remained indifferent as I ushered the bewildered arrivals towards folding chairs that Guisante had arranged in the semi-dark living room.

'Please sit,' I told them breezily, 'take the load off. Enjoy our candlelit atmosphere, everybody, it doesn't cost extra, ha, ha.' My attempt at levity fell flat and everyone remained standing. Guisante's wife, Rosa, rushed in with tumblers of red wine, which were snatched up without ceremony.

Olympia stalked into the kitchen. 'Only wine? After being soaked to the bone to get here, I deserve a proper drink. Guisante! Where's the vodka bottle?'

'Welcome!' I repeated doggedly. 'Here's the wife I promised. Meet Ellen, all the way from New York. Ellen, this is Gus and Karen Bang, Grace Pennington, Maggie Potter, Henry and...'

Henry shook Ellen's hand and offered what sounded like a routine apology. 'I'm sorry, but Serena sends her regrets. She has the sniffles and felt...'

'What a shame,' Ellen consoled. 'Another time, perhaps?'

I came near to dropping my wineglass as I listened. Ellen? Solicitous? Heaven help me, she sounded genuine! Remaining acutely alert, I added, 'I invited Doreen and Ernst Baker, but...'

Olympia, trailing splashes of vodka, rushed from the kitchen to hug my wife. 'Darling!' she greeted. 'So happy to meet you. I'm Olympia, friend to all in need. If the need be alcoholic, of course.'

Ellen shifted her gaze from the half-dozen diamonds on Olympia's fingers. 'How do you do?' she replied, as civil as could be. 'So considerate of you to face this horrid storm to meet me. I do hope you aren't put off by this disaster of a house.'

'She's right,' I agreed. 'It's obvious why the Bakers aren't here. Too embarrassed, no doubt, as they should be.' I explained to Ellen, 'They sold this house to me.'

Olympia lit a cigarette. 'It isn't their fault, darling, they were simply the agents. However, they might have informed you that your tile floor will sprout reeds and your roof will leak torrents until you install aluminium-backed sheeting under both. You will have to add cavity walls to prevent constant dampness, and provide drainage for the patio. You must treat all ceiling beams and window frames for active woodworm and dry rot. Your plumbing is ancient lead, and your cheap wiring is extremely dangerous.' She drew hard on her cigarette, leaned back and offered a little '*tsk, tsk,*' implying pity or triumph, I couldn't tell which.

'You knew!' I cried. 'Everybody must have known. Yet nobody warned me. A fine lot of friends I've found in this sweet little mountain idyll.'

Maggie Potter, the grey-haired botanist, scolded, 'We *did* warn you! We all *told* you that Ben Beardsley, the TV set decorator, restored this house. Remember? We assumed that you would understand that this house is a *film set*, with nothing behind. In fact, we call it "Casa Potemkin", after the Russian village consisting of facades only, built to impress Catherine the Great.'

I turned on Henry. 'Henry, you knew this, why didn't you warn me of Ben Beardsley's reputation?'

He made no effort to defend himself. 'Dear boy, I was in England when you bought this house. You had already signed the contracts when I returned.'

'And Olympia?' I faced her squarely. ' "Friend to all in need"?'

My guests tensed and strained forward in their seats, drinking suspended.

Olympia drained her glass and handed it to Rosa for a refill. 'Oh, pooh,' she downgraded my question. 'I could have warned you, Roberto, but that might have jeopardized the sale. Which, I must stress, would have triggered the biggest family row since Diana ditched Charley. Benedict Beardsley, you see, is my son, by my second husband.'

Guisante invaded the hushed room to announce that the *paella* was cooked. He served it in on plastic plates by candlelight, guests balanced them on their laps, and each held up a glass for more wine. Everyone sat eating, chatting and drinking, steadfastly avoiding any mention of the indoor deluge, while my mind tallied the cost of rebuilding the house for habitation. It had been carefully dried out before I viewed it; if only this rain had come before I signed on the dotted line! Should I abandon it now and accept the loss with good grace? Good riddance? A lesson learned?

An ingredient I hadn't anticipated now reared its illogical head. Having lived in this house for only a few weeks, I had developed a case of old-fashioned sentimentality. The Roman walls, the antique, if leaky, tiled roof, the ancient beams, and the patio with its massive olive crushing stone; its uniqueness outweighed the expensive repairs I foresaw. Ben Beardsley had played me for a sucker, which I couldn't deny. I would have to postpone into the future any thought of buying a new Porsche. Casa Potemkin, however, would remain mine.

Guisante, plying the guests with second helpings, frowned at my untouched plate. '*Señor* Roberto, you no like my *paella*?' he complained.

'It's delicious,' I assured him, suddenly at ease with my future. I took a mouthful and washed it down with the robust Rioja. 'You've produced the most enjoyable party I can remember.' It was true. The cost of building repairs diminished with each bite and swallow.

Guisante's dinner menu finished on an English note, cheese and port, then coffee. Conversation turned to the weather when the guests readied to leave and lined up for him to help them into their rain gear. My candlelight-with-water-music party would be a village joke for weeks, I suspected, although each guest complimented me on transforming disaster into a delightful evening. They all expressed pleasure in meeting Ellen, vied for dates to invite us to dinner and groaned disappointment when told that she was leaving tomorrow. Departing in a group as they had arrived, they screeched and yelped when stepping from my door into the driving rain and flashes of lightning.

The party over, Guisante and Rosa set about clearing the kitchen, packed their gear and stowed it for future collection. They thanked me profusely for the extra pesetas I paid them for mopping up the rainwater, and sang out '*Buenos noches*' as they left on the run. Now the house was quiet, except for crashes of thunder and the water concert upstairs, buckets with a metallic rhythm more in common with a marimba band than with Handel.

Ellen finished the last of her wine and sagged into a chair, eyes closed as if saturated with contentment. I knew better. She had been gracious, listened to local gossip, added topical tit-bits about life in New York and made favourable comments about Spain. She had radiated Boston charm rather than New York cynicism and no one could have guessed that her softness was padding for steel. But I knew.

She said nothing. Better not tempt her lapse into civility, I figured, and made up my small bed in the living room for her, with blankets borrowed from Henry. I spread piles of newspapers on the floor and placed a pallet on them for myself, beside my drawing board on the damp entrance-hall floor. Aware that the buckets could overflow during the night, I went upstairs to empty them, and while there, went into the bathroom that I hadn't used before. Seconds after I flushed the toilet, a scream resounded from the living room below. I leapt down the stairs, to find Ellen dragging her bed across the room in a frantic attempt to avoid the sudden shower from the ceiling.

This is surely the final blow, I moaned. Ellen will explode. What a mistake, allowing her to visit before I had the house under control. Her famous demand for perfection, her rejection of apologies, versus Ben Beardsley's three-ring circus of greed – oh, God, please, did Olympia leave any vodka?

I sat, slumped and miserable, in the candlelight, drinking my Smirnoff solace. Ellen made her way to the downstairs bathroom. She returned wearing a nightgown, spread her khaki suit on a chair to dry and, after a cautious look at the ceiling, placed her safari bag on a chair as well. Without uttering a word she sat on the narrow bed, shed her slippers, shoved her feet under the blanket and fell heavily onto her pillow.

Was she exhausted, I wondered, which was understandable, or disgusted with my performance tonight? Also understandable. I blew out the candles in the entrance hall, then the candles in the living room, and in the dark offered my apology, simple but heartfelt: 'I'm sorry.'

Hardly surprising, Ellen's response was non-committal. 'Believe me, I do appreciate your efforts.'

I couldn't see her face. Was she genuinely sympathetic, or more likely, was she wearing a pleased smirk? 'If you wish to laugh at my paradise, be my guest,' I offered. 'Yes, I admit that moving to Spain and buying this house, was a stupid mistake. Meanwhile, goodness me, you're making it supersonically in New York. Isn't your victory a laugh? Hot dog, a real belly laugh? Ha, ha! Hee, hee! Ho, ho!'

Her bedclothes rustled as she sat up, a little fire in

her voice. 'Robert Brooks, you're still the silly ass, aren't you!' I heard her lie back on the pillow, her voice growing softer. 'Contrary to your ironclad belief during our marriage, I never strove to out-succeed you, only to be your equal. You'll swear that's claptrap, but it's true.'

'Well, my love,' I conceded, 'there's no denying that you've accomplished that, with room to spare. Bingo! I bow to you.' Thunder rolled against the nearby hills.

Forgoing New York *kvell*, she expressed uncharacteristic charity. 'Come off it. When you were way up there, a star in advertising, and I was a lab assistant baking profiteroles in a microwave, whether you realized it or not, you made me grovel.' Again, I wished that I could see her face as her improbable spiel continued, 'Now that this disaster of a house has brought you crashing to earth, we are roughly on equal footing. For example, were we to share this narrow bed, I would demand, unconditionally, that you not usurp an inch more than one-half.' A flash of lightning revealed her open arms. Yo! I dropped my clothes onto the wet floor and leapt into her bed. The bucket symphony upstairs magically picked up the beat, orchestrating my own Ode to Joy.

The music swells dramatically: its dynamic, galloping theme emphasizes movement and violent outbursts of instrumental intrusion. A slower section recalls the calm at the end of the adagio, and the flute arabesques at its close accentuate quiet recapitulation. The galloping scherzo is repeated.

The next movement is similarly bracing. Woodwind echoes the lively opening theme. The ensuing conflict builds to an overwhelming conclusion with a long drumroll and a triumphant series of brass fanfares. The crescendo ends, collapsing into a mood of happy serenity.

Lord, what a symphony! Who needs Handel?

Next morning was business as usual. The rainstorm continued unabated, Ellen grumbled that her wet safari suit made her look like she had swum the Zambezi. 'I don't know what possessed me to wear this gear,' she said, tossing toiletries into her canvas bag. 'Perhaps I was Stanley come to rescue Livingstone. Well, surprise, surprise, the people I met here last night are more civilized than many of my business acquaintances in the jaded jungle of New York City. Do I get points for admitting that I no longer think you're a freak for coming to roost on this mountain crag?'

The pleasant two-hour drive to the Malaga airport was easy chat about work, the rain, the view. We circumvented our tempestuous past, our futures, our lovemaking in bed last night. When I saw her off on the plane to Madrid, she gave me a peck on the cheek, as good friends do, and waved goodbye.

12

Except for the few gauzy clouds that crowned distant Gibraltar, the mid-morning sky remained dark blue right down to the treetops. There appeared, however, another cloud in the distance: Olympia, who caught me entering the post office two days after my wife had left. She had stuck the knife in at my party, now I expected her to turn it. She did, with all the skill of a surgeon. 'Did Doreen Baker explain *escrituras* to you?' she asked, her concern suspiciously generous.

I tried to remember. 'I think so. She said that I would receive mine when the house deed was recorded by the registry office in Malaga.'

Over a glass of vodka that she demanded I buy her at the Bar Suerte in exchange for 'vital information', Olympia dispensed her sugar-coated torment under the guise of 'I want to help you, darling'. Usually she dismissed technicalities as tedium, today she delighted in imparting shards of wisdom in pointed detail. 'For centuries,' she informed me in an officious voice, 'properties in Alciguna have been handed down from father to heir, without legal papers. Take your house, for instance. My scatterbrained son never got a clear title deed for it. Like everything else, he waited for mama to do it.'

I sputtered into my coffee, 'And mama never did?'

'You know I'm creating my own house, don't you? My busy schedule didn't allow time. Besides, against my advice, he called in Jules Reemrev, a *macho* British artist, to supervise the restoration of your house. He was instructed by my son to employ the cheapest peons and to use only second-hand building material. Worse, they both tried to seduce the workers' wives when they delivered *desayuno* to their husbands. The builders, constantly trying to protect their wives, made a proper cock-up of the construction. Naturally, I washed my hands of the whole distasteful affair. With my promiscuous history, how dare I censure my son's morals? Now, you, darling, are stuck with the consequences.'

'Let me get this straight,' I said, gripping the table. 'I paid for the house, yet it's not legally mine, or what? How the hell do I get a clear title?'

'Benedict's solicitor, *Señor* Coronado, has worked on it, so to speak, for three years. Claims he is trying to buy off one of the original owner's cousins, who lives in Estremadura and owns one-sixteenth of your house.'

I leapt up, temporarily interrupting the noise of Bar Suerte with my demand. 'I damn well want to meet this Coronado guy! Now! Right away! Now!'

'Get control of yourself, darling,' Olympia shushed. 'Spanish legal wheels grind extremely slowly. Some people wait five years for an *escritura*. Although I'm working night and day on my own house, I'll introduce you to *Señor* Coronado ... buy me another vodka?' She smiled primly.

Near purring over her new drink, she explained that *Señor* Coronado's wife had converted her parlour into a *supermercado*. When Olympia had finished her drink, she led me there.

Señora Coronado sat sorting onions as we entered her mini-supermarket; neat and aloof, she answered our enquiry with a nod towards stairs to the next floor. '*Este semana el es Ovidio.*' Olympia's Spanish, limited to present tense, left her unable to translate '*Ovidio*', so I accepted it as an irregular verb beyond her. We climbed the stairs, and before settling on wooden chairs in the waiting room, I pushed a button labelled EMPUJAD near a door. We heard a buzz in an adjoining room and waited. I pushed it again. This time we heard an annoyed, *'Tranquillo!'*

I noticed Olympia watching me when the door opened. Seeing my eyebrows arch to my hairline, she barely concealed a wicked giggle. *Señor* Coronado, tall and willowy, floated into the room, draped in a loosely woven toga. He had a white beard, white hair pulled back into a ponytail, and bushy black eyebrows. His feet were shod in goatskin sandals, his arms embraced rolled parchments tied with green ribbons. He greeted us warmly in a lilting language that I took to be the English equivalent of poetic Spanish. 'When I compose poetry, I become my subject. Today I am a herd of sheep in a storm,' – he cringed, buffeted by cruel winds – 'and then, oh, paradisiacal sunshine!' He fluttered his hands in its heavenly rays. 'You arrive as I am completing *"Oda de Ovidio"*. Melancholic sheep are my analogy of Ovid's misery in the court of Augustus. Their good fortune represents his happiness at being granted exile.'

At least, I think that's what he said. Yet, I would not be sidetracked by poetry, however epochal. '*Señor* Coronado,' I demanded, 'I am here to enquire how long I must wait for the *escritura* on the house that I bought from Ben Beardsley.'

He stroked his beard, trying to remember. 'Ah, *Señor* Beardsley. I had but a glimpse of Virgil. Oh, unadorned simplicity and blushing modesty.'

Olympia shrieked, 'My God! Are you referring to my son?'

I insisted, 'I've heard that there's a problem with my title deed.'

The poet-lawyer rested his hand on my shoulder, his tone sympathetic. 'Yes, an unformed and confused mess.'

To hell with politeness. '*Señor!*' I ranted. 'If you spend all your time writing poetry, I'll never get my *escritura*.'

With an angry flourish he pulled one of the rolled parchments from under his arm and opened it for me to read, reproof for interrupting genius. '*Señor!* A faithful study of the liberal arts humanizes character and permits it not to be cruel.'

Ill prepared to compete with Ovid's wisdom, I signalled Olympia that I must retreat to seek advice. We said our *hasta la vistas* and left. On the street, I barked, 'It's patently obvious that my *escritura* is not among *Señor* Coronado's literary priorities. How serious is this? Could I lose my house?'

'No, no,' Olympia soothed. 'The only restriction is that you can't sell it without a clear title deed.'

'Why not?' I fumed. 'I bought it from your son without one.'

She offered one of her wise smiles. 'There you are, you see.'

I should have hated Olympia. Yet I had to rely on her advice, vital at this stage, no matter how many vodkas it cost me. 'By damn,' I told her, 'I'll get my own lawyer, or "solicitor", as you British like to say. Until this ownership thing is settled, I won't be able to concentrate on my work.'

She pursed her lips. 'The seller pays the solicitor's fee; hire your own, you'll have to pay for him yourself. If you wish to do that, I'll contact *Señor* Alba. He'll settle your case within days. But be warned, darling, although he's excellent, he's also expensive.'

'Why didn't your son hire Alba instead of that nut, Coronado?'

Olympia stated the obvious. 'I just told you. Alba costs.'

'I might have guessed,' I muttered. 'More of Ben Beardsley's money-grubbing. He pays nothing if Coronado does nothing, which could go on forever. It would appear that Coronado's wife is the man of the family.'

Olympia shrugged. 'Rumour has it that Coronado can be seen in bars late at night wearing womens' clothes. However, with nine children, I suspect he's wearing a jock-strap under his toga that's mistaken for a dress.'

Arranged by Olympia, *Señor* Alba knocked at my door two days later. Spruce, spare-boned and bald, he appeared all business. Since Guisante had collected the party chairs, Alba sat on my work stool and spread his papers over my drawing board. He took a fountain pen from his coat pocket and handed it to me with a quick comment, 'It took one telephone call to clear your title deed. I've brought papers for you to sign. Also, my bill.'

'Hallelujah!' I cried. 'I'm now the uncontested owner of...'

Alba punctured my euphoria without a hint of compassion. '*Escrituras* are hand-written in classic script. There is only one scrivener in the Malaga office, therefore you won't receive yours for another six months. At best.'

I signed the papers, the lawyer gathered them up and pocketed my cheque. He paused, spoke low, taking me into close confidence. '*Señor* Brooks, I've looked into the possibility of your purchasing the little house on the cul-de-sac next to you. Converted into a garage, it would increase the value of your property notably.'

'I've already checked that out,' I bragged. 'It adjoins the rear of Casa Grande, the big house that stretches to the next street, whose owners would certainly have bought it were it on the market.'

'They can't buy it. But you can.'

His interest bothered me. Could he be another conniving Ben Beardsley perhaps? I asked, 'And why is that?'

He adjusted his perch on my work stool and delivered a morsel of legally correct gossip. 'Casa Grande was built by Hortensia del Busto, owner of a famous bordello in Algeciras until she married one of Franco's generals, Manuel del Busto. They moved here, had two daughters, he died.'

'Does Hortensia still own Casa Grande?'

'Until she died five years ago, at age eighty-seven. She entertained lavishly, always wearing a bikini. One daughter died. The surviving one, Delores, lives there today.'

'So Spanish,' I put in. 'Everyone dies. Delores forever after wearing black, I assume?'

Alba rasped, the closest I had seen him come to an outright laugh, although he didn't elaborate. 'That's another story. Now, about the little house. Delores offers one-and-a-half million pesetas for it, but her offer has been repeatedly rejected. You, *Señor* Brooks, can have it for one million.'

'Wow. Seven thousand US bucks for a garage, when my rusty old banger has never known cover? Too rich for my blood, I'm afraid. But tell me, why can't Delores buy it?'

Alba, impatient with my questions, snapped, '*Señor* Campo, who owns it, remembers Hortensia and refuses to sell it to Delores because her mother was a *puta*, or whore. Simple as that. *Señor* Brooks, I recommend that you buy this property.'

I countered, 'I planned to use the last of my savings to buy furniture.' A practical enough reason, I thought. 'Sit on the floor,' Alba urged. 'Sleep on the floor, eat on the floor. But don't miss this opportunity. Buy the little house before someone else snaps it up. Ben Beardsley, for example, is very interested in buying it.'

'Ben Beardsley wants it?' I clasped Alba's shoulder, revenge in the air. 'Hot damn! I can't pass up a sweetheart deal like this, now can I?'

On the date set for the exchange of contracts on the little house, I arrived early at the agreed meeting place, a gloomy bar in an apartment complex on the outskirts of San Roque, near Gibraltar. I ordered coffee, alone in the nicotine-tinted *venta* except for a short, dumpy Spanish woman sitting at a bare table. Her reluctance to look at me indicated a fear of being mistaken for a pick-up, until my accent emboldened her. '*Señor* Brooks?' she asked, voice timorous, eyes shy.

I answered with breezy assurance, to put her at ease. 'That's me. Are you here for the paper signing?' Her instant smile was bright, despite protruding teeth and exposed gums. Her hair, pulled back into a knot, accented high cheekbones in her round, puffy face. Overweight, her legs sausage-shaped, only her smiling eyes could be called attractive. She told me her name was Maria.

Noting my limited Spanish, she pronounced words slowly and used pantomime to put across a complex statement. Too bad about her looks, I thought, her kindness deserves better. I bought her a coffee, and we were soon discussing the little house, which she remembered from childhood when she, her two sisters, brother and father had shared its one room. 'Life was happy there,' she told me, 'except for *Señora* Hortensia del Busto! Her noisy parties for gentlemen in Casa Grande kept our family awake until dawn.' Maria rolled her eyes for emphasis. 'So much money, yet the *Señora* never gave a peseta to the Church, indeed, never even attended Mass. Our father wouldn't allow us children to speak to her.'

I wanted to hear more of Maria's family history, except that the lawyers' arrivals created a bustle that precluded all else. *Señor* Amador, representing the seller, *Señor* Campos, appeared first. Then came *Señor* Alba, who greeted me with an anxious whisper, 'Did you remember to bring the money?' He had warned that *Señor* Campos demanded cash only. I thumped the bulging envelope in my jacket pocket, breathed goodbye to a new Porsche, and nodded.

Maria led the three of us to a grey apartment building nearby, identical to others in the high-rise cluster, ground floors like gaudy billboards of spray-can slogans and sexual graffiti in Jackson Pollock layers. Old cars as dilapidated as mine stood parked at random over pools of oil, while nearby children romped on a muddy playground.

Scarred elevators looked accustomed to heavy traffic in marauders. On the fourth floor, Maria led us down an airless corridor, through an even darker parlour to reach *Señor* Campos in his bedroom. His bed supported a heavy oak headboard and he lay under a black sateen coverlet embroidered with red roses, with tassels that reached the floor. A picture of the Madonna smiled from high on the wall and a bare lightbulb in the ceiling barely lit a table that stood in a far corner, laden with bottles of dark medicines.

Maria arranged chairs around her father's bed and pushed pillows behind his fleshless shoulders. She brushed his wisp of hair with her hand before introducing us. White stubble gave his face a frosted glow, his contrasting dark, sunken eyes lingered on me. 'Ah, *Americano*,' he rasped through a toothless smile. 'Are you John Wayne? *Bueno*. Then I can trust you never to sell the little house to that *puta*!'

His words expressed a compressed hatred that made we wonder how many years he had held Hortensia del Busto in such intense contempt. I winced, thinking, when a Spaniard hates you, you're really in deep trouble. Maria smoothed the shiny coverlet for the lawyers to spread their legal papers before *Señor* Campo. Alba explained the transaction, Amador nodded agreement and handed the old man a ballpoint pen and pointed to the space to sign. *Señor* Campo dropped the pen onto the coverlet and grunted contemptuous rejection. '*Donde esta el dinero?*'

'Where is the money?' Alba repeated. I thrust my envelope containing a hundred ten-thousand peseta notes into his hand. He passed it to *Señor* Campo, who counted each bill with taut concentration. Again Amador offered the pen, again it was ignored. We waited until a second tally finally confirmed the correct amount.

Alba threw in a touch of sarcasm, 'It's all there, is it?'

'Just barely,' *Señor* Campo answered, and signed a jagged 'X' on the proffered documents. The transaction at last concluded, he wheezed, 'Maria, my angel, bring the bottle of *fino* that I have saved from my wedding feast.' She brought from the parlour a green bottle, its Jerez label yellowed with age, and prized out the cork with tender care. As she passed around ornate wine glasses ringed with faded gold, the old man caught her hand in his and squeezed it. 'And one for yourself,' he instructed.

She filled each glass with the cloudy amber liquid. *Señor* Campo raised his with trembling effort and nodded to his guests. His voice crackled, 'We drink not to celebrate the sale of the little house, but to the happiness of my sweet and loving daughter.' Again he reached for her hand, placed the bundle of peseta notes in it and pressed her fingers around them. He murmured, 'Now you can buy yourself the fine husband that you deserve.'

Maria kissed the old man's forehead and crossed the room to the table covered with bottles, packets and a steel kidney bowl holding a syringe. She dried her fat cheeks and then turned to us with a quiet apology. 'I am sorry, but it is time for my father's medicine.' She led us through shadowy rooms to the front door, where she bade us '*Adios*' with a timid wave. Her eyes were soft with the acceptance of God willing the level on which her life was pegged, and her smile was genuine.

13

Polita called from upstairs, 'Come! Come and see!' She giggled like a schoolgirl on ecstasy. 'Come and see!'

Doreen Baker had recommended her to me and I hired her for six hours a week at three dollars an hour. Her one stipulation: she would not be called a cleaning lady, but *Ama de llaves*, my 'housekeeper'. She at once took over the running of my house as her private fiefdom, and, had I allowed it, my life as well. A buxom widow of around sixty, she was brisk, candid and had dyed hair approaching orange. Her permanent smile verged on cynicism, her eyes danced or condemned with equal focus. Her name was Amapola, Polita for short, my little poppy.

'Come and see!' she insisted. Not sure if her cackle signalled alarm or amusement, I rushed upstairs where she stood pointing from my bathroom window at the back garden of Casa Grande. Her finger directed my eyes to a sparkling swimming pool lined with flowered tiles, beside which stood a woman, naked as a jaybird, her arms stretched to embrace the glorious morning sunshine. Polita sniggered at my unabashed ogling of the gorgeous body glowing in the soft light, then grinned broader as she shifted her pointing finger. A well-built young man jogged from the big house and did a couple of turns around the pool. He was also nude, with the most enormous penis I had ever seen flapping at his knees. I have showered in football changing rooms, spent time at a 'naturist' beach in Maine where dozens of us romped fully exposed. But this youth cavorting below my window took first prize. Polita tiptoed from the window as if to avoid disturbing a rustic idyll. Embarrassed by my own amazement, I followed her.

Olympia invited me to dinner on Saturday night, insisting that we 'go Dutch' at a local *venta*. Frankly, her background intrigued me; the widow of three millionaires, certainly she had colourful stories to tell, and I wanted to hear them. We met at my house, she downed two vodka-tonics, and by ten o'clock we were settled in the tiny Red de Seguridad restaurant. The *venta* contained six tables jammed close together, which got new paper covers after each set of customers. Its local recipes were plain and invariably delicious, the vegetables homegrown. A three-course dinner, with wine, cost roughly four dollars. Usually by ten-thirty every table was taken, and we grabbed the last empty one.

Olympia drank another vodka-tonic and I described the scene I had witnessed that morning from my bathroom window. 'Couldn't be more than twenty,' I reported in a whisper, aware of the nearby tables. 'And she was fabulous, I kid you not. What a body!'

Olympia took up the frayed, hand-written menu, rattled her jewellery and snorted cigarette smoke. 'That was Delores del Busto. In her fifties. Goes to Madrid every year for a body tuck. You're not very observant, young man, or you'd have spotted the seams.'

I reached for my wine glass. 'Fifties!' I gulped. 'I can't believe it. Then from what I saw, she goes for studs half her age.'

'Oh, you've seen Peter, have you?' Olympia concentrated on her menu. 'Frightful chap. Phallic elephantiasis. Permanent erection. Hm-m-m, *Gambas de pil-pil* is recommended today. Delicious. Have you tried it?'

'It wasn't an erection, Olympia,' I assured her. 'It just hung there.'

'Careful, Roberto,' she wheezed loudly through a tobacco cough. 'Aren't you showing too much interest in another man's willie?'

Patrons at two nearby tables halted their eating and twisted to stare. Relieved that they were total strangers, I whispered to Olympia, 'Nobody can be expected to ignore a freakshow, now can they!'

She drained her vodka glass, reached for a cigarette. 'Call it freakish, whatever. Delores seems deliriously happy with it, hneh, hneh hneh.'

I was into my third glass of wine. 'Was her sister as demanding?' I hoped Olympia would open up. She did.

'My God, you're becoming as nosey as Henry. Next, you'll be conducting your own loopy crusades.'

'It's just that Delores is my next-door neighbour. I should know what's up, what's going on, shouldn't I?'

Olympia looked at the ceiling and feigned defeat to disguise her joy of a gossip-fest. 'All right,' she sighed, 'what do you already know about Casa Grande, across the back garden from you?'

I recalled the briefing by my lawyer, Alba. 'Only that it was owned by Hortensia del Busto, ex-madame, who married a Franco general and had two daughters by him, one of whom now frolics naked under my bathroom window.'

'Well, since I can't avoid it...' She called, '*Camarero! Otro* vodka-tonic, *por favor!*' Suitably primed, she began her florid account. 'When Hortensia died, Delores and her sister, Veronica, finding themselves suddenly wealthy and fancy free, set out on a worldwide quest for – you guessed it – men. Delores found the Peter you saw, on the "meat rack", London's notorious stud *marché* in Piccadilly Circus. Veronica bought herself a real Texas cowboy, and they all lived happy as rabbits in the "big house" – until the tragedy. Veronica...'

'*Si, Señora?*' The waiter was standing on one foot then the other, his pencil poised over his order pad.

Olympia ordered a starter and main course, I echoed her choice to save time, to keep her talking. 'The "tragedy"?' I prompted.

She finished her vodka, reached for the wine, 'Oh, yes, very sad,' she continued, after sampling it. 'Veronica developed breast cancer, you see. Since the del Bustos never trusted western medicine, Veronica took her cowboy and flew to India for treatment. The family faith healer removed the cancerous breast, some say with a machete, then returned with her to Alciguna to administer post-operative care. Despite his continuous dancing around her bed and playing a reed flute, Veronica's condition worsened. The Texan built a box for her to lie in, with a small hole in its roof to focus a ray of sunlight onto the cancer. This cosmic therapy also proved ineffective, and Veronica, poor wretch, died.'

Wine came free with dinner at the Red de Seguridad and Olympia barely touched her food. After coffee, which she ignored, she said, 'There's more to that story, of course. But I need to jog my memory. Shall we go to the bar next door for a liqueur?' Her coy act was redundant, of course. Already a willing moth in her web, I agreed at once.

On our way out, a man, an Australian tourist, according to Olympia, called, 'Ai, mite, yeu live 'ere?'

'We do,' I said, remaining noncommittal.

His female backpack companion clanged, 'Chiange from a fiver for dinner! Gawgous but unbelievable. Yeu're living in a fantasy world 'ere, yeu realize thet?'

The man emphasized, 'Yeas, this 'ere Camelot, mite, it cawn't last.' We laughed at their wine-inspired blarney, wished them a pleasant stay, and moved next door.

Immediately upon entering the long, noisy bar, Olympia started berating the bartender, one of the few people I had seen who failed to jump at her commands. His lack of kowtow seemed to annoy her. 'This bloody Baileys has gone sour,' she stormed. 'Take it back and open a fresh bottle. *Pronto, camarero! Va!*' The young, square-jawed bartender sauntered away, opened a new bottle and returned with a refilled glass at his leisure. She tasted it with haughty suspicion before accepting it.

'The del Busto saga,' I reminded her, as I paid for her drink.

'Have you seen our *Cementerio Municipal*?'

Wondering what the hell, I answered, 'Well, yes, it's that garden of cement file cabinets. Each drawer contains, or will some day contain, a body.'

'Correct. Our town owns the cemetery; the mayor refused Veronica a vault because she had no death certificate. No doctor could be found who would issue one, because only the faith healer had attended her.'

'Were there enough ice cubes handy to preserve the body?'

Olympia went on. 'During the night, the cowboy and the faith healer crept up the hill and dug a hole behind the cemetery...'

'Hold it. That hill is pure granite.'

The story seemed to tire Olympia. She admitted, 'All right. More accurately, they took the body in the box that the Texan had constructed, stuffed it into a crevice, and then covered it with stones. That took place a year ago. Veronica still rests there.' Story concluded, she called to the bartender. 'Another Baileys, *camarero*.' Again she barked at him. '*Nunca!* Never again try to pass stale Baileys off on me. Understand? *Nunca!* I'll report you to the landlord if you do.' The young man smiled, accepting her tirade with the equanimity of one planning sweet revenge. I learned later that only that day he had been appointed Alciguna's new traffic cop, and Olympia was a notoriously bad driver.

When we left the bar, a balmy breeze wafted music from some distant source in the night. Olympia's pace quickened as she led me to another bar, where a TV played opera to empty tables. The proprietor met us at the door, waving his arms. 'We are closed. Now it is two o'clock, I must sleep.' He reached up and clicked off the TV set that hung over the bar, shrinking Maria Callas to a silent dot on the screen. He closed the door and bolted it with force, apologizing as he did so.

Olympia fumed, 'Callas, my favourite singer. *Tosca*, my favourite opera. I must see it. Come, let's go to Jesús Maria's bar.'

'Olympia, it'll be closed too, at this hour.'

She punched my ribs with her elbow. 'Money answereth all desires, Roberto. Jesús Maria has been my Man Friday for years. He supervises the construction of my house, among other – duties.'

'But if his bar is closed...'

'Don't be dense. My money bought him the bar. He'll open. It's just here.' She pointed down an unlighted alley, took my arm and pulled me along. She halted before a dark building and knocked on its door with echoing force. A window banged open on the floor above. Jesús Maria leaned out. '*Jode!* What do you want?'

Olympia shouted, 'Open up, J.M., it's me.'

'*Señora* Olympia!' His voice softened. 'Is there a problem?'

'Open up!' she demanded. 'There's a programme I must see on your telly. Make haste!'

Within seconds the door swished open. Jesús Maria, wearing trousers only, no shoes, leapt onto a stool to switch on the television set above the bar. Callas was singing '*Vissi d'arte*'. Olympia swooned into a chair, moaning in uncontainable ecstasy. Jesús Maria's pregnant wife crept down the staircase from the quarters above and offered us a drowsy smile. 'May I get you coffee?'

'No!' Olympia, eyes glued to Callas, waved silence. 'I want 103!' The wife shrugged and waddled back upstairs. Jesús Maria hustled behind the bar to fill two glasses. The recorded concert ended too soon for Olympia's liking. 'I'll not have it!' she howled as a news programme usurped the screen. 'I'll ring the station and demand a replay. 'I'll...' Her anger subsided when Jesús Maria handed her the brandy, even more so when he stretched his lithe, tanned body to switch off the television.

I thanked him for opening the bar, and apologized for our intrusion on his night's rest. His answering smile was at odds with his dark eyes. Yet they expressed no annoyance when Olympia spoke. 'J.M., will you escort me home? I've drunk *mucho* too *mucho* firewater tonight.'

'I'll take you home,' I offered, figuring that Jesús Maria had remained the gracious host longer than politeness required. He glinted a cold 'mind your own business' smile that cut me dead.

Ignoring my offer, Olympia whispered to him, 'Your wife won't miss you for a couple of hours. Come along, sweet Jesús.' So that was it.

The three of us left the bar, a strained silence broken by my inane remarks about the bright stars, the warm weather. At the turn-off to my Casa Potemkin, Olympia offered both cheeks with her usual 'Um-wah, um-wah,' and thanked me for a fun evening, her upper-class requirement. Her jewellery jingled like the goat bells at her front door as she and Jesús Maria walked on. I couldn't see her as they disappeared into the shadowy street, but two-bits says she was aiming her inimitable humour at me as she croaked an off-key version of that capitalist paean, 'Money makes the world go round, the world go round, the world go round...'

14

'Never complain, never explain,' is the closest Olympia came to an apology for her abrupt departure with Jesús Maria. No problem. Her private life was her own, I readily conceded, and over time we drifted effortlessly into weekly dinners together at the Red de Seguridad. The arrangement developed quite naturally, our age difference precluded any hint of *rompey pompey*, except to Alejandra. Olympia wasn't dull, and her company was a change from spending Saturday evenings with only my drawing board to talk to. She, in turn, liked being escorted by any man more interested in her personality than her jewellery, although she never complained about the numerous quests by fortune hunters seeking her favour. Rumour had it that she exploited would-be suitors, usually obtaining amorous satisfaction from their attempts before ditching them.

Another diversion was Trivial Pursuit Night at Doreen and Ernst Baker's La Casa Vic bar every Thursday; dinner, ample and cheap, followed by the game. The event took place upstairs above the bar, a room with beamed ceiling and a bank of windows that viewed the valley towards Gibraltar. On game nights, bountiful bowls of mixed green salad and bottles of wine were spaced along the paper cover of the long table, its twenty unmatched chairs usually occupied by nine o'clock. A separate buffet table held the main course, usually curried chicken with an over-abundance of rice. Olympia always arrived alone, ate dinner with the players, but joined the game only when she found the bar empty. Technical Trivial Pursuit questions betrayed her scant formal education, whereas subjects concerning mysticism, homoeopathy, black magic and royalty were her meat. However, her irrefutable authority in all categories determined the answers, rendering the answer cards incidental.

If the Alciguna post office served as clearing house for gossip, Trivial Pursuit Night at La Casa Vic existed for airing complaints. A favourite subject was our erratic electricity; blackouts during rainstorms and high winds, fun rides at carnivals that gobbled the town's kilowatts, wreaking havoc with television sets and electric tea-kettles. Since all major social events required a *raison d'être*, Doreen and Ernst donated the profits from Trivial Pursuit dinners towards capping the waitress's teeth, which were black due to medicine administered during a childhood illness.

A typical game night found the usual people present, the paper table cloth splotched with dribbled wine and olive oil from the self-serve green salads. Olympia, having picked at her food between swigs of wine, slipped away to the bar to see if any of her drinking friends had arrived. Paul Jones-Jones, always the first to begin eating and last to finish, crossed his swabbed plate with his knife and fork and blotted his lips with a paper napkin, his mouth, at last, empty enough to ask, 'What about your protest march, Olga? Any results?'

Permanently incensed about one catastrophe or another, Olga Campbell barked her answer, 'It was an important night football match, so naturally, the town's lights went out. I led a torch parade to the house of the electricity franchise owners, but couldn't rouse them, surprising no one.'

Maggie Potter whispered to me, 'Thirty years ago a Franco supporter was awarded the franchise; his heirs refuse to upgrade the power lines, even though the town has doubled in size. Olga does have a point.'

'The problem is foreigners!' Olga raged, piercingly impassioned. 'Tourists! They steal our electricity and plunge us into darkness. Well, we must combat the Vandal hordes, or next we'll have tour buses. As we all know, that's just one step ahead of, God forbid, donkey rides!' Her weekly soapbox oration delivered, she drained her wineglass and slammed it down, but being a Campbell, was careful not to smash it to make an expensive point.

The Nurembergs, Manfred and Ilsa, an autocratic, some said arrogant, middle-aged couple who had recently built a luxury home on the outskirts of Alciguna, stared aghast at Olga. Had he worn one, Manfred would have dropped his monocle.

Olympia, having found the bar vacant, returned to join the game. I whispered to her, 'Wow. Olga's a high-strung lady. My guess is, what she needs is a good man to calm her down. Like urgently.'

Olympia shushed my crude observation. 'Highly strung, granted. But that lady is exceptionally brilliant, well informed and talented.'

'All that?' I smiled, assuming that she was joking.

'You see, she is my sister. My maiden name was Campbell.' Olympia crossed her lips with her finger. 'Now, sh-h-h-h!'

Jan van den Burg, a Dutch house painter, was labouring to read the first Trivial Pursuit question. 'Vich seventeenth-century poet wrote, "Through ze rare red hetter ve danced togetter, O love my Villie! and smelt for flow-vers."?'

Unimpressed, Olympia shrugged. 'Oscar Wilde. Who else?'

Everyone strained to hear Jan struggle with the answer, which he read like an apology. 'Zis card says it vas somevun called "Caverley".'

'Nonsense,' Olympia corrected. 'I am a relative of the Marquis of Queensberry, Willie Douglas, and I know that he was Oscar Wilde's lover.'

Receiving no objections from cowed opponents, her team racked up its first point. Throughout the evening Olympia overrode the answer cards, her counter-intelligence guaranteeing vanquished opponents.

Game over, the players traipsed downstairs and through the bar, noisily exchanging 'Good night' or *'Buenos noches'* as they reached the street. Manfred Nuremberg had drunk too much brandy, and his *'Gute nacht'* sounded much like he was gagging on something.

La Casa Vic was suddenly quiet and deserted. Olympia grasped my arm and halted me at the bar. Ernst poured 103 and set it before her. Expecting this, I had brought pesetas, and ordered coffee. Olympia tapped my shoulder, nodded towards a couple slumped in a dark corner, elbows planted on the table, funk style clothing indicating more money than taste. I resented her assumption that I would be interested. Then it dawned. 'Good Lord!' I whispered. 'I didn't recognize them with their clothes on.'

Her eyes crinkled with mischief. 'Yoo hoo!' she called. 'Delores and Peter! Yoo hoo!'

Unsteady, confused and dimly annoyed, the couple rallied to raise their heads and mutter, 'Hello, Olympia.'

She held up my hand as if I were the Statue of Liberty. 'Meet your new neighbour, Robert Brooks. He's American. There goes the neighbourhood, what? Hneh, hneh, hneh.'

Peter winced at her laugh and stared from under weary eyelids, pupils like spatters of dark paint. He raised his hand, then let it drop. 'Hiya, mate,' he greeted, faking a smile.

Delores made the same effort. 'Yesh, I've heard of you. Mush come to my house for drinks, or whatever. Not tonight, *muchacho*, we've had a real hell day with city hall. Come tomorrow. OK?'

Olympia and I finished our drinks and started for the door. Delores roused briefly to call, 'You, *muchacho*, without Olympia, OK? Around sevenish-ish. OK, *muchacho*?'

As we left, Ernst advised from the side of his mouth, 'And leave your American morals at home, OK, *muchacho*?'

Outside the bar, I laughed. 'So that's Delores del Busto. A little on the nasty side towards you, wasn't she?'

Olympia coughed a plume of cigarette smoke. 'Yes, that's Delores. She knows I disapprove of her lifestyle. When her eighty-seven year old mother entertained in a bikini, it was accepted as eccentric chic. When Delores tries it, she's yobbo Benidorm. The poor cow lacks taste, in spite of her inherited millions.'

'Well, I can forget that invitation. She's too stoned to remember that she invited me.'

'Oh, no,' Olympia warned. 'I advise you to go. Locals remember her father as a Franco general, which even today carries an aura of authority. They jump when Delores sneezes. With her money, she ignores the police, walks all over them. Oh, she still has power, that one.'

'Sounds like I'd better accept, then. I'll fill you in on the gory details later.' We left La Casa Vic. 'As for now, since it's after midnight, I'll walk you home. That is, if you don't have Jesús Maria waiting in the wings.'

'I don't need an escort, darling,' she assured me, as she trod on alone. 'I've walked on these streets at night for seven years and never been raped yet. Damn it.'

I'm behind schedule! My week's design work remains unfinished. I must phone Malaga and swear to deliver it on Saturday. With no interruptions I might be able to...

There came the inevitable knock on the door. Henry, of course, and he was exuberant. 'So you're having drinks with Delores del Busto this evening. Excellent! She has long been on our list of prime suspects. A foot in the door at long last. Excellent, dear boy. Excellent!'

Without missing a brushstroke, I told him, 'Henry,

you're downright spooky. How the hell did you know that I'm invited to Casa Grande?'

He answered with a non-committal smile. 'For months I've tried to get a peek inside that house, now you succeed. You know what to look for, locked doors, hidden storage space, excessive telephone or electric cables, clues of traffic in any type of photographic material, anything at all that might suggest child pornography –'

I had to laugh. 'Do you really think that hippy couple would be involved in anything requiring work? They're in perpetual paradise, man, with enough money to maintain an address there.'

'Don't be flippant, Robert,' Henry snapped. 'It's Delores who's got the money. Peter has to improvise. In the past, he thrived as Fagan to a gang of local Artful Dodgers. Our police generally ignored their petty thievery, until Peter became greedy. Then whammo!' Henry knew where I kept the instant coffee, and went into the kitchen to make himself a cup. I waited, paintbrush suspended.

He returned, sipped his brew, and approved it. 'There is a chapel behind the castle ruins that contains a statue of El Niño, the town's patron saint. Local widows make offerings by draping it with strands of semi-precious stones and placing valuable rings on its fingers. One night Peter's merry thieves stripped it. As you can imagine, the town erupted in holy uproar, angry burghers demanding quick action. Peter was arrested on the coast when he attempted to sell the jewellery, was tried, convicted, and sentenced to six months in Malaga prison.'

I whistled. 'Wow. Six months. Did he return a reformed man?'

Henry shook his head. 'The prison, being filled at the time, sent him home without serving a day. Ah, but not for long. Peter made the more serious mistake of goosing the mayor's daughter while she was leaning over the

Roman fountain in the town square. The mayor bypassed local law and called in the *Guardia Civil*. This time, Peter got instant prison – one year.'

'Rough. How did Delores take it?'

'With high drama, as you can imagine.' Henry tried to conceal a grin. 'When Peter was apprehended and handcuffed at Bar Suerte, she demanded that she provide him with "protection". Knowing that upon entry into Spanish prisons every male is issued a half-dozen condoms to prevent AIDS, she demanded that the officials wait while she ran to the *farmacia* for a gross of them. You see, Peter has a permanent er, er, erectile condition, and she didn't want it returned as damaged goods.'

'I know. I've seen it. Enormous.'

Henry's eyebrows shot up.

I led him to the upstairs bathroom window and pointed to the Casa Grande garden, with the swimming pool of flowered tiles. 'There,' I explained. 'Peter and Delores often play around that pool bare-ass naked. They...'

A flute shrilling across the garden halted us. Henry leaned from the window, one ear directed like a television dish, disquiet creasing his brow. He winced. 'Oh, oh, oriental music. That signals something nefarious over there. A celebration for a new shipment of pornography from Bangkok, perhaps?' He gave the scene a learned glance. 'H-m-m-m. Standby to telephone *Guardia Civil*. I'll reconnoitre the far side of the house. If a van is parked near a door – wait for my signal.' Henry left the house on tiptoe, the classic gait of the Pink Panther on the prowl.

Within minutes he returned, breathless with frustration. 'Nothing being loaded or unloaded,' he puffed, 'however! There are numerous bizarre vehicles stationed out front. Casa Grande is shut bung tight, yet its closed curtains are agitated, indicating a cyclone of action inside. What with that exotic flute music going up and down the scales, up and down, could they be filming a sex orgy in there?' His cunning eyes narrowed on me, his voice dark. 'Delores invited you for seven, right? Surprise them. Arrive at six. Catch them in the act!'

I checked my watch. The day was already shot, I would have to finish my design work on Sunday, for Monday delivery. Henry aside, there existed powerful oriental mystique behind that wavering flute, and I felt caught in its uncanny draw. Or, could it be that Henry's meddlesome genie has jumped from his shoulder to mine?

15

As Henry had described, a welter of crude jalopies flanked Casa Grande, each a junkyard escapee. I worked my way between their crinkled fenders to the towering front door and banged the 'Fatima hand' brass knocker. At my third rap the door swung partially open, a man's hand reached out, grabbed my arm and hauled me inside.

The door slammed shut behind me, the hand vanished, leaving me blinded by the room's dark contrast to the late afternoon sunshine I had just left. A flute wailed with deafening intensity. Far worse, a smoky reek heavy with putrefaction assailed my nose like the swat of a boxing glove, and my watering eyes at last focused. A candlelit scene of kinetic shadows staggered me. Scruffy male figures with wild hair, women ranging from Ophelia to Scheherezade, were elbow-locked in a wide circle, dipping and swaying in a jerky rhythm around a wooden box propped on two chairs in the centre of the room. A *dhoti* clad Indian, green turban knotted around his head, sat cross-legged on the floor at its base, lost in the hypnotic plangency of his flute. The macabre carousel rotated to a moaned dirge, which stood my hair on end.

No! This can't be! I told myself. Next door to my house? Am I caught up in a nightmare? That is one possible explanation. Another is, could that wine I drank with lunch have been hallucinogenic? I felt better at seeing Delores and Peter across the room, sitting on floor cushions, with out-of-it expressions and double-glazed eyes reflecting the gyrating action before them.

A thin, swarthy woman left the ring of canting forms to approach me, maroon lips parted, questioning my confusion. Her black hair was centre-parted, a white pelisse reached her bare feet, silver bracelets cordoned her arms and ankles. She placed her palms together above her head and wobbled it, a kohl-eyed metronome. Her reedy voice pierced the haze. 'Who are you, o sober one?'

I croaked, 'Delores invited me.' The woman's face turned doleful. 'Then you knew Veronica?' She twirled away to rejoin the undulating circle and began chanting with renewed grief.

The potent smell was getting to me. I saw no one with drinks in their hands, even though Delores had invited me 'for a drink', and my sudden need was dire. I slipped past the swirl of zombies, headed down a long hallway hung with sagging, nicotine darkened tapestries, woven versions of grotesque Goya paintings. Finally I reached a large kitchen lined with glass-fronted cabinets and Arabic tiles, a large orchid flower design on its mosaic floor. Just inside the door stood a tall blue and white porcelain birdcage, the type made by Delft I had seen in a museum, except this one was filled with liquor bottles. Dusty with age, they must be leftovers from Delores' father, Franco's general, I figured, since her friends plainly preferred kicks from a source more spatial than alcohol. I unfastened the birdcage door and extracted a bottle, which I almost dropped when I read its darkened label. 'Mendeleyev ВОДКА, 1902', it said beneath an engraved two-headed eagle with one crown, gold wings spread. Since this cache had been ignored for years, I told myself, Delores and Peter wouldn't miss one bottle. No doubt they would even suggest that I put it to good use. I admit to blatant thievery, but with my nostrils smarting from that sweet-and-sour stench in the other room, it seemed excusable – of which I was easily convinced.

I broke the imperial seal and selected a grease-filmed cut-glass tumbler from a shelf. I filled it with the clear liquid. Pre-revolution vodka! I breathed with appropriate awe, and sampled it. How did it taste? Instant ermine! Bottled monarchy! Long live the Tsar!

Finding ВОДКА a neat antidote for the pervading odour, I gulped down more of the Russian joy. I felt inspired to toss the empty glass over my shoulder, but didn't, so that I could refill it, and savoured every drop of the second glass. The vodka's instant firepower emboldened me to investigate the scene of action. I must find out what the hell is going on. *En garde!*

But on the way – zap! I was clobbered by a bolt of fission straight from Chernobyl. Hooray for ВОДКА! I reeled into the main room, and found myself at once entangled in the arms of swirling, chanting robots. The spooky cartwheel spun to the flute *fortissimo*, my head spun faster. I was swaying towards the wooden box. It had no lid. I looked inside. I was face to face with a rotting corpse.

Dead flowers and decaying tulle surrounded the body, its neck black, its leathery face fallen into crevices of the skull. Protruding teeth were locked in perpetual hilarity, black eye holes stared, amused by my horror. I broke free from the circle and bolted for the nearest door.

Back stairs led down to a garden. I had barely cleared the last step when my ВОДКА did a reverse flow. The evening had grown dark, nobody witnessed my proletarian dispersal of royal elixir into the shrubbery. Ah, but I was not alone. A man in a grease-spotted T-shirt and with pony-tailed blond hair, appeared from beyond the swimming pool. He fumbled with a tangle of rope, and since his own voice floated in juice, he was uncritical of my up-chuck disgrace He asked, 'Did you come to help, brother?'

'Help do what?' I answered, noting the garden's high wall, and beyond it the vague outline of my bathroom window.

'You got a car, like, big enough to haul a casket?'

'You plan to take that upstairs body someplace?' I moved towards the wall.

'Don't you know?' he answered with yet another question.

'I'm a friend of Delores, from out of town. Clue me in.'

'Sounds like way out of town, brother,' he replied, with football fluency. 'Yesterday the Alciguna town hall ordered Delores to remove Veronica's body, like, from her hillside grave, you know, because the town is going to enlarge its cemetery. Our soul sister, Veronica, said on her deathbed that she didn't want to be stuffed, like, into one of those cement drawers, you know, but the nearest actual graveyard is in, like, Malaga. After we finish celebrating her resurrection, we'll take her there. Around midnight, you know, like when there's less traffic on the coast road. You going with us, brother?'

'Must look after a sick friend,' I told him. 'Lives next door.' He did not look up from untangling his rope when I clambered up the lumpy stone wall and slid over its top. After a short drop, I staggered the few feet to my front door, hoping, praying, that Henry would not be there. His inevitable questions about the party would set off another eruption of royal booze, I was certain. Inside, my house slowly revolved and the floor took on an alcoholic tilt, even in the dark. Having experienced the probable cause of the fall of imperial Russia, I tumbled into my humble bed, fully clothed.

Later, I'm not sure how much later, insistent pounding on the front door awakened me. Damn! It would not be ignored, no matter how many pillows I stacked over my head. Thus forced to lift the *rustico* door latch, I stood back when Henry flounced in, hopped a victory dance and trumpeted, 'By George, we've got them! Quick! Telephone the *Guardia*. Tell them we've caught the buggers with the goods! A whole box full of child pornography. Has to be the real thing, because its being carried by an army of perverts wearing beads and earrings. And at midnight! They're so obviously guilty, it's laughable.'

'Hey, slow down. How do you know what's in the box?' Then I froze. 'BOX?' I shouted. 'Henry, leave that box alone. It's...'

Henry stormed back, 'Are you loco? The prize that's eluded us for months? Hurry! The phone! I'll go and keep the paedophiles covered until the *Guardia* nabs the lot of them! Make haste, dear boy.' He charged off like a cheetah closing in on a doomed gnu.

'Wait! Wait!' I warned, as he disappeared into the dark street. Following on the run, I rounded the corner and the scene halted me. The wooden box was resting on the pavement in the dim light of Casa Grande's front window. Seedy images were gathered around it, rumbling heated concern. I ducked into a recessed doorway and listened to the protests and mounting confusion. 'She won't fit into my car!' several voices declared.

'Nor mine!'

'Nor mine!'

'We can tie her, like, on top of my VW,' said the man I had left untangling rope in the back garden. 'It's parked on the next street, like. I'll go fetch it.' The men agreed and dispersed towards their vehicles, followed by their women in multi-culture dress, with a few barefoot children wearing long, grimy smocks. The box was momentarily left alone in front of Casa Grande.

Suddenly Henry darted from a shadow. He pounced

on the box, tearing rotten boards from its top. From the doorway I warned fiercely, 'Henry! Don't do it! Henry! No!'

Heaven inspired and purpose driven, he yanked open the box and poked vigorously through the dead flowers and rotten tulle. Ignoring the smell, he peered down to inspect what he had discovered. Old filmmakers liked to shock by depicting a sudden disappearance: a person is there, and then he isn't. That was Henry. I didn't see his face, nor could I describe his reaction. He simply vanished into the night air. I backed into the shadowed doorway and watched an ancient VW clatter up the street. Men gathered to lift the wooden box onto its top and secure it with rope supplied by the driver. They didn't bother to replace the boards Henry had pulled from its top, leaving the box's contents exposed to the stars. The mourners returned to their cars, motors hacked to life, and the cortège set off towards the coast. When the little old VW's brakes proved near helpless to impede its wild career down the mountain road, I wished it well. Wind picked at the open box, whipping its lighter contents into the air. I imagined a sombre trail of pale flowers and shreds of tulle following Veronica all the way to her Malaga grave, her final fix.

I checked the street, right and left. No one was in sight; it appeared that Henry and I were the only witnesses to the evening's funereal event. Yet, dollar to a doughnut, for weeks to come it would be topic number one, in various versions, at the post office, Bar Suerte and Trivial Pursuit.

Returning home on my dark, quiet street, I figured Casa Grande was now a spent cause and could be struck off Henry's list of suspected distribution points of pornography. I also knew that tonight's face-to-face contact with a dead hippie would not deter him from manning his missional barricades tomorrow morning. Tomorrow I would also learn that I had written off Casa Grande too soon. Much too soon.

Same as I had foolishly dismissed that vague but insistent word, 'Developers'.

16

In California, the stock claim of wanna-be Hollywood actors is that they turned down the role that made Bruce Willis or Mel Gibson a star because the gay director demanded 'compensation'. His counterpart on the East Coast is the playboy whose yacht in Chesapeake Bay never quite sails into port. These arch phoneys have musician brothers all over the globe – including Alciguna.

Breathing in gasps after her climb up the stairs to my terrace on Saturday evening, Olympia puffed her way to the drinks trolley, mixed a vodka-tonic, settled into a chair and overrode her cigarette rattle with praise for Peter. I wondered where this opening gambit would lead, compliments not being her forte. She announced, 'Peter is very talented, you know, could have been a famous composer. Wrote a song that made millions, but...'

'Let me guess,' I helped, and repeated the old cliché. 'His song was plagiarized by a crooked agent and Peter didn't get a penny for it. Right?'

Olympia blinked at my worldly knowledge and turned back to view what had reminded her of Peter. 'That new construction,' she said, pointing ominously towards Casa Grande, 'Oh dear, oh dear.'

I followed her gaze, looked back at my own construction. After the faith healer had taken his flute playing to the coast, where he opened a breast cancer surgery, I installed an awning over the flat roof of part of my house. It converted into a quiet, pleasant terrace with a terrific view, perfect for lunch and drinks. Olympia had become a Saturday evening regular, for vodka-tonics before our dinner together. Her fund of adventures appeared endless; her tales of early Alciguna, habit-forming. Except tonight, her story was growing too pregnant for comfort. The framework taking shape on the roof of Casa Grande, just across the garden from mine, seemed to intrigue her. She couldn't wait to describe its wonders.

'Delores is building it in order to prevent another theft of Peter's talent.' She pointed again. 'That's to be his private recording studio.'

I mixed myself a hefty vodka-tonic and studied the six new Roman columns supporting a terracotta roof. No walls. I pointed out, 'Can't be. A recording studio must be insulated from outside sounds.'

As usual, Olympia knew it all. 'The most common complaint in Spain is about excessive noise. Yet, this part of town has always been eerily quiet, which will allow Peter to record in the open with no sound contamination.' She poured herself another drink, added an ice cube, swirled it and took a protracted sip. 'Such being the case, his noise will make this terrace unbearable.'

'No it won't!' I exploded. 'I'll call in the law!'

Olympia reached for a cigarette, leaned back and related more unpleasant Spanish facts. 'The *Guardia Civil* respond only to physical violence, which sound is not, no matter how loud it is. And the local police are still too traumatized by the del Busto name to interfere with any disturbances in Delores's house.'

Grasping for straws, I bubbled, 'Maybe Peter will compose tuneful melodies that we will enjoy as background music.'

Olympia gave a negative laugh. 'I hate to disillusion you, Roberto, but today I saw a lorry parked in front of Casa Grande. Its crew was unloading reams of cables and piles of serious looking electronic noisemakers. Background music? C'mon, baby, light my fire.'

Our Saturday night dinner proved a glum affair, with me matching Olympia drink for drink.

On Monday, I delivered my weekly assignment of artwork to Malaga. On Tuesday morning, I settled at my drawing board to study the new assignment. My coffee suddenly leapt from its cup. A blast of temple bells, at least half a million decibels of them, shook my house to its foundations. Electronic notes roared up and down the scale as if accompanying planets in cosmic acrobatics. Windows flew open, my porous roof rattled ominously. I charged up to my terrace, ears pinned to my skull, to find glasses bouncing on the tabletop, the awning flapping. And that was only the lightning. When thunder struck, the whole town jounced a seismic rumba. Chickens squawked and scurried for cover, dogs scratched their ears and howled, villagers poured into the streets, scanning the heavens for Gabriel. I looked across the garden at the rooftop studio and saw Peter composing on a small electronic keyboard, lost in creative rapture. All this havoc created by one man? I thought. Heaven help us when he starts recording 'loud stuff' with a whole nuclear band!

I raced to Casa Grande, grabbed the heavy brass doorknocker and banged it furiously. Even so, no one heard me. I dashed for the town hall. On my way, I met Enrique, a neighbour. 'We must form a committee and go to the mayor,' I shouted, hoping he could hear me over Peter's one-man blitz.

Enrique's shrugged response verified Olympia's warning. 'I agree, Roberto, but there is nothing we can do. Delores is the daughter of General del Busto and no one dares cross her.'

In the town hall, I found Josefa shuffling tax billings, trying to ignore the volcanic notes clacking her closed windows. She led me to Mayor Prudencio's office, and remained to translate. Sitting at his desk, before him a marble penholder and three silver framed photographs of his wife and two children, he looked up over a *SUR* newspaper and frowned. '*Si!*'

'The noise...' I started to say.

'*Extranjeros!*' he barked. 'Foreigners! Forever fermenting trouble, then they expect the mayor to step in and remedy it. Now this disturbance; you create it, you damn well curb it, before I raise all your taxes. *Extranjeros!*' he repeated, which Josefa didn't bother to translate. He returned to his reading. I noted the newspaper article I had interrupted concerned the influx of foreigners buying property in White Villages. 'And Still They Come!' it read.

For the first time in my life, I realized the pitfalls of being classified a minority. Jan the Dutchman, Gloria the Australian, Maggie Potter the botanist, Peter the perpetual stud, Paul the ageing stud, Olympia the millionairess, and me, Joe Blow; all lumped together in one category. If one *extranjero* ruffles the feathers of authority, we all feel the eagle's peck.

The following week's sonic barrier was shattered repeatedly. New 'musicians' arrived daily to add heavy metal to the fury. When Olympia breezed in as usual on Saturday evening, I led her up to my terrace that now shook, rattled and rolled under sustained aural assault. Earlier in the afternoon, Peter had discovered Big Ben. Now he was composing the rhapsodic equivalent of a jumbo jet take-off. Olympia crinkled her eyes and assumed her combative look. Unable to hear her words, I tried to read her lips, which muttered some sort of edict. 'I'll not have it,' I think she pronounced, 'I work all week building my house, then this no-talent yobbo ruins my only relaxation, my weekly vodka-tonics on this terrace. Well, we'll see about that, Mr Permanent Hard-On!'

Olympia and I left my house under a hail of pizzicato

bomblets. Against all odds we enjoyed our dinner, for Red de Seguridad stood on the far side of town from the Casa Grande rooftop recording studio, and only the occasional polytonal scale ricocheted over our heads.

I heard the knock on my front door early on Monday morning because Peter sleeps late, and hadn't yet started composing. Jesús Maria, Olympia's second in command, had parked a truckload of bulky black boxes in front of my house. He informed officiously, '*Señora* Olympia says these go on your terrace.' He and two helpers shoved past me and began transporting crates through the reception hall, across the patio and up the stairs to my roof.

Olympia arrived, wheezing from too many smokes. 'I know what I'm doing,' was adequate explanation for her early morning invasion. 'Do these boxes contain live ammunition?' I asked, guardedly optimistic. She headed for the kitchen, poured herself a straight vodka and waited for me to follow, if I wanted to be clued in. This had better be good, I thought, and joined her. She turned windbag after her first swallow, suggesting something big was afoot.

'When I lived in the Congo,' she began, as enchanting as a panting Hans Andersen, 'my husband, my second, I think, owned a plush hunting lodge in the bush. Sometimes I accompanied him there on weekends, but I never went on safari with him. Oh no, back then when I hunted big game, trousers, not tiger skins, were my trophies. Once my husband forgot to hire a guard when he went on safari, I was left alone at the lodge. Well, that night there was a celebration in the surrounding jungle, which seemed to require an awful lot of drums. I assumed that the natives were having some juicy enemy for dinner or –

dear, oh dear! *Me?* Drums! Drums! Boom! Boom! The tempo grew more ominous as the night thundered on. The beat was driving them into a mindless frenzy, and as you can well imagine, that just wouldn't do.'

'Being alone, how could you prevent it?' I asked, from the edge of my chair.

'Wagner,' she said, simply.

I had to confess. 'You've lost me.'

'My husband had installed in the lodge one of the early hi-fi contraptions, because he always dined black tie, classical music and candlelight, insisting on the niceties of culture whether it be in Kinshasa, Ulan Bator or Mayfair. So this night I pushed his big speakers beside the open windows, turned up the generator and released Wagner's opera, *Die Walkure*,' full volume. Did you know that Wagner makes palm trees abort? There was a sudden deluge of green coconuts.'

'How did the natives react to Wagner?'

She reached for a cigarette. 'Their drums went silent. And they remained silent. Next day my husband learned from his dragoman that the previous night's sacrificial offering of chicken blood had been interrupted in mid-ceremony by some angry gods that screeched powerful curses at them. As a result, they stoned their witch doctor to death and sold the headless chickens to a Mercedes-Benz salesman.'

'Ah, so,' I said. 'Now we're going to call in angry gods to put a curse on Peter, right? My only fear is that I might suffer the fate of the witch doctor.'

Olympia was annoyed that I guessed her plan so early, but carried on. 'Right, then, smart-ass. The black boxes that Jesús Maria brought are sound-blasters borrowed from one of his disco friends. Fight fire with sauce for the gander, or some such folk wisdom.'

'Oh, no!' I protested. 'That would devastate my

neighbours. They've suffered enough from us foreigners, without more pandemonium.'

'Come off it,' Olympia scoffed. 'You know that short, sharp punishment is preferable to hanging by one ball.' I had to agree.

Jesús Maria learned of a recording session scheduled for Wednesday morning, so Olympia ordered him into quick action. He arrived on my terrace soon after dawn and hastily strung cables between turntable, pre-amplifiers, amplifiers, speakers, woofers, tweeters and various other electronic gadgets I couldn't identify. He aimed the monumental speakers with cannon-range precision and stationed himself behind a fortress of knobs, switches and gauges, his fingers twitching with anticipation. I figured either Olympia had paid him well, or he held some long-standing grudge against Peter that needed settling. Olympia arrived, settled beside the drinks trolley, and fortified herself for Armageddon.

At mid-morning we saw Peter's band troop onto his rooftop-recording studio, armed with weird-shaped stringed instruments, batteries of drums and a formidable phalanx of brass. A truckload of recording equipment was heaved into position and plugged in. Six performers in grunge uniform settled around Peter's keyboard command centre, which was bolted into place like a howitzer. Sound meters measured instrumental boom and crash as if fine-tuning thunderclaps. Technicians positioned microphones like radiation detectors for an atomic bomb blast.

At last satisfied with the recording arrangements, Peter stood from his electric console and gazed approval at the spike-haired ensemble that sat or stood poised like an artillery squadron awaiting an assault order. He assumed the vaulted authority of a tank commander, one hand on the keyboard, the other rising slowly. Those villagers who could watch, and I, held our collective breath.

Peter slashed the air to establish downbeat and bawled, 'A one, and a two, and a – go for it, mates!'

'HOYA TAHOYA! HOYA TAHOYA!' Jesús Maria launched his pre-emptive strike, the same Brunnhilde that Olympia had commissioned to bombard the Congo, the same singing warrior maiden who later dispersed musical mayhem in the film *Apocalypse Now*.

The cyclonic discord from Casa Grande groaned to silence like a hundred punctured bagpipes. Peter's musicians lowered their instruments and stamped across the rooftop to glare in Brunnhilde's direction, disbelieving that anyone could have out-thundered them. Yet, her full-throttle jet across the sky had swamped their recording equipment, no contest. The punk group jeered 'Pagan!' 'Degenerate!' 'Barbarian!' until Peter ordered them back into position, saw that the recording tapes were untangled and rethreaded, once again assumed his directorial stance and chopped the air like an aggressive duellist.

'A one, and a two, and a –'
'HOYA TAHOYA! HOYA TAHOYA!'

After their fifth failed attempt to override Brunnhilde's heavenly romp, Peter's musicians, finding themselves stereophonically vanquished, packed their equipment and decamped in sullied confusion. For the hell of it, Jesús Maria accompanied their retreat with a Wagner victory march, full mega-decibel. Then silence. I looked for Olympia, expecting to find her stationed on the barricades, waving a flag, singing 'La Marseillaise'. She had not witnessed her triumph. Certain of what the outcome would be, she had left to take command of another discord; her architect's refusal to tackle her fourth redesign of her dream house.

After a week, with no further recording sessions attempted, Peter seemed safely demoralized into silence and Jesús Maria packed up his sound arsenal and returned it to the disco from whence it came. Townspeople greeted me on the street with smiles and slaps on the back – apparently Olympia and I had proven ourselves good *extranjeros*. She dismissed all praise with, 'Oh, pooh. It was Wagner that won the day. Those young dudes didn't stand a chance against that old rock daddy of them all.'

She never bragged about her second triumph over the natives, accepting it simply as how things should be: Alciguna the Quiet, Alciguna the Tranquil. We resumed our Saturday evening drinks on my quiet terrace, and I never objected to the amount of vodka she drank after that.

Only the Nurembergs complained. Although their house was outside Alciguna, they had heard our Wagner and at the next Trivial Pursuit Night came near to demanding that he be played on a regular basis.

17

Henry joined me and ordered coffee at Bar Suerte, his mind involved elsewhere. 'Saw Winthrop Harvey at the post office,' he mumbled absently. 'He wonders why you haven't visited him and his wife. They both have interesting backgrounds, big, expensive house...'

I sensed that Henry had more urgent cards up his sleeve and asked that he show his hand. He moved closer, his conspirator tone reserved for crises. 'A local schoolgirl was found with a snapshot of explicit sex involving children. Questioned by the police, she said only that Alejandra had given it to her. I confronted the old crone, who, I might have known, didn't know what I was talking about. If, indeed, she did give the child the snapshot, she is not sane enough to remember where she got it.'

'So you've reached another dead end.'

'Alejandra might lead us to –' Henry paused, a light bulb flashing above his head. 'Oh, ho! Alejandra runs errands for the Harveys, same as Olympia. I've already got Olympia under surveillance, so...'

Putting two and two together revealed conspiracy. 'I am to visit the Harveys, "to get acquainted". With you along, right?'

He didn't bother to deny it. 'Winthrop Harvey comes from a Canadian banking family, Ilka is Hungarian. The idle rich. Both are world-weary enough to be intrigued by something different, something illegal. Interested?'

Ignoring the *café con leche* that the waiter served him, Henry didn't wait for an answer. 'Ilka comes from

Hungarian landowners, very wealthy until the communists confiscated everything – they thought. Before the communist Prime Minister Rakosi took power, her family had rushed paper assets abroad. When Rakosi learned this, her father was imprisoned and soon died under 'unexplained circumstances'. The mother fled with Ilka and her sister to live in a fashionable world of grand hotels and spas. The daughters grew up associating only with the wealthy and the famous. Exclusive schools in Switzerland, and so on. Get the picture?'

Having learned not to swallow Henry's stories with one gulp, I asked, 'Then why is she living in this isolated village a million miles from café society?'

Henry stirred his tepid coffee. 'She married into an ancient-name family in France, and had three daughters before discovering that her husband was a notorious womanizer. After a quick divorce she met Winthrop Harvey, an artist, and fell in love as only Hungarian women can. They now live in Alciguna, for its inspirational scenery.'

'Wait,' I said. 'You say he's an artist, yet they have a big, expensive house? Unless he's a Picasso, that's an oxymoron, Henry.'

'The Harveys don't need to worry where their next hundred thousand comes from, I assure you. Winthrop was living in Paris when he turned twenty-one and inherited a million Canadian dollars. A tall, young, good-looking Canadian flashing all those dollars, you can imagine the attention, the adulation. During all this, he fell under the spell of Bohemia and chose the artist's life. This flew in the face of his banker father's plans, who showed his disapproval by severing Winthrop's income. The million dollars didn't last long, but Winthrop had a doting grandmother in Italy who kept him flush, so he went on to study art under some of the leading names of the day, even Braque and Brancusi.'

Again, I questioned Henry's extravagant briefing. 'If he's that good, why haven't I heard of him?'

Henry turned pensive over his coffee. 'Winthrop has great talent, drive and passion, and yet...'

'His muse deserted him?'

'He hasn't suffered.' Henry took a sip of coffee, frowned, and pushed it aside. 'Life was handed to him on a silver tray. He's never experienced that primeval struggle for survival, the requirement that ignites genius...'

'Whoa, Henry!' I raised my hands as a shield. 'Don't wax poetic on me. OK, I'm convinced, the Harveys sound worth a visit. That is, if you promise to keep your snooping to a minimum.'

He cleared his throat to delay explaining, 'There's one thing you should know. Mention anyone of note, Ilka claims to know him. This is to warn you that she probably does.'

'No problem,' I assured him. 'I can dredge up some famous names of my own. Did you know that I once shook hands with Boy George?'

'Act your age,' Henry said under his breath, and stood.

Mid-afternoon, Henry pushed the buzzer beside a blue door that distinguished the Harvey house from its whitewashed neighbours on a hillside street overlooking the town and valley. There was no response.

'We should have telephoned first,' I told him. 'You know it's rude to arrive this way, unannounced. I doubt if they'll see us.' He pushed the button again.

The door speaker clacked an irate female voice. 'Yes? Who the hell is it?'

'Henry. Henry Perry-Smith. I've brought Mr Brooks. I thought you...'

'Go away!' the speaker rasped. A moment later it added,

'But come back in half an hour. I'm just finishing my bath.'

Thirty minutes later the door opened at the first push of the buzzer and a maid escorted us up a staircase of classic Moroccan tiles, into a bright room whose large windows framed the spectacular view below. Hand-woven white curtains gave the terracotta tinted walls a cool spaciousness; a host of small bronze statues stood on shelves, stands and in crannies. Mammoth white lounge chairs were clustered around glass-top coffee tables that held more statues, mostly Balinese girls squirming in dance poses. Ilka Harvey was resting on one of the chairs, beside a giant vase of flowers that heightened the radiance of her round face, flushed from her bath. Skin glowing with a hint of gold, she was plump to the degree that most Hungarian men prefer. Her moist hair was pearly, with a Zsa Zsa Gabor wave that fell across her brow; a baby-doll smile revealed perfect white teeth. Henry introduced us and she raised her hand. I accepted my continental duty and kissed it, aware that Henry was already eyeing the walls for hidden wiring.

Ilka's voice was dark, smooth Tokay. Had Henry not told me of her Magyar background, I would have placed her accent as top-drawer English. I noticed her lips were slightly pouty. 'You should have rung first,' she scolded. 'I would have prepared small eats.' Instead, she graciously offered coffee, tea, gin and tonic, vodka, whatever.

'Thank you, no, we just had coffee,' Henry answered for both of us, adding, 'Is Winthrop about? Robert would like to see some of his bigger projects ... his studio...'

One step further, I thought, and I'll belt you one, Henry.

Ilka answered, 'Winthrop is working. He's doing a child's figure in clay before having it cast in bronze.'

Henry's ears went radar. He sucked in his breath. 'He's doing a child?'

'Yes,' Ilka said, evincing soft pleasure. 'A beautiful little girl. Winthrop has been commissioned to do her by a very dear friend of mine, Justine Valderic.' She turned to me. 'You've seen her on television? Star reporter for CNN?'

'Of course,' I said, remembering Henry's warning of Ilka's name-dropping. 'Is it her daughter?'

'No,' she smiled, 'it's the daughter of a very dear friend of mine, the world famous economist, Gennadi Melikov, Russian Commercial Attaché to the Court of St James, London. I met him at a birthday party given by the Duchess of Kent for Luci Pavarotti.'

Henry was near speechless. 'R-Russian, did you say?' He glanced at me, 'Mafia' flashing in his eyes. 'While you two talk, I'll go to the loo. Don't bother, Ilka, I know where it is.' He left for the bathroom, but veered towards the stairs leading to where I imagined Winthrop's studio to be.

I tried to distract Ilka. 'Wow. The Duchess of Kent? Luciano Pavarotti? Too much!' From the corner of my eye, I watched Henry easing himself down the stairs. I shuddered.

Ilka explained, 'I met Luci in London at the Plaza Roma, where I stay as their guest. Its owners are related to a very dear friend of mine, Omar Patan, who owns the largest chain of hotels in the Middle East. We attended the same school in Geneva, you see.' Our conversation progressed pleasantly until we heard a sudden ruckus below stairs, like the bellowing of an angry animal. Ilka and I rushed to peer down the stairwell, expecting flames or a flood or at least escaping gas. It was Henry being roughly shoved upstairs, pop-eyed from being throttled by a bear of a man shouting indecipherable gibberish.

'Gennadi!' Ilka shrieked. 'That man is a very dear friend of mine. Let him go immediately!'

Gennadi's enormous, bristling black eyebrows didn't relent. He switched from Russian ranting to English. 'This creep is perwert! I find him spying on my sweet little Tatiana while she is posing for Winthrop to do her sculpture!'

He gave Henry's shirt collar a vengeful twist. 'You like leetle girls, ha? You get off your rocks by spying on them weeth no clothes on? You are peed-file, ha?'

Ilka pulled at the Russian hand that was choking Henry. 'I will vouch for this man, Gennadi,' she calmed. 'I'm sure he has a perfectly plausible explanation.'

Gennadi relaxed his grip, allowing Henry to breathe and rub his neck to re-start the circulation. His excuse grated in his throat like gravel. 'I wanted to see how Winthrop works with clay. I hid behind a column so as not to distract him.'

Gennadi scowled and gestured at me. 'He is perwert, too?'

Ilka smiled soothingly. 'Gennadi, may I present Robert Brooks? He is a commercial artist and a very dear friend of mine.'

Gennadi merely glanced in my direction as she led him to a chair and directed, 'Sit! I'll pour you a Stolichnaya, your favourite vodka.'

'Not my favourite,' he growled. 'But is the only brand worthy of name wodka in the West. Ha! Except American embassies. They keep biggest selection of Russian wodka in the world. They have discover the power of our national drink. Give client wodka, he will endorse any document. Enough wodka, a captive will confess any crime. Wodka is most valuable tool in world's diplomatic cubicles. Wodka is...'

'Does the Russian Mafia employ it as well?' Henry asked, recovered enough to act the fool.

Gennadi threw him a furious glare, tossed down his

tumbler of Stolichnaya with three hydraulic gulps, wiped his mouth with the back of his hand and spoke only to Ilka. 'I haven't had chance to tell you that the American ambassador sends to you his regards. Also Duchess of Kent and Elizabeth Taylor send their love. Dame Judi Dench says she will visit you soon, but first I must warn her about perwerts you have in Alciguna.' He shambled towards the stairs, staring icily at me from under heavy, free-fall black eyebrows. Words not needed to express his loathing; guilt by association. I thanked Ilka for her hospitality and stood to leave. Henry followed. Saying our good-byes, Ilka extended a dinner invitation to me, which I accepted. She did not invite Henry for a return visit.

Henry headed down the street, I took the opposite direction. He didn't notice, so engrossed was he in sorting out and evaluating, I imagined, the afternoon's discoveries. His conclusion? The Russian Mafia, plus a little girl being sculpted in the nude – an evocative combination. Poor Henry, always on the roll. Yet, I shouldn't complain, for without him, I might not have met the Harveys. He was right about Ilka dropping names, although she obviously knew on intimate terms the famous people whose names she so casually scattered. Her dinner party should be amusing, even exciting. Recalling East End irreverence, I mused, who knows, I might even bump into Lizzy Windsor there.

18

Paul Jones-Jones's anecdotes about his past profession in Hong Kong (stocks and bonds) did not prevent him from being entertaining, on occasion. Of fleshy build, with a flushed round face and grey fuzzed scalp, his distinguishing feature was the rich crop of hair that hung from his pear-shaped nose. The nose hairs merged with his salt and pepper moustache, a drooping mass that snagged a toll of food at each bite. Paul was a professional bachelor, despite an ex-wife and six daughters. From Olympia I learned that he was the bane of housewives, always appearing at the moment lunch or dinner reached the table. His rare idea of paying back was to invite choice friends to his cramped living room for hours of Haydn's *Creation*, or Bach's *St Matthew Passion*, CDs screeching full volume through miniscule speakers, mice tortured to roar. He served wine from pre-opened bottles, its quality seldom matching the fancy labels. And yet, being a treasury of local history embellished with colourful scandal, he was seldom missing from the better dinner parties.

Paul proved one of the few in town who could calm Olga Campbell, a perennial guest perhaps owing to her famous bank account. During her diatribes bemoaning Alciguna's fate, when she invariably railed against the next great peril, donkey rides, he shook his head and advised with astute neutrality, 'Let's wait and see what the future holds.'

'Or what it holds for thee,' she usually shot back.

'Historically, a stockbroker's top priority is the bottom line, a base standard, indeed.' Having had the last word, Olga usually sat back to allow Paul to sing for his supper; a boom or bust economy prediction, or juicy revelations about the mayor's newest mistress. Paul was an oracle, Paul was a barrel of laughs.

I had seen him walking on the street with a woman, next month he would be escorting a different one. During dinner the next Saturday night, Olympia avoided my query about Paul's changing parade of female companions and instead described digging her new swimming pool into a mountainside of pure granite. Finally she grimaced and answered, 'He runs adverts in the "lonely hearts" columns of British publications. Such as, "Sensuous widower of means, early sixties, to share dream casa in Southern Spain with attractive lady of taste".'

Recalling the number of women I had seen on his arm, I reminded her, 'Well, obviously, his bait snags 'em.'

She crackled over a hefty swig of vodka-tonic, 'Obviously, it's a disgrace. I blush that some of my gender, otherwise intelligent women, fall for his old wolf's mating call. They arrive in Alciguna all aquiver, expecting to be met by Don Juan who will whisk them to a bougainvillaea-draped cottage. Instead, they find Colonel Blimp panting to rush them to bed in his dinky little walk-up.'

'Oh, boy,' I laughed. 'I have trouble picturing Paul Jones-Jones as a Latin lover. Still, I admire his perseverance, chasing females at his age.'

Olympia affected compassion, in her way. 'Poor wretches. They seldom endure more than two weeks of him before fleeing back to the British Isles.'

Absorbed in Olympia's love and romance narrative, I was taken by surprise when Winthrop Harvey approached our table and tapped me on the shoulder. He told us that we were invited to La Española for dinner on Thursday night. 'Paul Jones-Jones is going to announce wedding plans.' He left without further comment.

'Speak of the devil!' Olympia choked on her vodka and took another swallow to quell a fit of coughing. 'Wedding plans? Paul Jones-Jones? Never! Not once since his wife divorced him has any affair reached that point of no return. Invited to dinner? I assure you, it will be Dutch. Paul never pays. He is not known as *El Avaro*, the miser, for nothing.' Ah, but Paul did pay, and at a hefty interest rate.

La Española, where I lodged on my first visit to Alciguna, had over the years become an institution. Olympia said that its history reached back three hundred years, when it was a day's horseback or carriage ride from Gibraltar during Spain's intermittent periods of peace with Britain. This stopping-off place provisioned traffic from Gibraltar through to Madrid and points north. Until recently La Española had possessed an ancient reception desk register, with names and comments such as, 'A welcome respite after a perilous mountain ride from Ronda', or 'Never have I encountered such lumpy beds, I should have slept better on straw in the stables'. Unfortunately, the register had been confiscated by the government as 'of historical interest', with only faded photocopies now available to interested guests.

Since before the Civil War, one family, which included a large proportion of the town's population, had owned La Española, whose kitchen was Mecca. It resounded with laughter and the clink of wine glasses, a far jollier place than the public dining room, where bare ceiling lights cast a mantle of gloom over the painted fake marble walls, giving the effect of dining in a funeral parlour.

Its manageress, miniscule Camelia, all dimpled smile

and dyed red hair, was a sweetheart. She rose on tiptoe to kiss the cheek of each of our party as we entered, except Manfred and Ilsa Nuremberg, who ignored her greeting. She directed us to the long table bright with white napery, gleaming cutlery and upside-down goblets for wine and water. A bottle of wine and a vase with one rose stood between each four place settings.

Paul's chosen guests speculated in hushed tones about his upcoming announcement as they settled around the table. Triumph flashed in his eyes when he introduced his new lady friend, Sarah MacDonald, without further comment. Sarah's face, bonny enough, appeared long under the harsh glare of the overhead lights. She was slightly built, with reddish blonde hair pulled back and tied with a black ribbon. Her blue eyes were downcast, as if acknowledging that she knew everyone was wondering how she could have been duped by this overripe Romeo. She ignored Paul's hand stroking her shoulder. Her face remained passive until waitresses righted our glasses and filled them with red wine. Foregoing ceremony, Sarah seized hers and took a long drink, then another. Only then did she offer a tepid smile in recognition of the well-wishers beaming at her. Waitresses placed large bowls of mixed green salad along the table, customary, except that these were topped with red radishes arranged in the shapes of hearts, and Camelia stood in the kitchen doorway to receive compliments for her romantic gesture. Venison was served with the inevitable chips, and bowls of cooked vegetables in help-yourself fashion. Sarah barely sniffed at the venison, nibbled at the chips, refilled her glass repeatedly and quaffed her wine in silence.

The dinner hummed, with occasional shrill laughter from Clara Cornwallis. According to Olympia, Paul had once pinched Clara's bottom during a Anglican church service, since then she claimed that she couldn't stand the sight of him. Yet he had invited her, and she had come. She was born in Kenya, her first husband died from a fall from a tree house, her second was killed by the Mau-Mau. Now in her sixties, she lived with an eighty-year old Sicilian whom she called her toy-boy. She often acknowledged, with regal aloofness, that she had been a Tsarina in a previous incarnation.

No one looked directly at Sarah, yet each of us was aware of the amount of wine coursing down her Caledonian throat. Dinner ended, plates were removed, Camelia served a cream pudding with coffee, and free brandy to those who wanted it. Manfred Nuremberg requested that she leave the bottle on the table. Winthrop Harvey rose to his feet, the waitresses paused and stood by with an air of expectation. The table's buzz subsided when he tapped a wine bottle with his spoon, and spoke through a broad Canadian grin. 'We all know why we're here, so I'll make it short and sweet. Paul Jones-Jones wishes me to announce that he is engaged to be married.' Before anyone could respond, he sighed a theatrical, 'Thank God. At long last.'

Paul rose to acknowledge a few sanctions of 'Hear! Hear!' and applause hampered by the holding of raised wineglasses. He glowed with smugness. 'I agree with Winthrop, but it took a lot of sampling to find the right woman.' He fluttered his fingers towards Sarah, who failed to respond. He went on, 'Sarah and I invite you all to attend our wedding ceremony at her family kirk near Kelso, Scotland, and afterwards to the reception, which will be held in my love's manor house.'

Olympia nudged me under the table. 'Bingo!' she whispered.

'We will not have a honeymoon, *per se*,' Paul continued with weary regret, 'there's much work to be done on her large farm, her riding stables...'

'You must be joking!' Through Sarah's thick Scottish brogue, her meaning radiated lucidly over the table. 'I came to Alciguna with an open mind. If things worked out with Paul, fine, I am a lonely widow, I could use a man. If not – well, it hasn't. Firstly, he sent me a thirty-year-old snapshot of himself. Secondly, he expects to be pampered, the colonial *bwana*. A month's collection of dirty clothes was waiting in the bathtub, there is no washing machine. The fridge was mouldy. There is no dishwasher, and he expects gourmet meals from his dark, medieval kitchen. Thirdly, dear God, I won't go into what he demands in the bedroom.'

Olympia couldn't sit still. 'Paul! Don't tell me you can still get it up?'

'Marry you?' continued Sarah, administering the *coup de grâce* with style. 'Up a wee cat's anus, I will.'

Pretending not to stare, everyone pivoted to see Paul's reaction. The poor guy was pressed into his chair, gut sucked in as if receiving punches. His face had gone ashen, except for the varix blue of his nose. Surprisingly, I felt a tug of sympathy for the sad old clown, caught off guard by Sarah's drunken rejection being spewed before his friends.

He cringed as she expanded into ridicule. 'Paul intended to use me, but ork! I turned the tables on him! You see, for a long period I'd wanted to buy a house in southern Spain, so when I saw Paul's seductive advert in the love press, I seized on it. This way it cost me nothing, except for a few nights of his walrus rooting in bed. Meanwhile, I looked for a suitable property. Noo I have found it, and the search hasn't cost me a penny. So Paul can go fist himself.'

Half the stares around the table focused on Paul, the other half on Sarah MacDonald. Maggie Potter's enlarged eyes oscillated, following a one-sided tennis match. The atmosphere of the room turned frosty. Karen Bang lifted her empty coffee cup to her lips. Gus Bang looked relieved, happy that, for a change, he was not the butt of tonight's cabaret. Gloria the Australian looked confused. Ernst studied the middle distance, Doreen Baker smiled, pleased with the evening's entertainment. Ilka Harvey yawned, Winthrop studied the ceiling. Manfred Nuremberg, who had gulped a number of free brandies, rested his face in his cream pudding, as if rehearsing for a B-grade movie.

Clara Cornwallis was inspired by the unscheduled drama, and demanded a vodka refill. She raised her glass to the Scotswoman. 'Welcome to Alciguna, my dear. To you I offer congratulations! You have vindicated the long queue of ladies who were lured into Rasputin's lair, unfortunates who had no opportunity for revenge. Voz snoz ka pop!' Clara drained her glass and hurled it over her shoulder. Camelia smiled as she watched the 'glass' bounce off the wall. Familiar with Clara's periodic lapses into her former incarnation, she served only plastic tumblers to the Tsarina.

The party ended on an awkward note. No one was sure what to say. We had come to congratulate Paul and now wondered if condolences were in order. He remained bereft of words. Although we paid our own bills, we complimented him on a fine dinner, and angled across the dark foyer to the street. Outside, glistening cobbles reflected streetlights haloed by a fine mist.

I turned up my coat collar and hunched for a quick walk home, when, for some reason, I remembered Henry. He wasn't at the dinner. I waited for Olga Campbell to catch up, and said, 'Strange that Henry wasn't here tonight. I thought he was one of Paul's close friends.'

Olga stopped, dug her fists into her sides. 'You, of all people, don't know why Henry wasn't invited?' Her accusing tone worried me, suggesting that she had found an issue more dreadful than donkey rides. 'You mean you really don't know?' she repeated, affecting disbelief. I hadn't been fond of Olga Campbell, now I hated her.

'OK, I surrender. "Know" what?'

She stared into my face, I suspect to witness its shock. 'Henry Perry-Smith is a paedophile! Caught spying on a nude child that was modelling for Winthrop Harvey. The pervert should be run out of town. Think what this scandal could do to the town's genteel reputation!' She stalked on.

Stunned, I rushed to Henry's house, called him out of bed and repeated Olga's allegation. Trying not to sound too alarmed, I warned him, 'That story must be all over town. You must do something to squelch it.'

Henry wiped sleep from his eyes and listened to my report. 'Good!' he responded, self-assured as usual. 'We must be closer to the pornography operation than I suspected. Trying to destroy my credibility by charging me with the very crime they're perpetrating? A common ploy, dear boy. Most encouraging, this.'

I had intended to suggest to Henry that he cool it, now said to hell with it. If he lost no sleep over the accusation, regardless of its poisonous potential, then why should I? As I walked home the question persisted: should I distance myself from Henry? I knew that he was innocent of even the slightest moral lapse, yet the town didn't know that. Guilt by association was already tainting the air, and I didn't have the resilient spirit to turn troubles into bubbles, as did Henry.

But abandon Henry?

19

Early on Sunday morning I hunched in earnest over my drawing board, a full day's design work ahead. My Malaga boss had landed me with a promotional job for a bottled water company, not an easy task. What design or which colours would induce *Señora* to select one bottle of water over another? Since I was limited to four colours ... green mountains to give it bucolic freshness, blue sky for purity, a yellow sun adds cheeriness, black logo. OK, mountains, jagged but friendly...

My new doorbell rang. I already regretted having the damn thing installed, it had become Henry's favourite toy. It rang again. I washed the green from my brush and dried it, knowing full well who the caller would be.

I lifted the *rústico* door latch and Henry rushed in. 'Drop what you're doing,' he panted, as if winded from a long run. 'I've got proof that our Turk owns a high-speed motor-boat, capable of delivering contraband from Morocco.'

Last night I had seriously questioned Henry's campaign and was still undecided whether to follow him. Where would it lead? I said, 'I'll bet my Aunt Nellie that you have no proof that "our Turk" is involved in anything illegal. Besides, I'm on an assignment that must be delivered to Malaga tomorrow morning without fail. I must, repeat, must, finish it today.'

'But he's home now,' Henry urged, adding a hint of intrigue, 'Oh, you would be most impressed. Stable full of horses, racing cars, yacht, beautiful wife. My question is, did he bring his money from Turkey? That is doubtful, given the political climate there, so how does he finance his lavish lifestyle? Ah, ha! By distributing child pornography from Morocco?'

'Not interested,' I said. 'Now if you'll excuse me...'

As is known, Henry can be annoyingly persistent – and persuasive. He sort of hummed, 'I hear he's just returned from Istanbul with a cargo of females. Knowing his taste, I can well imagine their, ah, measurements. Belly dancers? Dear, oh dear.'

'Control yourself, Henry,' I told him. 'You say they're from Turkey? Veiled or unveiled?'

'If you can finish your art stuff by twelve o'clock, we can pay them a visit and find out. I'll call back then.'

I hoped the *Señora* buying water would forgive my suddenly peaked mountains. I rushed through my assignment and was tidying up the logo when Henry reappeared on the tick of twelve o'clock.

We took my car, as usual. While Henry spouted directions, he added a rundown on 'our Turk'. 'Yahya Barmakids,' he quoted, from either homework or gossip, I could never tell, 'born in Ankara, educated in Chicago, builder by trade. Turn left at the next junction.' Henry rattled on. 'Married. Plenty of money – from who knows where – his wife's from Latvia.'

'Strange combination,' I commented, following his command to take a precipitous track, crags on one side, a hundred-foot drop on the other.

'Strange, indeed,' Henry agreed. 'He's Muslim, she's Russian Orthodox. After that tree ahead, take a sharp left.'

The steep road climbed, we opened and closed two cattle gates and dodged a cluster of boulders to reach the modern stone, glass and wood house that protruded from the mountainside like a natural outcrop. Reflecting *Architectural Digest*, it was surrounded by boulders blotched with flowers and vines and its front balconies overlooked much of southern Spain. 'Ah, what a warm and welcoming scene,' Henry sighed, inducement for me to enjoy my spying tour.

Except that the house was guarded by a platoon of slick and shiny guard dogs that charged my car head-on. Henry and I cranked up the windows to prevent slavering teeth from savaging our throats. I sounded my horn, which drove the brutes into greater fury. They gnashed at the tyres and dug at the windows with hyena claws. It was clearly time to get the hell outta there.

Henry reached to grip the steering wheel. 'Hold on. There's someone coming from the house. Looks like our Turk.' A man stepped from the veranda and shouted a command. The dogs froze into obedience and slunk back behind the house, while continuing to study us, poised with suspicion. I cautiously lowered my window to greet the man lumbering towards us. He was wearing khaki shorts, chest exposed, hairy arms and legs. His feet, clad in sandals, were immense. A stack of unruly black hair topped his strong-featured face and a stubbly beard completed his Smokey the Bear image.

Before I could speak, Henry explained our intrusion. 'Yahya, meet my friend Robert Brooks, a newcomer to our town. He's an artist, and I suggested that he meet you, our outstanding builder in residence.'

Yahya's heavy lips stretched into a gigantic smile. Big, white teeth gleamed from his tanned face. Handshake rough and firm, he frowned. 'Alciguna? I'm not very popular there at the moment.' Offering no explanation, he raised a questioning eyebrow towards Henry. I watched his penetrating Turkish stare probe beyond Henry's eyes for clandestine motives. If Henry felt violated by the laser zap he didn't let on, being more anxious to get to more weighty subjects. 'Yes, I've heard about your little scrap with Ilka Harvey. By the way, Yahya, I hear you've got a new speedboat. Ever go to, oh, say, Morocco?'

Yahya's face lit up like a happy puppy. His broad hand fell playfully on Henry's shoulder. 'Hey, you like boats?' he beamed. 'I am on my way to my boat now. Come. I have a short trip to make, and I will take you and your friend on my boat. I will show you what my boat can do. Leave your car here. My four-by is ready to go.'

He faced the house and cupped his hands to his mouth to amplify, 'Dawn! I'm leaving for Marbella. Dawn! Do you hear me?'

A petite young woman came running across the veranda, drying her hands on her apron. So small, I thought, and Yahya so big. Indeed, opposites attract, but in bed? My schoolboy conjecture was interrupted by her harsh, Latvian accent. 'Oh, dear!' she laughed, facing us. 'Have you got caught up in Yahya's boat crazy?'

'We – we're interested in his boat, yes,' Henry answered, truthfully.

'Then we're off.' Yahya directed us into the rear of his Jeep and loaded equipment into the space behind us. He called Jinn, the largest of the guard dogs, to sit beside him in the front seat, and told Dawn, 'Don't wait lunch for me, I'll eat in Marbella.'

'Agree by me,' she said, 'I have to cancel Ronda, so I exercising the horses this afternoon.' Ringlets of pink hair bounced as she turned to me, her green eyes friendly. 'Hello, I'm Dawn. You have been to the bullfights in Ronda as yet?'

'No, but I have a ticket for next Sunday. I bought it off Doreen Baker, who has sudden business demands.'

'Great fortune!' Dawn said. 'Yahya's two aunts and I have tickets for next Sunday, but my Maserati sick, so is waiting for a spare part from Italy. Is possible we ride with you? Can your car three passengers carry?'

'Be my guest. That is, if you don't mind riding in my fabulous Japanese rust bucket. Er, I hear you have some guests from the Middle East?'

Yahya started the motor and swung the car towards the gate. 'My two aunts are our guests,' he grunted. Henry studied the scenery.

Dawn sang out, 'It's a date! Next Sunday, about three o'clock? We will be ready, I promise to you.'

'Close the gate after us, will you, sweetie pie?' Yahya called to her as we drove out. 'I'll miss my appointment in Marbella.'

Expertly dodging most of the road's potholes, Yahya got us to the Costa del Sol in half the time that it usually took me. We arrived at Puerto Duquesa, a marina whose piers had turned the bay into a marine labyrinth. We parked, and Yahya and Jinn led us unerringly through the maze to reach the *Sting Ray*, a flashy speedboat with lines angled to make it look full throttle even when stationary. Yahya grinned with boyish boastfulness as he waved Henry and me aboard. He swung into the cabin, and before Henry could ask his first question, Yahya was at the instrument panel thrashing at levers and buttons and switches. The engine fired at first stroke.

Henry and I positioned ourselves on low seats ranged against the railings, hard plastic for durability rather than comfort. The *Sting Ray* swayed from its moorings and lurched forward, throwing Jinn hard against the back railing. Neither Henry nor I offered a helping hand, for fear of not getting it back.

Gaining speed at a dizzy rate, Yahya appeared seized by ecstasy. Salt spray buffeted his face as he held the wheel steady ho, and within seconds we zoomed from skimming the water to flying over it. The motor settled into medium thunder. Our speed sliced the waves with hardly a ripple as Puerto Duquesa dropped below the horizon and the shoreline sped past like a jet-engined freight train. We covered some thirty miles in a flash, then I felt our speed diminish and we were veering towards shore, headed into a bay. A beach littered with bright umbrellas and exposed human flesh lay ahead, backdropped by an impressive skyline of pastel-coloured buildings. Yahya slowed to a chug-chug. Bathers rushed to water's edge to watch the *Sting Ray*'s graceful approach. There was no pier, I noted, as he dropped anchor.

Youths in pedalboats raced to meet our craft, working their legs like pistons as if expecting us to toss out trinkets and beads. Yahya shouted to Henry and me, 'There are plenty of restaurants on the beach, you have lunch there, OK? I've got an appointment, see you back here in two hours, OK?' He hailed the pedalboats, lowered Jinn onto one, then himself, clad only in khaki shorts, onto another. He pointed to us and the happy natives pedalled in our direction.

'We're wearing street clothes!' I called to Yahya. 'They'll get wet!'

'Do what I do,' he answered, raising a dripping bare foot from the water. 'Take your shoes and trousers off and leave them on the boat.' He and Jinn headed for land, leapt from the pedalboats and waded ashore with playful splashes.

I was willing to wait on the boat, Henry was not. 'Where's he going?' he worried. 'We must follow him, or this whole trip will be a wasted effort.' He rolled up his trouser legs, left on his shoes, and lowered himself onto one of the waiting pedalboats. I removed my shoes, placed them on the deck, rolled up my trouser legs, and followed.

We were deposited within wading distance of the beach by the helpful pedallers. Our audience had lost interest; swimmers returned to the sea, sun-worshippers basted themselves with more quick tan or sun block lotions. We saw Yahya ahead, greeting a pretty, dark-haired woman; her skin heavily tanned and shiny, she looked about eight months pregnant. They clasped hands and strolled towards a row of beach houses, followed by Jinn, dancing and leaping, delighted with the beach scene. He did not like being staked out to guard the small, intimate building that Yahya and his friend entered.

We saw Yahya's 'appointment' close the door, and made our way across the sand to a boardwalk, where Henry removed his shoes to empty the water. Barefoot, he stood in deep thought, muttering, 'Misused day. We've accomplished nothing.' But his dark moment passed. 'Well now, it's just possible that Yahya stores contraband below decks, where he hasn't allowed us to go. Our mission may not be wasted, after all.' Henry's reprieve was brief – real fear keened his voice when he remembered. 'Oh, crikey – my wife! She'll kill me. She expects me home for lunch.'

There was nothing to do but find a good *tapas* bar and kill two hours waiting for Yahya to complete his appointment. We settled for a 'south seas' restaurant, palm frond roof, stainless steel interior. A pleasant enough place, with a good selection of *tapas*, yet my stay there was made memorable by sudden unease. Alarm bells warned that I was becoming Europeanized.

We found a table with a view of the beach and the *Sting Ray*, near three Americans who were concentrating on their menus. How did I know their nationality? I hated myself for viewing critically the man's flowered shirt, the woman's diamanté-studded sunshades, hair dyed to imitate a bleached haystack, her middle-aged bulge straining within a too-tight blouse, hips likewise in electric-blue spandex trousers. She spoke from the top of the mouth, more a quack than a voice, each statement descending into gravel. I assumed the younger woman with them was their daughter. Like her parents, she wore sunshades, but unlike them, she was beautiful. A Candice Bergen lookalike; classic lines, aloof, Gucci attired.

What's this? I cautioned myself. Could I be turning flip about my own people? The American phoney who goes to London for a weekend and returns with an Oxford accent? No, all three of these people are beautiful. To criticize them would be like giving my own mother a hotfoot. They are the salt of the earth. American gothic.

Henry and I dawdled over our *tapas*, while the Yankee trio ordered and were served hamburgers and cans of Coca-Cola. The hamburgers were multi-layered, authentic replicas of the US original, and I watched to see how they would be tackled. Simple. The hamburger was lifted to the mouth, the mouth opened and took a bite. Which was impossible, because the hamburgers were five inches thick. It dawned on me that through rapid evolution we Americans have developed anaconda jawbones, which can be disengaged from the skull at will to accommodate a mammoth morsel. Poor Candice Bergen. Her elegant profile shattered, I would forever remember her engaged in the reptilian act of swallowing a whole pig with one bite. Oh, Candice! Candice!

Two hours later, Yahya and his appointment reappeared on the beach with Jinn bored and restless, as were Henry and I. We pushed from the restaurant to join them. Sunbathers were still thick on the ground, while all the pedalboat operators had disappeared, probably overtaken by *siesta*. With growing misgivings, I remembered that Yahya's boat was some twenty yards off shore. He said goodbye to his companion, then laughed at my concern. 'No problem. I brought ashore a rubber dingy. Look, it's just here, in the sand.' Of course Henry wanted to reach the *Sting Ray* first, to get a peek below decks before Yahya came aboard. He helped drag the dingy to the water's edge, jumped into it and sat on its flat bottom, waiting for a wave to sweep him out to sea. Waves flowed and ebbed, Henry and the dingy remained planted firmly in the sand.

'No, no, no,' Yahya instructed. 'Wade out and float the dingy first, then get into it.'

Henry stormed, 'My clothes! My shoes are already soaked!'

Yahya, waist deep in the water, yowled raucously, 'Hey! Didn't I tell you to leave your clothes on the boat?'

'And face the world in my Y-fronts?' Henry shot back.

Yahya laughed, 'You could pretend you are wearing the South Africa national flag.'

Henry removed his shoes, placed them in the rubber raft, rolled up his trouser legs and waded out until the raft bobbed in the water. An obliging wave rolled in. He hoisted one leg on board, and pulled himself onto the craft. It skittered like a frightened mustang and flipped, dumping Henry into the briny up to his neck, along with his shoes. I worried that he might not be able to swim, but hadn't counted on his tenacity. He snatched the boat back under control, and in rhythm with the next big roller, threw himself across the craft. This time, it bucked forward. Henry again tumbled into the sea, and for a moment disappeared under its surface. He came up snorting with anger. Even more determined, he conjured up gymnast strength to spring higher, and with the next wave landed in the centre of the rubber square. Meanwhile, beach loungers interrupted their leather tanning to cheer and hail his spectacular success. Yahya swam out and pulled the raft to the *Sting Ray*, where the sodden Henry clambered aboard. Yahya then swam shoreward with the raft to collect me.

I was determined not to be as entertaining as Henry had been. I couldn't afford to be, what with the papers in my pockets that my company recommended I carry at all times: my passport, my *residencia*, my Spanish and American driving licences, my hospitalization papers. There were also my credit cards, a few pesetas, and a snapshot of Ellen that I hadn't got around to discarding. I was a walking identification kit, and it was imperative that I stay dry.

Seizing the raft, I waded into the surf with masterful determination, then proceeded to match Henry's comic performance, splash for splash, until I boarded the obstinate craft. Like him, I also received applause for my trapeze act when I reached the *Sting Ray* and swung aboard. More encouragement followed in the form of whistles and shouts of 'Take it off' when I tugged off my dripping trousers and hung them on the railing. Now there were two stripteasers on view, until Henry scuttled below decks to search for child pornography.

Yahya's final trip ferried Jinn to the *Sting Ray*. He swung the mastiff up to me and I seized the dog's forelegs to lift him aboard. He lost his cool and started snapping at my hands. Naturally I let go, which triggered a spate of boos from the beach when he hit the water. They resumed their cheering when Yayha lifted the mutt up a second time, and Jinn graciously accepted my hesitant assistance.

Yahya pulled himself and the rubber raft onto the deck just as Henry appeared from below with an expression of blighted hopes. At once Yahya attacked the *Sting Ray* instrument panel, and within seconds we were flashing towards the horizon. I felt a tug of regret at leaving such a rapt audience, yet they should be happy with the lavish entertainment we had supplied for free. In return, I appreciated the memorable hamburger disappearing act performed by my fellow countrymen, as gratifying as a visit to Middle America.

We docked at Puerto Duquesa and loaded ourselves

into the Jeep for our homeward journey. Henry, having found nothing suspicious on the boat, launched his usual interrogation. 'Yahya,' he began, 'how often do you go to Morocco? Which ports do you use? How long do you stay?' Innocuous questions on the surface, yet I knew Henry's system.

Yahya grinned with schoolboy openness, but his voice was hot with intrigue. 'Aha. You want to go with me to Morocco, Henry?'

'I was just wondering if ... if...' Henry sputtered.

Yahya glanced around to ensure privacy, even though we were on a deserted mountain road. Once more he impaled Henry with his Turkish stare, then aimed a knowing wink. 'Hey, my friend,' he beamed, 'you don't have to pussyfoot with me, I read you loud and clear. I hear that you like little girls. I know of a place in Morocco for twelve-year-olds, or younger if that's your cuppa, every one a virgin. Hey, Henry, me and you can go to Morocco together. You set the date, and by zingo, we're there. I'll introduce you and even pay for your first visit. What do you say to that, my friend?'

Henry didn't flinch. Instead, a smile of accomplishment crept across his face as he cunningly set his trap. 'What about pictures, Yahya? Any – child pornography we can look at?' His smile hardened in anticipation of the incriminating evidence that was about to jackpot before him.

Yahya turned his mouth down to defray insult. 'Pictures! You like pictures, Henry? I don't. That's nasty. To use pictures for ... for ... and all, Henry, is sick. You'll go blind. Much better to go for the genuine, the real Turkish delight. So what about it, my friend? Want to go to Morocco with me? Hey, just me and you in my boat?'

Now Henry flinched. 'I'll let you know,' he answered, exuding bitter disappointment. 'Right now, I must get home and into dry clothes. And find some shoes. Oh, crikey, Serena will kill me.'

Leaving Yahya's house and driving home in my car, clothes clinging like band-aids, both of us sneezing, I silently detested Henry and his whole do-gooder campaign. I would have to replace every official paper now a soggy paste in my pockets. But, for what it was worth, he could now scratch another name off his list of suspected porno literature traffickers. I delivered the barefoot Sherlock to his door, and gave a deep sigh, relieved that I had seen the last of Yahya Barmakids.

Like hell I had. His name identified with discord, like 'Developers', both of which I would hear again.

20

Dawn rang on Thursday morning to confirm my agreement to take her and Yahya's two aunts to the bullfights on Sunday. I promised to wash my car for the occasion, even though that would expose more rust. Dawn laughed and told me that when Yahya picked them up at the airport in his Jeep, the stately ladies admitted that they had never ridden in anything but a Rolls-Royce, except once, in an emergency, a Mercedes. 'It'll add to their education to see how we peasants live.' I couldn't understand why she put herself in my category, except, perhaps, to distance herself from her in-laws.

Ilka Harvey invited me for dinner on Friday night. She apologized for the short notice by explaining that the 'Director of BBC Television' had unexpectedly arrived to assess Alciguna for a travel feature, and she wanted him to meet some of the town's more outstanding talents. A Harvey dinner invitation, plus flattery, is an irresistible combination for the vain. Good Lord, yes. Of course I would be there.

I arrived on foot and found construction in progress next to the Harvey house – columns, beams and rafters stacked on piles of bricks and cement bags. From somewhere in the jumble I heard female shouts. Surely not part of the construction process? I joined several villagers hidden behind a mound of gravel, who were watching an extremely agitated Ilka waving threatening gestures and screeching what sounded like potent Magyar cuss-words. Next, we saw Yahya Barmakids reverse his Jeep from the building site. Driving away, he smiled, stuck out his tongue and waved it at Ilka. She gasped, whirled around and, still gesturing, stamped into her house and slammed the door. Wow, I thought. And she's giving a fancy dinner party tonight? Recalling what frozen dinners there might be in reserve in my refrigerator, I waited a few timorous minutes before pushing the doorbell. The Harvey maid, all smiles, admitted me and pointed upstairs. I found the living room extravagantly appointed with splashy bouquets of fresh flowers, Winthrop's dancing-girl statues numerously displayed. A few earlier guests stood chatting in groups. Ilka, reclining on a *chaise longue*, temporarily suspended her Madame Récamier pose of world-weariness to raise her limp hand to me. Astounding! Could she possibly be the wild woman I had seen outside just ten minutes ago?

More guests arrived: Olympia, drink in hand as if conjured by magic, complaining that none of the gold plumbing fixtures fit in her new house; Paul Jones-Jones looking miserable without a girlfriend; Olga Campbell predicting imminent calamity for Alciguna; Clara Cornwallis shrieking laughter and looking wild-eyed for a fireplace in which to hurl her vodka glass. The Bangs arrived without stir, Karen demure, Gus sizing up Gloria the Australian. Grace Pennington, always diplomatically punctual, stood at the centre of a group of Spaniards whom I hadn't met. Mollie Potter fussily rearranged the bouquets of flowers. The Nurembergs made their usual austere entrance, Manfred at once in full chase, tracking down the brandy bottle.

Ilka rose to greet more guests, and introduced me to Allen Spurko. Not quite the 'Director of BBC Television', I discovered, but an impressive title all the same. He asked the customary question of visitors, 'What brings you to Alciguna?' to which I repeated Mollie

Potter's stock answer, 'Once you visit Alciguna, you always return.'

'Very apt. I'm enjoying this area,' Allen agreed. 'I find its ambience fascinating. Ilka is taking all her guests to the Ronda bullfights on Sunday. Do you go to bullfights?'

Before I could comment, another guest elbowed between us, a man in his early forties, military build, middle height, crew-cut dark hair, his blue eyes flashing alert aggression. I had seen him on the street, but we had never talked.

'Excuse me,' he said, his speech a T-less hint of Cockney. 'I'm Jules Reemrev; Cambridge, local artist, construction engineer. Couldn't help overhearing your discussion, and, if you don't mind, I would like to add a little self-promotional spin.' He patted my shoulder, the one that Carlos the electrician had left purple, and explained to Allen, 'He's here because he found a house with so much charm it overwhelmed him. I know the house and its merits, because I supervised its renovation.'

'You!' I bristled, almost dropping my glass of *cava*. 'You admit, bald-faced, to having supervised that fiasco? My Casa Potemkin?'

His eyes sparkled private amusement. 'Should have had it surveyed before you bought it, mate. Ben Beardsley instructed me from London to cut every possible cost; no insulation under roof or floor, cheapest wiring, used plumbing, no doors on bathrooms –'

'Damn it, I know all that,' I sputtered. 'A half-assed disaster!'

'Oy, don't blame me, mate. It was lack of time what blew the job. As part of me duties, when Ben Beardsley was here he demanded that I drive him to the nude "nature beaches" on the coast every afternoon. Meanwhile, without supervision, the builders mucked up your house right royally.'

'I suppose it's poetic justice that I get the royal shaft,' I muttered into my drink. 'Ben Beardsley. Olympia's son, class gone agley.'

'Oh, there's more to that jolly story,' Jules added. 'When he arrives in town from London, local blokes threaten him in bars and shout at him on the streets, "Leave my wife alone, puto!"'

I told Allen, 'Sorry you're hearing the seamy side of our village life. There's plenty of virtue here if you search for it.'

Allen hadn't missed a word. 'Oh, do carry on. I'm receiving vibes that this town has all the daft ingredients of an Andalusian *Coronation Street*.'

Jules agreed. 'But keep in mind, mate, Alciguna's *modus vivendi* is as faithful to reality as Miró's abstracts. The Cambridge Cockney has spoken.'

A maid called us to the dining room. Everyone was seated by place card around a glimmering table. Pink napery and arrayed silverware reflected the glow of black candles in crystal candelabras, guests admired the elegant outlay before them, blissfully unprepared for the fireworks I would ignite before the meal was finished. Into the second course, beef Wellington with baby vegetables, accompanied by a rare Ronda red wine, everyone concentrated on eating. Conversation was reduced to purrs, only cutlery rattled. I saw it as an opportune opening for relating a sea saga I felt would amuse everyone. It began, 'Last Sunday, Henry Perry-Smith and I were invited for a "cruise" on Yahya Barmakids's speedboat. We...'

A sudden and violent crash stopped me. Ilka slammed down her knife and fork, her eyes screwed up in distress. 'Don't *ever* mention that name in my house!' she stormed, words quivering abhorrence.

All movement in the dining room ceased, all eyes trained on me. Olympia broke the silence with a whisper to me that was heard by all, 'Roberto, you just stepped on your willy.'

'Sorry,' I gulped, 'I didn't mean to offend...'

Ilka sputtered, 'That troglodyte! Calls himself a builder, and has taken on the construction next door. Dumps his trash on the street. His building waste covers my terrace. His loud mouth disrupts the whole street, starting at eight in the morning. Most beastly of all, he has usurped my parking space and when I ask him to move his car he shouts obscenities and makes rude Turkish gestures at me. He's uncivilized! An animal!' Ilka paused, took a sip of wine.

Storm over, black clouds gave way to rainbows and sunny tranquillity. She retrieved her knife and fork and asked sweetly, 'Has anyone heard the new Michael Tilson Thomas CD of *Pelleas and Melisande*?'

To minimize my disgrace, I manufactured a red herring, 'No, but I saw Thomas conduct *Nixon in China* in New York.'

'*Querido!*' she exclaimed, reaching across the table for my hand. 'I know the composer. John Adams is a very dear friend of mine.'

'Whass wrong with Wagner?' Manfred wanted to know, now that he had switched from beef Wellington to brandy Napoleon.

I had averted certain exile in a flash. Easy. Yet, there was neon flashing in my head, warning that I had promised Dawn that I would take her and relatives to the bullfights on Sunday. Ho boy. The Harveys and the Barmakids. If I allowed those two high voltage cables to cross on Sunday, the short circuit would provide a sizzling first chapter for Allen Spurko's *Calle Coronasion*. With me, *el Butt-Head*, its star.

Ellen had been appalled by my rusty automobile; Yahya's two aunts were horrified by it. Dressed in *haute couture* as if attending a state performance at the Paris opera, they refused to enter the car until oriental carpets layered the floor and silk shawls draped its tattered seats. They had little to say to me, the chauffeur, so Dawn and I chatted in the front seat as I dodged with elaborate care potholes and corrugations on the road to Ronda. The Barmakids were met at the bullring and escorted to special seats on, of course, the shady side. Doreen's ticket placed me in the blazing *sol* section, where only a vendor passing my row every fifteen minutes, selling tepid beer in plastic cups, averted dehydration.

As for bullfights, I fall into neither the Like nor Dislike columns. I've read stacks of books in praise of the spectacle, and have attempted to absorb their passion. The medieval pageantry of a *corrida* is marvellous to behold, and the mass '*Olé*' of the spectators is moving. I thoroughly appreciate the artistry and courage of a matador, and understand that these bulls are bred to fight and would be disgraced by old age. Yet, when *el toro* charges from his dark confinement into the bullring's bright sunlight, his primeval rage challenging the world, I have goose bumps, knowing that this magnificent creature will die by a sword thrust to the heart, if he's lucky, within thirty minutes. Or, if the thrust is not true, and killing the beast degenerates into clumsy butchery, I can lose control of my last frozen dinner.

When the last dead bull was dragged ignominiously from the arena by two nags under the guidance of sombre-attired attendants, I was more than ready for a proper cold drink, and rushed to grab a table in the nearby sidewalk café where the Barmakids and I had agreed to meet. Yahya's two aunts were already there. They informed me that when the first bull met his moment of truth, they declared Spanish culture barbaric and had left the *corrida*. They were now recovering by drinking Coca-Cola from champagne glasses.

Dawn arrived and we both ordered cold beer and sat discussing the balletic footwork of one of the matadors. I made certain that my face was turned from the crowds leaving the arena but, oh God, oh God, that ploy wasn't good enough. The trilling laughter heading in my direction belonged to none other than Ilka Harvey.

She left her entourage of six to rush to my table, arms outstretched for embrace. 'Roberto!' she greeted effusively, and offered her cheek. But in the midst of her 'um-wahs' she spotted Dawn.

She stiffened. Aversion distorted her face into a tragic mask. But no explosion, as I had feared. Her expression simply went blank. She retreated as if having made a slight mistake, rejoined her group and led them on with cool detachment. I had ceased to exist.

'Zap, you're dead,' Dawn laughed. 'But with seriousness, had I known Ilka Harvey is here, I wouldn't have sit with you. Associate with me has sent you to the Siberia. Welcome to Alciguna gulag, comrade.'

'Stay clear of her,' warned one of the aunts, diamonds flashing. '*Nouveau riche.*'

'Po' white trash,' agreed the other, and sipped her Coca-Cola with Middle Eastern *hauteur*.

'Is it total war between the Harveys and the Barmakids?' asked the innocent sheep caught in crossfire.

Dawn explained, 'Since Yahya started construction next door to Ilka's house, she criticizes no end. Her Hungary ranting grows louder, Yahya's hand signals that he learn as boy in Ankara grow more vulgar. This row has become hottest attraction in town. Citizens drive miles, fight for best view. Yahya loves it.'

Driving back towards Alciguna, I thought of my position;

caught in a village feud not of my making. I couldn't shrug it off, because it was basic – I could live without Ilka's breathtaking tales of celebrities, but as a bachelor lacking culinary expertise, I would sorely miss her dinners.

Yet, salvation is within reach, I assured myself. I'll simply smooth things out at next Thursday's Trivial Pursuit. Easy.

Not at Trivial Pursuit, I wouldn't. I arrived with fulsome greetings and bubbled with 'ho, ho, ho' fizz, yet glances from my old friends could be taken as censure. All evening Ilka radiated high spirits; animated in gesture, shrill in speech, her stories of Budapest's eccentric characters never more amusing. While to her, I wasn't there. Well, then, had I, like Henry, become an outcast in my own community through no fault of my own? Is this what living among expatriates was all about? Did they all have shallow minds, or had I truly blundered out of step?

As for Olympia, nothing had changed. There were far more crucial issues at stake. One of her new bathrooms had been tiled heliotrope instead of her selected persimmon. My crisis paled by comparison.

This was not my night. During Trivial Pursuit questions, I couldn't name the capital of Bashkirskaya. Olympia, of course, knew the answer straight away. Although at odds with the answer card, she claimed first-hand knowledge and swore it was Baryshnikov, where one of her husbands had had his vodka custom distilled. The only dissenter was Manfred Nuremberg, who claimed it was Stuttgart. But, mellowed by after-dinner brandy, and since his name obligated *noblesse oblige*, he graciously declared no contest, and Olympia's opposing side won the game.

21

It was the usual Alciguna summer morning; bright, salubrious, silent except for a few roosters crowing and sheep bleating on their way to pasture. A breeze, fresh and warm and perfumed by hillside flowers, floated up from the valley. Sitting on my terrace with a first cup of coffee, determined not to let social problems spoil my bucolic bliss, I was rocked by the doorbell. It rang insistently. I descended the stairs, crossed the patio and shuffled through the reception room-cum-art studio, wondering who could be up at this hour. In summer most Spaniards go to bed after midnight and sleep late. Henry? I couldn't dismiss that probability. Annoyed by the untimely intrusion, I flung open the door. One of the postman's children thrust a yellow envelope into my hand and scampered away. What the hell? A telegram arriving at first birdsong? Mail is delivered only in the afternoon. Weirder still, it was from New York. I ripped open the envelope, began to read, and leaned against the door.

> Dear Ex, > Clear the decks. Said NO to my boss, who replaced me with an anorexic who said YES. I'm fired. Sacked. Need a place to recuperate. Share your eyrie with a singed chickadee who tried to ape Icarus? Yes or no immaterial, arriving Malaga Flight 209, Wed., 2:40 PM. > Meet me. > Your Ex

Did my heart skip a beat from joy, or was it fear of being trapped? As I was learning to accept bachelorhood as a preferred state, this development was damned inconvenient. First off, what about my expurgation by Ilka Harvey? She did not allow neutrality, so Ellen would be branded with me, restricted to the 'other side'. The Barmakids were lively and hospitable, but horses, speedboats and barbecues were not Ellen's uppermost choice of social activity. Until I settled my dispute with Ilka, this was not the time for visitors.

All week I pondered the pitfalls. As I drove to Malaga airport my emotions remained ambivalent; cold, then hot flashes blurred my vision all the way. Ellen emerged from customs distinguished from other travellers by her smart attire, a light blue business suit cut to stress her curves, its formality softened by a flowered scarf at her neck. Her smile was radiant. My blood pressure surged like a hot geyser. At that moment, it hit me that if she wanted to make another stab at wedded harmony, then boom, boom! Of course I would meet her more than halfway.

On our drive to Alciguna, the chaotic traffic on the coast road was incidental. Ellen kick-started a homely conversation, during which we avoided mentioning the vacant interval in our marriage. There were no expressions of guilt on either side, no finger pointing, no *mea culpas*. Instead, she asked if there was a supermarket on our way.

We arrived home, my car sagging with basic cooking utensils, bags of groceries, fresh, frozen, canned and bottled. At once, Ellen changed into her laboratory smock and started setting the kitchen in order. I watched her prod the dressed carcass of a fat chicken, chop garlic and olives. Soon the smells of properly prepared food were wafting from my kitchen for the first time, and my stomach danced.

Ellen served dinner in my unused dining room. We ate quietly, content and relaxed by candlelight, wine bottles serving as candelabras. After the chocolate mocha mousse and dessert wine, she countered my elaborate compliments with a warning. 'Just wait. You may tire of being my guinea pig. Your kitchen is destined to become a famous culinary laboratory, did you know that? I intend to capitalize on what I learned during my late employment by writing a cookbook. It will be called, *Traditional Microwave Dishes of Andalusia.* How does that sound?'

Sugarplums pirouetted before my eyes, a future diet of experimental cuisine, devoutly anticipated. Yet, I detected a false note. Determined not to sound negative, I mentioned, 'I don't think microwaves are a Spanish tradition, my love.'

'Then it's high time they became so.' She thought for a moment. 'Then what about, *Andalusia Goes Microwave?*'

'It'll sell a million,' I assured her. Now I knew why I had ripped out Ben Beardsley's rotten plumbing and wiring to install a usable kitchen. 'How many more microwaves do we need?'

Ellen registered only tepid interest when I explained my pariah status with Ilka Harvey. 'You'll survive,' she said, 'It's a big world out there.' Now was not the time to tell her that expat living can be extremely restrictive, and that a society of foreigners can be as prickly as a basket of cactus pears. And Henry, how would I explain to him that, with Ellen here, I no longer had time for his crusade? Frankly, I felt sorry for the guy. Since he was unjustly charged, by whisper and innuendo, of spying on a little girl in Winthrop Harvey's sculpture studio, there was a trace of concern on his face, hidden under his mask of purpose and determination. He was shunned. He walked alone on the streets and avoided Bar Suerte. I invited him to have morning coffee with Ellen and me. He accepted immediately, and reported with enthusiasm his latest progress in his pursuit of evil. He also reminded me that he sorely regretted my absence on the job.

Ellen agreed with his quest for a crime-free Alciguna, but when I described the adventures I had shared with him in the search for child pornography distribution, she thought that our over-the-top actions bordered on the puerile, although her Boston taste didn't allow her to tell Henry that. I got the message and promised to stay at home and work on illustrations for her cookbook. Soon finding that sketching baked potatoes lacked the excitement and intrigue of chasing malfeasance, I wavered. Was it, then, to be a choice between Henry and Ellen? No contest. Ellen could cook.

22

No longer a 'very dear friend' of Ilka Harvey's, I felt guilty that my social blunder had labelled Ellen 'untouchable' as well. To our great fortune, rewarding diversions were at hand. It was the era when the Bolshoi and the Kirov theatres found themselves abandoned by the Russian government, and from sink or swim financial necessity, fanned out across Europe to perform song and dance on any available stage – even Alciguna's. We could see performances for peanuts in this little village which would cost a month's salary in their original houses in Moscow and St Petersburg. Most of the older villagers hadn't a clue what they were watching at the ballet, but not so the younger set. A makeshift stage was erected in the square, and a plank runway was slung between backstage and a next-door window, into which the dancers could scurry between their performances. During the second act of a scaled-down production of *Swan Lake*, the makeshift curtain came crashing down. Not by accident, it turned out, but to make a point. Zorro and his two assistant policemen were called in. They rushed underneath the plank runway and seconds later emerged with several young boys in tow who looked sheepish, frightened, and a little dreamy eyed. Oddly, Manfried Nuremberg was among them, helping the police, everyone assumed. The curtain went up, the swans soared again in balletic flight. Came the interval, we heard that the ruckus was due to ballerinas complaining that a gang of the town's *chicos* had positioned themselves underneath the plank runway, where they enjoyed unobstructed views up the tutus that passed overhead. *Chicos* will be *chicos*. Manfried, Manfried.

Another touching component of the ballet occurred between acts, when dancers manned display stands in the plaza to hawk Russian strawberry jam and jellied cherries, embroidered shawls, waistcoats, hand-woven coverlets and Russian dolls. On display were bottles of vodka boasting exotic names, but of suspect quality, since there were no seals on the corked tops. Ellen and I tried to imagine stars of the New York City Ballet having to peddle hand-sewn quilts, home-brew and Barbie dolls for their livelihood. Never mind, the dancing was superb.

A week later, a poster at the post office announced a state-financed concert by a popular Spanish opera singer with pianist, who would perform at the cathedral on Thursday night at ten o'clock. We invited friends to our house for pre-concert drinks, and were preparing to leave when the doorbell rang. The mayor had sent runners to inform all that the performance was postponed until eleven-thirty. With luck, we had extra canapés and plenty of alcohol, so our party settled back for a further session of cocktail small talk.

The extra drinks made our climb slow up the hill to the church. We arrived at eleven twenty-five. The pews were mostly filled. None of the villagers seemed unduly upset that no preparations had been made for a concert: no piano, no singer, nothing. Perhaps another runner would say that it had been cancelled? Too much alcohol generates impatience, and I felt my cool dissipating. I was ready to say to hell with it, and stamp home and fume over a wasted evening. I hadn't taken into account the Spanish talent for improvisation.

At exactly eleven twenty-eight, a van backed up to the front door of the church. A man and woman jumped from its cab to open the van doors. They rolled out an upright piano with stool on top, down the van's ramp and up the aisle to the base of the lectern. The man placed the stool before the piano, sat, opened the lid and began to play. The woman started to sing, at eleven-thirty on the dot, Albénez, Granados and Falla. Wonderful!

Ellen's joy at testing the limits of microwave cooking, and my appreciation of her efforts, made staying home a pleasure. With varied productions on our local stage, *flamenco* and *cante jondo* under the post office, first communion dinners and weddings, plus Henry and Olympia in high profile, we found our entertainment calendar near complete. Only my rift with Ilka Harvey, and the suspected presence of the Russian Mafia in Alciguna, muddied the waters.

Even faster than bad news, word spread that Ellen's experimental dinners were superb. Paul Jones-Jones duly favoured us with visits that coincided unerringly with mealtimes. Ellen didn't mind; her microwave recipes produced more food than the two of us could consume. I was gaining weight. Polita, our *Alma de llaves*, all the while complaining about extra kitchenware to clean, was growing more obese by the day.

One night we received a visit from Viktor Berki who, surprise, surprise, hadn't come for dinner. He apologized for his intrusion, explaining that he had heard Ellen was writing a cookbook, and since cooking was his hobby, he would like to compare notes. I wondered why I had never met him, why I had not been taken to his house by Henry, why he was not suspected of being Russian Mafia as was everyone else.

Viktor was tall, slender and graceful, ready with a quick smile, but hesitant with laughter. His brown eyes and complexion were Middle European, his accent French.

Neatly dressed, he was handsome in a slightly effete way, his manner near formal. Ellen, always impressed by impeccable manners, invited him to stay for dinner, and instructed Polita to add a fourth plate to the table.

If not the laugh-a-minute dinner guest, Viktor was well travelled and well read, droll and entertaining. Paul, sitting across the table from him in his usual chair, was a ready straight man. 'Tell us about Hungary,' he proposed, between mouthfuls of canapés. 'How you escaped the communists.'

Seeing that Ellen and I were eager listeners, Viktor easily slid into his past, his French accent adding colour, his dark looks lending intrigue. 'Fortunately, or unfortunately, we were of a certain class,' he began, 'on par with Ilka's family. Her father and mine, being land-owners, were imprisoned when Hungary became a "People's Republic", and met unexplained deaths. Since Ilka's family had sent holdings abroad, her mother stuffed her considerable collection of jewellery down a duck's throat, then took the 'pet' and her two daughters to Berlin, and then to the US. My mother wasn't so astute, and was forced to remain in Budapest with the most negative of assets – me. I was called back from school in Paris, where I was studying Islamic calligraphy and abstract tile design. Not, you'll agree, the most propitious qualifications for financing a luxury spoilt mother.'

Ellen, absorbed as I had seldom seen her, passed around a bottle of Penedés red wine. Paul swirled his wine in his mouth as if considering rejection, finally nodded approval. Ignoring him, Ellen concentrated on Viktor. 'Were you able to get your mother out of Hungary?'

Viktor sipped his wine without ceremony. 'When I saw what communism was doing to my country, I resorted to my one asset, education, to get her to the United States. I applied for a job in the Hungarian diplomatic service.'

Suave as he was, I couldn't picture the willowy Viktor as a Magyar 007. 'Wasn't that a dangerous move?' I questioned.

Viktor studied his wine glass. 'The communists were elated to sign up an educated turncoat, and posted me to New Delhi as cultural attaché. I was shadowed constantly, of course, every movement monitored, yet I discreetly transferred the family's hidden paper assets to America. That done, I threatened to blackmail a Russian official I had seen buying General Motors stock, and was able to get a visa for my mother to visit a "dying brother" in San Francisco.'

'Your plan worked?' breathed Ellen.

'Until everything went haywire. More quickly than I had hoped, my blackmail victim reported suspicions of my loyalty, and I was ordered to Moscow.'

'I say, this is a noble vintage,' Paul said, pouring himself another glass of wine. Ellen glared at him and turned to Viktor. 'Weren't you afraid?'

'Terrified!' His eyes squinted, reliving fear. 'Of course I pretended pleasure at such good fortune; to be called to mother Russia – hoorah! I prepared for my happy trip to paradise, whilst foreseeing the usual reward for communist disapproval, Lubyanka or a firing squad.'

'But here you are,' Paul said with dismissive cheeriness. He had yielded the table for far too long. 'Now. Have I told you about the mayor's newest proposal?'

'Let him finish his story!' Ellen snapped, and from a familiar script I read her thoughts: Paul Jones-Jones, enjoy your dinner. This is the last freeloader's meal you'll be having at Casa Potemkin.

Viktor was not interrupted. 'Meanwhile, I had informed the American Embassy in New Delhi of my plan. Oh, yes, I had a plan, but what does a specialist in abstract tile design know about international cloak-and-daggery?

On the day I was scheduled to return to the Workers' Paradise, plain clothed minders of the dreaded AVO Hungarian intelligence bureau, coats bulging with firearms, escorted me to the Indira Gandhi Airport. My meek and cooperative manner cajoled them into laxity, they didn't notice my desperate attempts to make eye-contact with anyone who might be an intercept, which the CIA had promised me. But no one was vaguely interested in returning my enquiring stares, no one. More alarming, I suddenly wondered, had my messages to the CIA been intercepted? Wasn't I naive to think that I could outsmart the AVO and KGB? Then I saw him, head tilted from behind a newspaper. His eyebrows rose with guarded recognition, his eyes flickered towards the men's restroom. That panicked me. Was this man an American agent, or was he on the make? It had happened before.'

'Only a Middle European would suspect that,' interjected Paul.

Viktor viewed him with an aloof toss of the head. 'I bolted from my AVO escorts and zigzagged towards the men's room like a charging football player. People that looked like Indian tourists suddenly pressed around my guards, preventing them from following. Two more men grabbed me and shunted me through a back door to a plane waiting to take off for Zurich. And, as Paul says, here I am.'

Ellen rocked forward. 'Was your mother waiting in San Francisco?'

'Yes, after I was interrogated, we were both granted US asylum. I bought a house in San Francisco, but shortly thereafter, she died. I went to Madrid, where I heard about Alciguna, and bought here also. Now I spend six months in Spain and six months in the US, thus avoiding taxes in both countries.'

The table was quiet, except for a sudden sputter from

Paul. 'Your mother died in San Francisco? You told me that –'

Viktor answered with a shrug. 'Which story did I tell you, Paul?'

'She fell from a tree –'

'Oh, yes, my favourite.' Viktor winked at Ellen. 'In Hungary, it is the custom that a woman must climb a cherry tree to have a baby. When my mother was having me, she fell from the tree. Killed her, and I, having landed on my head, have never been quite right since.'

'And you say you're a diplomat!' Ellen scolded as she left the table to help Polita serve an experimental dish of Serrano ham with wild asparagus. Paul, ignoring his recent snub, tackled his food before anyone else, and groaned satisfaction.

After dinner, Viktor removed cigars from his coat pocket and offered them around. When everyone declined, he asked permission to smoke. Ellen passed around Pacharan, a Navarra liqueur. The room became quiet with sated contentment.

Viktor blew out a breath of mild cigar smoke and pretended an afterthought. 'Oh, yes. Another reason I'm here; I'm on a peace mission.'

Ellen tilted her head. 'Peace mission? Who are we Americans at war with this time?'

The diplomat removed a blue envelope from his pocket and handed it to her. 'Ilka Harvey asks you and Robert to her house for dinner on Friday night.'

'That's impossible!' I snorted. 'We met on the street only yesterday, and her glare at me would topple the church tower.'

Viktor laughed. 'You must remember, she's Hungarian. Our women blow hot and cold. It's a national trait.'

I remained sceptical. 'What celestial event brought about this – this miracle?'

The answer was obvious, at least to Viktor. 'Ilka heard that Ellen once had her own TV show. In Ilka's eyes, that makes Ellen a celebrity. Therefore you, Ellen, are automatically one of Ilka's "very dear friends of mine".'

23

Ilka's dinner party was lavish, an excess of complicated dishes to demonstrate that Ellen didn't have a monopoly on *haute cuisine*. The familiar gallery of Alciguna faces were on display, and Ellen was moderately entertained by woeful stories of the town's decline, the encroachment of developers, inept servants – in short, the common litany of expats the world over. When we started to leave, around midnight, some guests asked if they might walk with us to the town's square. 'It's St John's Eve,' someone said, 'there's always a jumping contest over a bonfire to celebrate the longest day of the year.'

Olympia said that one wall of her new house had started to lean, and left to check if it was still standing. The rest of us tramped to the intersection of three streets where villagers stood intently watching a pile of burning debris, pointing excitedly, faces expectant. They suddenly turned silent. A bare-chested youth soared through the flames, barely clearing the awesome pyre. A soaked towel covered his head and his trousers were close to igniting from the heat. The audience applauded as attendant youths doused him with buckets of water, then heaved more logs and wooden boxes onto the heap to send the blaze higher. Again the crowd cringed. Another young man leapt through the fire, creating a spectacular spray of sparks when his bare heel struck the red-hot mound. There was louder applause. More logs were added, the flames thrashed and soared.

I pushed through the onlookers to peer behind the

bonfire. The group of young men facing incineration were not laughing with the giddy thrill of defying danger, instead, dread flickered on their faces. This was not a game. Each youth emptied a bucket of water over his head, and queued to run down a slight incline to gain speed for his leap over the crackling inferno.

I rejoined my group. 'Good Lord, this is madness!' I cried. 'Whose numbskull idea is this? Those kids could be seriously burned, and there's not an ambulance within miles.'

'It's traditional,' Grace Pennington informed me. 'Has been for centuries. But now, instead of a jug of wine, as of yore, the current prize is a basketful of groceries. As more wood is plied and the flames soar, the last contestant to jump over them gets the prize. Larry Garcia, that tall, lanky jumper coming up, always wins. He's got a widowed mother and four younger siblings to feed.' I recalled Ellen's complaint during dinner when she whispered to me that the Baked Alaska should have remained in the oven a moment longer to brown the meringue evenly. At that moment Larry streaked through the fire, the towel over his head steaming, his bare chest gleaming with sweat. One trouser leg snagged the jagged end of a blazing beam. Momentum carried him on, freeing his leg, but meteors of orange coals followed his foot. He rolled on the ground to quench the scorched trouser leg, and then raced behind the blazing tower to jump again. Meanwhile, more wood, higher flames.

'Hold on!' I yelled. 'I'll buy you that basket of groceries! For God's sake, don't jump again! It's certain death, can't you see that?'

'They don't understand English,' Maggie Potter told me. 'Which doesn't matter anyway, because Larry has won. Look. No one is game enough to follow his last jump.'

There was lots of backslapping. Larry's narrow face beamed as he dried his long black hair, took up his basket of food and pranced homewards.

Our group dispersed. On the dark street to Casa Potemkin, Ellen squeezed my hand and spoke with quiet concern. 'There must be other families in Alciguna who are as desperate for food as Larry Garcia's. I've been thinking, instead of adding more blubber to Paul's rounded bottom, why don't we donate my experimental left-overs to the needy?'

I answered by flaunting wisdom gained from living in old Spain. 'You must be careful. Ancient superstition won't allow the Spanish to wear second-hand clothing, no matter how poor they are. As for food, they'll accept it only as payment, never as charity. So between the uptight expats and the sensitive villagers, you must steer a tactical course through Alciguna, my dear. Else you'll find yourself relegated to the boonies before you know what hit you.' I laughed. 'Take my word for it.'

My mind went back to an elderly man I had recently met, who lived outside town and employed Larry Garcia as gardener. On our next encounter in the street, I explained Ellen's plan to help the Garcias with our redundant food, and asked his guidance on contacting them. He had commanded a battalion during the Second World War, and was known as General Coles. From a historically famous Cheshire family, he was treated with near reverence by the other English expats and I felt privileged to receive his advice. His counsel, I found, was direct and not very complimentary to the Spanish. 'Let them work for the food. Never give anything free to these natives, or they'll take advantage of you.'

I had plenty of work to be done, especially painting. But only Larry's mother, Maria Garcia, could do it, because painting is a woman's job – except a house exterior above ground floor where a ladder is required, thus giving a view up her skirt. After the flood at my welcoming party for Ellen, and since I had removed the roof and installed waterproofing, the mottled interior walls of my house were begging for paint. Polita, initially annoyed when another woman invaded her domain, accepted Maria when I explained my humanitarian reasons behind the painting project.

On Monday, Ellen and I went to Malaga, I to deliver completed design work and pick up a new assignment, and she to raid the coast supermarkets. The local shops, she had found, carried only basic provisions, and seldom stocked the ingredients required for fancy dishes. On our return home, a shock of *déjà vu* awaited us. 'Oh, no!' I moaned. 'Oh, crap! The living room floor is flooded again! Damn! I thought all of Ben Beardsley's handiwork had been replaced or repaired. What is it this time?'

In the middle of the living room lagoon stood a stepladder, on top of which Maria swung a paintbrush to the rhythm of her portable radio squawking *pasodobles*. '*Hola!*' she sang out. 'I deedn't expect you back so soon.'

'This water!' I sputtered. 'Where the hell did it come from?'

'The water?' She was amused by my question. 'Is necessary. You cover floor with water, and when paint drips, it no harm floor tiles. Everybody use water when they paint inside house. You never use water?'

'No!' I was highly annoyed. 'When the rains flooded my house, it took months to dry out.'

'That's why everybody paint in summer. It take only a pair of weeks to dry, you'll see.'

'Meanwhile, I'll prepare dishes loaded with vitamin C,' Ellen consoled, and unwrapped groceries for stocking the shelves in the downstairs lavatory, which she had recently converted into a larder. Olympia bragged that installing the convenience was her idea, when the house was being renovated. It was her favourite room, she claimed, and complained loudly when Ellen assigned it additional use.

Maria's employment proved short-lived. She completed the ground floor paint job then moved upstairs, to tackle the bedrooms. She spread newspapers instead of water on the floor, thank heavens, and used a pointed paintbrush, her way of keeping white paint from smudging the black beams in the ceiling.

I was on the patio with a cup of coffee when Larry charged into the house, without knocking or explanation. He ran up the stairs three steps at a time to reach his mother. I heard Maria scream. Sobbing and moaning, beating her breast, she staggered after Larry down the stairs and out the front door.

I rushed to the bedroom, to see if she had left a clue as to what had gone wrong. I found an overturned bucket of paint and a paintbrush hurled onto the floor. My first move was to clean up the paint, then I rushed to Polita's house to enquire if she knew what was happening. She yawned, resenting my intrusion on her *siesta*, but obligingly telephoned Maria's house. After a few words Polita slumped in her chair and moaned, '*Dios mio. Dios mio.*' She replaced the phone in its cradle with an unsteady hand, her eyes streaming tears.

Turning to me, her voice wavered in the falsetto register of grief. 'It's Maria's youngest son. He's been found hanging in a neighbour's garage.'

Polita, too distraught to answer further questions, next day was barely calm enough to give Ellen and me her impassioned account. In the kitchen, fumbling at shelling peas, she intoned, 'As you know, the Garcias are poor, so every member of the family must work. Except Jaimie, who at sixteen was still in school. Yet, he thumbed rides to the coast, and returned with money to help feed the family.' Polita halted, blew her nose, and addressed Ellen formally, '*Señora*, do you want to hear this? It is not a pretty story.'

Ellen paused over a stuffed guinea hen. 'Go on. I've been around.'

Polita's lips thinned, she spoke through her teeth. 'On the Costa del Sol there is a bar where young men go late at night to make money. It's a place for meeting older men in big cars. Maria didn't know where Jaimie got the money he gave her, but suspected something evil and forbade him to go again. But seeing his brothers working to support him, he went anyway. Until recently, when he became ill.'

Polita began shelling the peas faster. 'The doctor told Jaimie that he had AIDS. He couldn't face his mother after that, and so, took his own life.'

24

Everyone said that Jaimie was a personable, well-liked young man, and the whole town seemed in mourning for him. I wasn't sure if stopping at the near empty Bar Suerte next morning was being disrespectful to his memory, yet when General Coles hailed me, I had no choice but to join him at his table for coffee.

His pale, watery blue eyes were troubled, his face veined with displeasure. 'I'm desperate for help,' he complained sourly. 'I've guests coming, and my swimming pool filter is clogged. My gardener is not on hand to clear it, instead, has hit me with the excuse that he must attend his brother's funeral.' The General's thin shoulders were slumped, he brushed at his stubble of military-cut grey hair, a signal of deep annoyance.

'The Garcia death?' I was unable to follow his remarks. 'Yes, terrible, terrible.'

'Don't let it bother you.' The General waved his hand to order pastries to go with his coffee. 'Tragedy stimulates the Spanish character. Disaster drives them. They revere death, as evidenced by their morbid fascination with bullfighting. Their favourite colour is black, their folk chronicler is Goya, whose paintings all contain some malign aspect.'

I stood to leave, and offered solace. 'I sincerely hope that you find someone to fix your swimming pool drain.'

General Coles sat erect and enquired with military briskness, 'I say, I hear that you go to Malaga quite often. Is that correct?'

'About twice a month.' I wondered if I should salute and add, 'Sir!'

'Age hinders my driving,' he stated, an official report. 'Therefore, I should appreciate it if you would be so kind as to purchase a few items for me on your next trip, necessities that can't be obtained locally.'

'I should be happy to do so,' I said, then came near to biting my tongue, wondering why I should be happy; I hardly knew the man, except that I didn't like him. At that moment, a car, older than mine, rattled past the Bar Suerte, which gave me an idea. 'Dale Foster,' I pointed. 'He's the town's handyman, he can unplug your swimming pool drain. He's done jobs for me, excellent work.'

The General paused before sipping his coffee. 'Dreadful fellow. Working class, you know.'

I began to wonder why expats honoured the General with so much misplaced respect. The English class system, I had heard, is left at the Spanish border. I said, 'I've talked with Dale, and found him quite likeable. OK, a diamond in the rough, maybe, yet he's trustworthy, industrious and inventive.'

The General chuckled dry amusement. 'Hee, hee. Invented his own credentials, you mean. Did you know that before he came here the man was a stevedore in Grimsby? Now calls himself a "technician", would you believe.'

'He installed my satellite antenna very professionally.'

'So? Does that make him an acceptable dinner guest?' The General's tone proclaimed *'Touché!'*

I came near to informing him that my work in Malaga demanded all my time, and that taking his shopping list was out of the question. I wish now that I had. His lists, delivered by Larry Garcia, his gardener, grew longer each week, and sometimes the more exotic items took hours to locate. Ellen called me a 'patsy' and ignored the lists.

'But,' I argued, 'running the General's errands keeps us in his circle of Alciguna upper crust; the wealthy, whatever their nationality, or those of correct lineage, whatever their financial status. Admirably democratic.' However, I didn't mention, no 'working class' allowed.

In October, the shopping list was a mile long and I had to take time from my work to fill it. Then I heard, by a word dropped at Trivial Pursuit and another at the post office, that the General's birthday was coming up. 'To celebrate,' Maggie Potter told me, 'he always throws an elaborate dinner party, for local friends and people who fly in from distant places. It's a highly prestigious occasion.'

'See?' I told Ellen. 'As a General Coles groupie, we'll attend the most exclusive event in Alciguna's calendar. I've heard that he erects a colourful tent in his garden and dinner is a *folklórico* production. A sheep is roasted on a spit at his poolside and everyone is served *tinto* in bulls' horns by Gipsies in traditional costume. It takes place this coming Friday. I can hardly wait.'

On Thursday, I checked my mailbox twice. I found bills and the usual Spanish versions of 'Congratulations! You have won –' but no invitation to the General's bash. Nor on Friday. I was puzzled. Could the post be to blame or would the invitation be hand delivered? I wouldn't believe that after all my fetching for the General's party, we simply hadn't been invited. When Friday night came, with no sign of an invitation, I chalked up another lesson learned in Spain: that an illustrious family name does not necessarily a gentleman make.

Since we had nothing else planned for the evening, I invited Dale Foster and his wife, Naomi, for dinner. It couldn't have been more pleasant. We discussed the autumn programmes offered on satellite TV, the upcoming choral concert at the cathedral, the recent mayoral election, the lack of progress on Olympia's mansion-to-be. Dale's wife proved well read. Despite no first name acquaintances with best-selling authors, her knowledge of plots and characters eclipsed that of anyone I had met in Alciguna. 'But that's cheating,' she laughed, 'since I read a lot when I spent six months in bed, with nothing else to do.'

Ellen said, 'Six months in bed! Whatever the reason, you look in the pink of health now.'

'It was a back problem. Had it for years until Olympia paid for my expensive operation. Dale has tried to repay her, since he took a course in electronics by post and is now working full time, but no, she won't hear of it.'

Ellen grew thoughtful. 'There is certainly more to the Fairfield legend than one reads in the funnies.'

'Oh, she's helped others as well,' Naomi added, 'mostly poor Spanish. But you'll never hear from Olympia that she steps in when the state refuses to furnish a wooden leg or a skin graft to conceal an ugly scar, among other things. She won't discuss her charity, dismisses it simply as "Olympia's Oblations".'

Toleration struck me. I would have to back up and reassess earlier thoughts about 'illustrious family names'. Never generalize. A red apple might conceal a wormy core, but that doesn't compute that all red cider is sour. Also, the Fosters made me wonder. If this be the 'working class', what is General Coles afraid of? Their conversation beats hell out of the bitchy gossip, bandied names and stories of inept workmanship or guffaws at the expense of 'quaint' locals, the kind of trivia prevalent in his circle's conversation.

I could imagine the General sitting at his party with his shoulders scrunched and his watery eyes merry, as he went 'Hee, hee, hee,' at putting us Americans in our place.

When the General sent his shopping list the following week, I filled it as usual. I wanted to prove to him that I didn't give a damn about not being invited to his party. Which was a lie. I did care, even if Ellen didn't. She had refused to consider going anyway, saying that such a party sounded much too lowbrow for her tastes.

25

Over a vodka-tonic on our terrace a few days later, after Olympia's usual litany of setbacks in her construction project, she told us that the General's birthday party had been a gigantic bore. Most of his visitors were intolerable snobs, she said, and the only comic relief was Manfred Nuremberg, who had drunkenly fallen into the swimming pool, taking the roasting sheep in with him.

Olympia was more positive about the gardener, Larry Garcia, who, she said, had won the town's admiration when he assumed the role of provider after a run-away tractor killed his day-labourer father. That had left Maria, her four sons and a daughter, with nothing except his burial expenses. Larry, as eldest son, took on odd jobs to feed the family and to keep the younger members in school. He excelled in many fields, among them gardening, painting, chimney sweeping and serving beer at carnivals. He also enjoyed a highly recommended reputation for escorting – Olympia changed it to 'servicing' – foreign ladies, chauffeuring their cars to out-of-town functions, on tours to the coast, or simply into the cork forest.

Thus few eyebrows were raised when a moneyed client, an English widow named Pauline, eighteen years his senior, bought him a van and financed his venture into operating tours for foreigners. She also married him. The happy couple built a house near the base of the castle, placing it higher than the church tower. Everyone in town could see the structure, its lines only a little more anglicized than its surroundings, and wished them well.

The marriage and the tour operation went well – until relatives on Larry's father's side heard that he had 'struck it rich' and returned from Barcelona to share his good fortune. Two uncles and a family of five crowded into the house with the newly-weds. At once, dissension developed beyond Larry's control and loud, drunken family fights erupted at night, once with blood. Pauline put the house on the market and fled back to England. Larry took his van and disappeared on the coast.

Three months later, neighbours were amazed when the SE VENDE sign came down and Maria with three offspring moved into the vacant house. Maria attended Mass in new, fashionable clothes. Speculations were confirmed that Larry had turned his van into a moneymaking industry. I was happy to see him zipping up from the coast, making quick pick-ups and efficient deliveries of people and merchandise wherever and whenever he was called. He easily out-performed larger delivery companies. Nothing seemed too arduous or too onerous for him to tackle, and he even began delivering Alejandra's weekly supply of food, absorbing her wild ranting and excited state with unruffled equanimity. 'Oh, Larry is supercharged with tact and momentum,' I heard at the post office. Olympia always added, 'That young man is headed for big time, I can tell.'

During the build-up to Christmas, Ellen and I learned early on to 'just say no'. To accept every invitation would mean attending at least three parties a day. We found that almost everyone throws a wingding during the festive season, each striving for the title of biggest, showiest or noisiest. How do you 'pay back'? You throw a party bigger, showier, noisier. We set a date for our own.

As the holiday approached, Ellen experimented with

local hams, cheeses, fish and relishes, until our freezer bulged with fancy hors d'oeuvres, canapés, dips and desserts. Salads and festive cakes completed our smorgasbord on party night, which everyone said was the most elaborate table in town. Added to that, we had seen a group of young girls perform in the school auditorium and hired them to sing at our party. Their final carol, 'Silent Night, Holy Night' sung in English, was charming, including their Spanish pronunciation of 'V', which made Mary a Birgen.

Every invited guest came. The mayor arrived, discreetly unescorted, our *practicante*, who runs the clinic, rode his horse decorated with red and green ribbons, and tied him at our front door. The postman came to hear his four daughters sing carols. The *gasolinera* owner brought his three station attendant sons, all eligible bachelors eyeing the female scenery, including Olympia. Camelia presented Ellen with a bowl of wild pig paté from her hotel. *Señor* Coronado, wearing a toga, brought his wife and a scroll of his poetry. Carlos Méndez, the communist electrician, offered his time and tool-kit in case my elitist decorations overloaded the fuse box. Gloria the Australian gave us a set of towels with 'Casa Potemkin' embroidered in a flower design. All my Spanish neighbours were there, plus most of the foreigners that I knew. But not Henry. He had declined, saying that since some villagers shunned him, his presence might blight my party. I appreciated his honesty, and since it was Christmas, felt even more sympathy for his grossly misunderstood campaign for good.

But the show must go on. Polita and two helpers wove among the guests and served drinks. Guisante was busy mixing them and pouring *cava*. He brought plastic 'glasses', so that Clara Cornwallis could drain a vodka glass and toss it over her shoulder without loss of crystal. I mixed two big bowls of punch, one labelled 'MILD', hardly touched, the other, loaded with 103, immensely popular. Manfred Nuremberg didn't leave its side until he was carried home, horizontal, and singing 'Deep In The Heart Of Texas'. The party, raucous but orderly, went smooth as silk; 'marvellous,' we were told repeatedly, a social coup that Alciguna would long remember.

The Harveys and the Barmakids ignored each other with refined disinterest. Paul Jones-Jones kept a room apart from Sarah MacDonald, who was now a resident of Alciguna. Olympia regaled those who could not escape with her report of installing a sauna in her new house, which she found burned only cedar boughs from Lebanon. Larry Garcia dropped in to wish us happy holidays. I offered him a cup of my punch, which he refused with a nervous twitch, 'No, *gracias*, I have to drive,' and left on the run. A few gatecrashers sneaked in, mostly foreigners. Well, there was enough booze for all. It was Christmas. Even that old fart, General Coles, would be welcome, had I remembered to invite him.

At around two o'clock the celebration rocked towards a crescendo, then, as if responding to some socially correct gong, it ended. As if by common consent, glasses were drained in near unison and a queue formed at the upstairs bedroom where Polita handed out coats and wraps. That's one good thing about European parties, when one guest leaves, they all leave.

Profuse exchanges of 'Happy Christmas' and '*Feliz Navidad*' progressed into the street, leaving the house silent, an abandoned banquet hall, except for Polita clearing the buffet table and Guisante and Rosa gathering up glasses, washing and storing plates and cutlery into crates for future collection. Ellen and I fell into chairs before the fireplace, its flickering flames dying to orange coals. Like Bill and Hillary Clinton on their first night in the White House, we congratulated ourselves. 'Well, we pulled it off!'

We had barely enough energy to lift our feet when Polita roared in with the vacuum cleaner, insisting that she set the house in order before leaving. At three o'clock in the morning, for God's sake!

Over the whirr, voices clamoured outside. Polita stopped the machine to listen. Shrill cries intensified as they approached my house and climaxed with a forceful pounding on the front door. Polita opened it. The whole party returned as they had left, except now they were shouting and waving their arms. One word persisted, 'Telephone!' I pointed, several hands lurched for it. I heard, *'Policia!'*

Through the cyclone of fragmented gabble, Maggie Potter managed an explanation. Pieced together, it translated, 'Larry Garcia was found near your house – slumped in his van – with a bullet hole in his head.'

26

My wardrobe from Boston included a tuxedo, a stupid mistake, I swore, until we received the invitation to the Harveys' New Year's Eve party. Neither did Ellen know why she had brought her best party dress, until now, *the* event of the Alciguna social season. Out of closets all over town came fancy gowns from their mothproof wrappers, and black suits, some verdigrised with age, from the farthest hanger. As guests arrived at the Harvey house, the subtle fragrance of Ilka's ceremonial mistletoe was swamped by what smelled like an all-out chemical assault on lepidoptera. Pots of orchids curled in revulsion at the pervading scent of mothballs. But nothing could depress the *felicidad* of the locals, nor the *présence* of Ilka's 'very dear friends of mine': several notables in the fields of art, theatre, business and government.

Without question, the reigning star of the evening proved to be Ilka's mother, who had flown in from Monaco for the occasion. Svelte and *très elegante*, she glowed with health-farm complexion, grey-blonde hair tinted and pouffed to cotton candy perfection, a black gown emphasizing her cultured figure. The breast of her low-cut bodice, her arms and fingers, sparkled with a none-too-subtle display of the jewellery famously smuggled out of Hungary in the intestines of a pet duck. Ilka had recounted endless times how her mother lost marriage to Orson Welles by the toss of a coin, when Rita Heyworth won. Never mind, La Comtesse, as she was called, went on to marry the late owner of a famous Paris jewellery store, and now a whole flock of ducks would be required to ingest her glittering collection for passage across a hostile border.

Ilka's trademark, chatter, always dominated her audience, large or small, but not tonight. La Comtesse left Ilka in the shadows, to handle details. The mother swanned about the candlelit room, brightening conversations as if waving an invisible wand, her teasing laughter prodding life into a sober group here, there raising howls of mirth by revealing the latest blunder or comic outrage by some international personality. Moving from group to group, vivacious and amusing, she constantly glanced at the Central Station-sized clock that Ilka had installed as tonight's centrepiece, its hands creeping towards the New Year. Olympia whispered to Ellen that there was a better party down the street, but didn't leave, since she didn't have time to reach it by midnight. She should have. At about five minutes to twelve, La Comtesse signalled the serving girls, who meticulously supplied each guest with a hand-cut crystal tumbler containing exactly twelve large, black grapes. Then she explained the ancient Spanish custom to us newcomers. 'One must eat a grape with each stroke of the clock at midnight, to ensure good luck during the twelve months of the coming year.' Her Magyar accent darkened. 'You must eat a grape for each month,' she said ominously, 'or the New Year will go very, very badly for you.'

The clock ticked the old year towards death. The room fell silent. The fateful hands merged under the Roman twelve, all breathing suspended. The clock's innards whirred. Everyone watched La Comtesse pluck a grape from her tumbler and hold it aloft, poised like an art nouveau bacchae. The gong struck. We all imitated her movement as she thrust the grape into her mouth.

Her eyes widened as she chomped on the grape and

reached for another. The clock struck again, she shoved another grape into her mouth, this time with difficulty. At once I saw her problem. As did everyone. La Comtesse made a futile effort to prevent spraying guests with grape giblets when she squawked, 'Ilka! You forgot to remove the seeds!'

It was like each grape contained a dozen seeds. Ilka had already discovered her oversight and tried to postpone disaster by popping another grape into her mouth with each gong of the clock. At around six, cheeks puffed, exquisitely painted mouth overflowing with juice, she admitted calamity and ran from the room. Those Spaniards who feared bad luck, or perhaps damnation if the ritual weren't completed, went on forcing the fruit into their mouths to the relentless rhythm of the clock. By gong ten, the entire guest list was choking and spewing and dribbling trails of half-chewed grapes towards the kitchen or bathrooms already overflowing with guests retching grape seeds into sinks and toilet bowls. Left alone in the big room, Ellen and I took the easier option of depositing our mouthfuls of pits into Ilka's pots of orchids. Manfred Nuremberg, who had substituted his grapes for brandy, couldn't puzzle out the commotion.

Gong twelve terminated the furore. Celebrants stumbled back into the main room with varied expressions, English guests pretending that choking on grape seeds was as natural as sneezing, the villagers nervous at having violated an age-old ritual. Ellen and I concentrated on our drinks. Ilka reappeared with vibrant sparkle, laughing, determined to resurrect the holiday spirit – 'More champagne! Join the conga line!' Despite louder music, the party was as dead as the old year, and remained so. La Comtesse was seized by a headache and retired to her room. Accepting her action as merciful release, all guests queued to tell Ilka what a perfectly marvellous party it had been, and left.

Ellen was silent on our walk home. I asked if it was because she felt sorry for Ilka. 'Of course I feel sorry for her,' she said gloomily. 'What a beautiful job of ushering in the New Year. She made so much effort to create that bubbly atmosphere, then one mishap, and bang, it's shattered. What chills me is that old misquote, "But for the grace of God, there go I".'

'Not only her,' I added, 'we're all due for a rough ride. We didn't complete that Spanish grape ceremony, you know, which means we're up the *rio* without a paddle.' What a trite way to express the events of the coming year.

'The future holds no dread for me,' Ellen sighed. 'It's the past year that echoes, echoes, in my brain. I can't forget poor Maria. During the last months two of her sons met horrible ends, Larry's death is still unexplained. Although the police, local and national, create a lot of noise and issue statements, what have they accomplished? Nothing. Only Henry seems genuinely involved, but since the whole town treats him like a leprous joke, he keeps his cards close to his chest.'

'Including us,' I agreed. 'I believe he is convinced that even we are sceptical of his so-called witch-hunt, however worthy his intentions.'

Ellen halted in her tracks, which halted me. 'Right!' she announced, reaching towards the stars, Joan of Arc dedicating her fate to heaven. 'New Year's resolution number one: we join forces with Henry in his search for evil! Onward and upward with his gung-ho crusade! To hell with what our neighbours think!'

My wife teamed up with Henry? Oh, joy. *Felez año nuevo!*

27

The young year began with the death of Ernst Baker, of a drugs overdose, it was whispered. Doreen announced that since she must go to Margate to scatter his ashes, La Casa Vic would be closed. That meant no more Trivial Pursuit evenings. The loss of that social event gave impetus to Ellen's New Year's resolution; something to do.

Our offer to pitch in with Henry Perry-Smith's search for child pornography purveyors brought a solemn nod, then a sparkle to his eyes and the first smile I had seen on his long face in months. Over coffee on our patio, he eagerly clued us in on his current thesis: 'Another delivery service company had Larry murdered to eliminate his expanding competition.' His antithesis: 'Not unless they were connected to the Russian Mafia, who laugh at the law.' Henry's synthesis: 'Aha! Larry must have been delivering child pornography in *competition* with the Russian Mafia!'

As usual, Henry had not one shred of evidence, yet suspects galore. He began, 'I've seen a swarm of technicians installing wiring in a house near here. Too many lines tapped into it already. Far too many antennas and TV dishes. I think the place needs checking out. What say you?'

Ellen, keenly professional, asked, 'Where is the house, who owns it?'

'One street west of here. It's on a *cul-de-sac*, like this one. Built around a patio, like this one. Shared by two Americans, both widowers. The house is divided, each has his own friends, but they have a strong common interest, entertaining with opera. Ha! And child pornography?'

'I know something about classical music,' Ellen offered, 'I'll see if I can wangle an invitation for us.'

'Without me,' moaned Henry. 'Their dinners always include a laser-disc opera, or some such. Personally, I prefer music with a tune. "Londonderry Air" or "Bridge Over Troubled Waters" is good listening music.'

'Very well,' Ellen agreed. 'We'll inspect the house, but you'll have to remind my husband and me what we must look for.'

Contriving to snare a dinner invitation does not indicate lapsed etiquette in Alciguna, rather, it is accepted as a compliment to the host. Thus, Ellen knocked on the door of the house of Elliot and David, stated that we liked opera, and was invited to dinner on Friday. 'It's Italian evening,' David informed her, as if she should know what that meant.

The invitation, being casual, left us unprepared for the elaborate dinner arrangements that greeted us. Neither did we anticipate the guest list. Olympia was there, glass in hand, 'bushed' from a hard day's work on her building; her sister, Olga, face screwed up more than usual, a jarring false note amidst the laughter. Grace Pennington and Paul Jones-Jones had come, Clara Cornwallis, Viktor Berki, and, oh, no! – that precious old fart with the fancy credentials, General Coles. I greeted him as a proper neighbour, and since he had shown no qualms about snubbing us at his birthday party, I felt no embarrassment at having ignored his recent shopping lists.

I enquired about the Nurembergs. David explained, 'They come only for Wagner. This evening's opera is *Rigoletto*, and they consider Verdi a degenerate.' I think I heard several sighs of relief.

We all crossed the patio and climbed stairs to what was called 'the music room'. The maid offered a choice of Lambrusco sparkling red wine or Soave Bolla, both from the Padua region, the opera's locale, so David informed us. He also served hot chicken liver canapés, *crostini di fegato di pollo*, during the first act, in keeping with the opera's opening banquet scene.

The abundance of electronic equipment in the room confirmed Henry's concern about so much wiring. Besides the large television set there was the laser-disc player, a CD player, a turntable for LPs, receivers for SKY and VIA satellite channels plus four mammoth loudspeakers, requiring powerful amplifiers and pre-amplifiers, ugly black boxes consigned to back cabinets. Ellen and I agreed to report to Henry that due to all that music equipment, there was no room left for receiving or transmitting contraband. Now sit back and relax, I told myself, and try not to fall asleep.

I was on the verge of questioning the ultimate sacrifice, becoming captive to someone else's musical taste, when the opera began. Its clarity of sound and image startled me. Why haven't laser-discs become more popular, I wondered, as the curtain rose on an orgy, Pavarotti performing a scene of debauchery straight from the pages of *Playboy*. The plot romped along, accompanied by great music, and the female lead's voice was fantastic. I found myself resenting the curtain at the end of Act One, when the TV screen went blank. Elliot stood and gave a drill instructor command, 'Chow time!' Spell broken.

We trooped downstairs to the patio where a large round table was set under a fancy tent, giving me dozens of ideas on how to decorate my own inner court. Even in January, gas heaters were adequate on this mild night. A fountain burbled in a corner, summer trees and a profusion of flowers adorned the walls softly lighted by hidden spotlights. Candles in the centre of the table made the arrayed wine glasses and silver cutlery sparkle; very showy. Heavy placemats under each plate were green, the napery red; very Italian. We settled into our assigned places, David offered a Bordalino with the antipasto, followed by escalope of veal wheeled to the table and served from a trolley by the maid. A red Merlot del Piave accompanied it.

I was dumbfounded to learn that Elliot, a bull of a man, who didn't look the type to cook anything more delicate than a boar barbecue, had prepared the dinner. Nor did his background suggest a complimentary connection with culinary art. Now retired, as an executive for an American oil company in Cambodia during the Vietnam War, he had driven a truck to deliver fuel behind Viet Cong lines. All this we learned from his booming account, which drowned out any comments or questions from guests. He was sort of a masculine Ilka, all palaver, except his forte was martial experiences. The other host, David, who had arranged the table and played the opera, was short, quiet and dull, contributing little except to keep our glasses full. Elliot and David, I decided, were the original Odd Couple.

After we scoffed the last scrap of veal, the maid cleared the table and set out a round of smaller plates. David pushed from the kitchen a trolley laden with accoutrements for preparing a further course. Elliot took charge of the operation with a commando's bravado while David, a trace of apprehension twisting his face, looked on.

'I know it's *gauche*, switching nationalities during a meal,' Elliot explained, 'but, with apologies to Verdi, I've decided to throw in a French dessert after our Italian dinner. Does anyone object if I inaugurate my chafing-dish that I received today from Paris? *Crêpes suzette*, anyone?' He glared over the table, daring dissent.

The response was predictably positive, with 'Oh' and 'Ah' thrown in to please the chef. Elliot scooped butter onto the *chauffe-plat*, checked the batter, stirred what he called the maraschino-curacao-kirsch sauce and poured paraffin from a bottle into the burner underneath. Everyone looked on, admiring his expertise in the exacting operation. A match failed to light the new machine and instead emitted a sharp smell of fuel that assaulted our noses. Elliot coughed annoyance, sloshed more paraffin into the burner, thrust another match.

WHOOSH! Flames shot up as high as the tent. The *poêlon* burst into blue blaze. Elliot stood back, mesmerized, watching napalm scorch a Vietnamese village. As if rehearsed, Olga sprang from her chair, pushed Elliot aside, placed a plate over the burner and covered the *poêlon* with her placemat. All fire extinguished, she reached up with bare fingers to quench the smouldering borders of the hole burnt in the tent. When we all applauded, Olga ignored our yelps of gratitude and instead used her central position to launch a new tirade. She wasn't ridiculous. No protests about donkey rides. Hell no, this time her complaints were more explosive than the chafing dish.

'I should have let it burn,' she muttered, rubbing her hands together to remind us that she had sacrificed her fingers to express gravity. Her gloom expanded into high drama, her voice crackled with doom. 'The whole town is about to go up in smoke, and I'm not speaking metaphorically. It's no longer a dreaded rumour, Morgan the pirate is upon us! Our Alciguna will be sacked, ravaged and pillaged!'

Paul asked, 'You mean the Morgan who developed great swaths of the Costa del Sol with cheap housing and turned it into modern slums?'

Olga ranted, 'The same Morgan whose name was

Montarelli in Palermo a few years back, charged many times with unethical practices, but never convicted of a punishable crime. He recently bought a large block of land on the southern border of Alciguna, and has obtained permission from our town hall to construct houses that will ruin Alciguna's view of the valley.' While we sat absorbing the shock, Elliot relaunched his Operation Chafing Dish, this time without pyrotechnic mishap. In no time, we were being served *crêpes suzette*. Delicious as they were, we ate in silence, mulling over the villainy at hand.

Coffee with sweet Moscato wine accompanied the remainder of *Rigoletto*, but I doubt if any of the minds present were concentrated on the musical tragedy. When the curtain fell and the TV was switched off, everyone stood, preparing to leave. General Coles, who had remained quiet all evening, remarked, ostensibly as an afterthought, 'Since my house is out of town it doesn't affect me, but I might also mention that the Pole, Mike Galuzin, is buying up all available houses in Alciguna, and plans to modernize them into up-market.'

'Mike Galuzin!' cried Clara Cornwallis. 'He's even more ruthless than Morgan. Buys officials right and left, so that he can ignore with impunity all building regulations. Poor Alciguna. Welwyn Garden City, here we come.'

'Oh, nothing so working class,' the General consoled cheerfully. 'He plans to brighten up the centre of the village with a beautiful new McDonald's.'

Speechless after the evening's one-two-three apocalypse, we all managed to mutter thanks for a marvellous dinner and opera, forced our 'Good-nights', then departed in sombre silence. Except General Coles, who, I'll bet you, chortled 'Hee, hee, hee,' all the way home.

Alciguna's destruction began almost at once. Seeing the village as a potential money-spinner, Madrid got into the act by providing a grant to restore the old convent. Despite its state of brooding abandonment, the *convento* remained structurally sound, a magnificent relic of Alciguna's past. Its medieval arches soared proud, its spires rigid, its empty bell tower dominated one end of town. Inside, stone saints meditated and ignored the leaking roof, carved angels and cherubim peered beatifically through their patina of ancient candle smoke. As a tourist attraction, the *convento* was a natural. The town needed only to open the ancient doors and charge admission.

In its wisdom, Madrid assigned a recently graduated architect to execute the renovation, who at once inaugurated a work of spectacular genius that would surely catapult him into the world order of Norman Foster and Richard Rogers. Gables were toppled, arches squared, rose windows reproportioned into geometric patterns; transformation of the building's exterior rendered it unrecognizable. Since the *convento* had been relegated the new function of community centre, his crew of university students gutted its old irrelevance with artistic zeal, obliterating its antiquity within days. Elaborate carved niches, figure sculpture and gilded screens were trashed and replaced by minimalist angles. Ornate panels gave way to stark planes, appropriate settings for *flamenco* and *cante jondo*, or concerts by the local brass band.

Mayor Prudencio, pleased by Madrid's attention, arranged a public inspection of the work in progress. Arriving with happy handshakes, he was staggered at finding Alciguna's architectural treasure being transformed into Pompidou Centre. He halted all renovation at once, and without ceremony dispatched the architect and his *avant-garde* Vandals back to Madrid. Too late. The half-medieval, half-Bauhaus structure was abandoned, and now stands dismal memorial to Alciguna's bow to 'progress'. Whereupon, enter the 'Developers'.

Dear Alciguna: *Never send to know for whom the bell tolls, it tolls for thee.*

28

February turned cold with rain, no sunny, diamond bright interludes such as had entranced me on my first visit a year ago. Alciguna was dismal in other ways, too, causing us to stop poking fun at the New Year grape ceremony foozle. Ellen sent a synopsis of her cookbook to a publisher where she had 'connections', only to receive a rejection slip by return mail. There was already a surfeit of cookbooks for Spanish microwave cooking, or that was their excuse. Neither were they enticed by my watercolor renderings of sumptuous dishes complemented by local flowers and *rústico* settings. Should we continue working on the book in hopes of attracting another publisher? Well, perhaps, but enthusiasm would be a missing ingredient in every recipe from now on.

Hillsides of almond tree blossoms were reaching the climax of their pink pearl brilliance, but, as I remembered from last year, spring was still a long way off. Which was just as well, I figured, since the developers couldn't begin their destruction of Alciguna until weather permitted. Despite inclement weather, new faces appeared, more foreigners buying houses, happy with the low prices, caring not a whit about developers' plans to update the village. Doreen's estate agency was booming. The leaden sky was countered by the enthusiasm of recent arrivals, whose warmth reinstated spirit into the continuous round of 'marvellous' dinner parties that had become old hat for us jaded regulars.

Thanks to Henry, I had met most of the expats who

lived permanently in the village, but not all. Lenti had attended Trivial Pursuit, but I never got to know her, perhaps because of her unique appearance. She had the face of a young boy: close cropped, unruly hair, but from the neck down she was outstandingly female; heavy breasted, wide hips, fleshy legs. Her style was frumpy housewife, flowered dresses with lacy collars, plus rawhide sandals.

Unlike most doorbells in Alciguna, mine worked, yet Lenti didn't trust it and knocked urgently on my front door one morning before Ellen and I were out of bed. I opened it, and Lenti stood waiting to inform me, in a pleasant English way, without preamble, 'I've been raped.'

'What?' I gasped, gently taking her arm and leading her inside to a chair. 'Are you all right? Can I get you a brandy?' I tried to soothe her shock. 'Have you notified the police? When did this happen?'

She shrugged. 'Oh, it happens all the time. And yes, I have reported it to the police, also to the *Guardia Civil*, but they do nothing. Now I hear that you have a typewriter, and I want you to write a letter of complaint to the Madrid government. Will you do this for me?'

'Ellen is the typist, I'll call her.' I was still shaken. 'You say you've been raped repeatedly? And the police refuse to help you?'

She nodded dismissively. 'The first time it happened, they came to my house and told me to put locks on my doors. I told them that I already had locks, but that didn't prevent the gipsy from breaking in to attack me.' I reached for her hand, held it in mine and patted it.

'Oh, he was a crafty one,' she said in a choppy voice, eyes slitted, teeth bared. 'First, he asked for a drink of water, humbly, as if I didn't know what he was up to. When I said no, he didn't leave, instead, asked if I lived alone. The reason for that question was so blatantly obvious, I slammed the door shut right in his face, I did.'

'He didn't take the hint? He didn't leave?'

Lenti shook her head. 'He just stood there, right outside my door, smiling, shirt open, flexing all his sweaty chest muscles. He was tall, and now breathing so heavy I became frightfully alarmed. Then it dawned on me that if I spoke harshly to him, he would go away. So I did the sensible thing, and insulted him. Oh, I did. Ever so rudely.'

'Good! What did you say?'

'I laughed at him. I shouted, "You've got no balls! You're not man enough to rape me!"'

I dropped her hand. 'Oh dear.'

'Anyone but a gipsy would have slunk away after that.' Lenti shivered and clutched her throat. 'But not this – this hairy animal. Instead, he seemed to explode. Kicked the door open, even though I had forgotten to lock it, and grabbed me. The rest, you might say, is history.'

I took a deep breath before querying further. 'You say there were other attacks? Different men?'

She sighed. 'The same man. The locks have been broken so many times, I don't have them repaired any more. He just walks in and rapes me at will.'

'Are you sure you want to complain to Madrid?' I asked, albeit hesitantly.

She tossed her head and pulled a hand-written page from a pocket in her skirt. 'Here is the pencilled letter. Should I wait for it to be typed, or come back later?'

I told her that Ellen and I were going to Malaga, and we would deliver the typed copy on our way home. She agreed, drew directions on an old envelope for finding her house, apologized for getting us out of bed, and strolled off towards Bar Suerte.

Our shopping in Malaga was lighter since Ellen's cutback on cooking experiments, and the back seat easily held all our purchases. Without General Coles' list, the car trunk held little more than my next artwork assignment, which was fortunate, because our groceries were shaken to shreds. We found that Lenti's map directed us up a steep, rutted track that corkscrewed down into a valley made green by a meandering stream. The formidable route ended at a square, unpainted cement blockhouse that was camouflaged by a lush growth of brush and trees. Scribbled letters on a slab of bark nailed over the front door named it 'Liver Bird Perch'. The corrugated iron roof held early spring weeds, screened windows were shuttered, no glass. Three dogs met us, but, unlike the Yahya Barmakids mastiffs, these were eager for a pat on the head instead of a leg bone. Chickens scattered, housecats observed us with languid curiosity, geese waddled up from the stream to inspect our intrusion. Lenti stepped from the front door onto the lean-to porch, its posts encoiled with last summer's ragged morning glory vines. She let the door slam behind her, a nanny goat grazing nearby jerked up her head to stare at us.

Lenti thanked us for the typed letter, then insisted that we have tea, to restore us after the stressful drive to her house. She brushed winter dust from a crippled wooden table, and tilted plastic chairs to clear them of leaves, for us to sit on. I asked if I might use her toilet, since we had been on the road for two hours from Malaga. She laughed, and pointed. 'You aren't bashful? Go behind that big tree over there. You see, I've got daffodils growing in the loo, where they get plenty of water. I sell them at the market for much needed pennies. You can't use the basin either, it's a nest for a broody hen, she'll be hatching any day now. And I used my pioneer inventiveness to turn my bathtub into a rabbit hutch, safe from the dogs. I bathe in the stream, when it's warm.' She disappeared into the house, calling over her shoulder, 'Back in half a jiff, soon as I put the kettle on. Relax. Consider yourselves at home.'

Ellen raised an eyebrow when Lenti served tea in delicate Aynsley china cups, with wooden, ice-cream paddles for stirring. There was brown sugar in an earthenware bowl, but no creamer. 'You take milk?' Lenti asked, and reached for Ellen's cup. She carried it into the grass and called, 'Madonna!' When Madonna approached, she held the cup under the goat's udder. 'Say when,' Lenti told Ellen, and squirted milk from Madonna's's teat into the cup. Since Ellen remained stone silent, her cup was nearly filled, leaving little room for tea. Strictly observing manners, Lenti added milk to my cup before aiming the teat at her own.

She watched Madonna return to her grazing, pulled up a chair and sat. 'A real life-saver, that dear goat. I get twenty-five Yankee dol-lahs a month for keeping her.'

'Twenty-five?' I asked. 'A month?'

'There was an American who lived in Alciguna for a while, claimed he owned a yacht in Chesapeake Bay. Bought this goat, slept with her, fell in love with her, but ran out of money and had to return home and get a job. He pays me to keep Madonna happy until he returns. These payments keep me ticking. Otherwise...' Lenti sighed.

I started to ask, but Ellen led, 'Have you lived here long?'

Lenti smacked her lips over her tea. 'Oh, about five years. The house was a gift. I always wanted to live in the forest, where I could be with animals, so my husband bought this place for me.'

Trying to picture Lenti as a blushing bride, I glanced at her. 'He did?'

Ellen asked more directly, 'Where is your husband, now that you're molested by this gipsy menace?'

Lenti set down her cup, leaned back and savoured a deep breath, ready to recount her life. Since she had no audience in these woods except Madonna, I saw at once that Ellen's question had entrapped us.

'I didn't always have these hips, did I,' Lenti began, and erected her shoulders in elegant pose. 'No, only a few years ago I was a slim and attractive waitress at the Lido, the most famous nightclub in Paris. Did you know that they employ mostly English girls there because our legs are longer? I wore my hair short, as it is now, and rumour had it that I was a transvestite. I didn't mind, oh dear no. It added to my *invididualité*. My sexy answers regarding my gender always brought enormous tips. It was all such a delightful giggle. I had borrowed to get to Paris from Liverpool, you see, and was approaching glorious liquidity, when – oh, shit! The Lido adopted a policy of more "ethnic" employees. A tart from Cameroon took my job.'

Ellen shook her head in sympathy. 'I see your problem.'

Lenti's eyes remained in the past. 'But along the way, I had acquired an aging admirer. Oh, yes, a real *papa gâteau*, more money than brains, who thought I was the greatest thing since penicillin. He was completely bonkers, you see, insisted without let up that we were meant for each other and should be married. I laughed and kept pushing him away, but he went on proposing until...'

Ellen helped, 'Until Miss Cameroon arrived?'

'I knew it would be a ghastly mistake.' Lenti raised a knowing eyebrow. 'Yet, money does have an aptness for putting things right, so I said yes. We went through the ceremony and at once, I mean on our wedding night, I discovered what a ludicrous bungle I had made. Prince *Charmant* faced an even bigger problem, when he discovered that I was not a boy. Our marriage was total disaster but he was a French gentleman, after all, and offered me a 'consolation prize' of my choice. I chose this house; he bought it for me, so good-bye Lido de Paris, hello Liver Bird Perch.'

I stood and placed my half-empty teacup on the table, where Ellen had already left hers, untouched. 'Sounds like one gipsy rapist has also discovered that you're not a boy.' I handed Lenti the typed letter. 'If you'll sign this, we'll mail it for you in the village. Madrid will surely send in the law to protect you.'

Lenti took the typed page and held it at arms length, as if struck with far-sightedness. 'This letter wouldn't do any good,' she crunched it into a ball and hurled it into a clump of oleander flowers. 'A complete waste of time to send it. I suppose I was a bit hasty this morning, the problem got out of hand when I heard that the gipsy had raped another woman on the coast road. The horror of it!' She hugged herself and shuddered. 'In the meantime, I'm awfully sorry to have troubled you, and I do appreciate your effort to help. More tea?'

Ellen and I said no together and stepped from the porch into tall grass. Ostensibly clearing a path for us, Lenti made a furtive effort to kick two objects under an oleander bush. She walked us to the car, apologizing again for inconveniencing us. 'But now that you've found where I live, perhaps you will visit me again? This is what I always wanted, living out here among the trees. But satisfying as it is, I sometimes get lonely, you know?'

The groceries in the back seat were near unrecognizable as such by the time we left Lenti's trail of seismic craters and banged onto the main road that climbed towards Alciguna. My car's rattles and squeaks subsided somewhat, allowing Ellen to ask, 'Did you notice that pair of men's sandals that Lenti kicked under a bush, as if trying to conceal them?'

'I did. They were placed neatly side by side, and were heavy duty gipsy, would be my guess.'

'QED,' Ellen laughed.

'Also, when I urinated against the tree, someone had

been there only a short time before me. Someone taller than I am.'

'Hearing that he had raped another woman, Lenti must have thought that her tormentor had moved on. Thus her letter of complaint to Madrid. Now that he has returned she no longer seeks revenge, so destroy the letter. H-m-m-m. That gipsy sounds like quite a man.' Ellen sighed, almost dreamily.

'Baby! You never told me! You like 'em rough? OK. One ghastly rape coming up.' I stamped the gas pedal. *The merry cuckoo, messenger of spring, was on the wing.*

29

The rains removed to northern Europe and my work schedule slackened. Ellen and I began 'spreading our wings', taking weekend drives on flowered back roads to government operated Paradors, usually mediaeval castles or monasteries refurbished into luxury hotels. Most were located in or near historic delights, all served excellent food, with tariffs within the confines of my budget. This being Spain, I could drive my shabby old car to a hotel's grand entrance, assured that I would receive a first-class welcome.

The state of my car, more aged and rusty than Olympia's Fiat, didn't deter her from setting a date for a trip to see her relatives in southern France. My company owed me two weeks' vacation, Ellen's plans for writing a cookbook were assigned back burner status, thus an interruption of routine seemed just the ticket. Besides, Olympia said that if I drove my car she would split the fuel costs, and once in her cousin's 'chateau' in France, our lodgings would be gratis. Too good to pass up, even when friends whispered warnings at the post office and at dinner parties. 'But I get along with Olympia very well,' I bragged. 'I know how to handle her.' I now choke when I think of the infinite stupidity of that remark.

To avoid any misunderstandings along the way, I set ironclad rules, times, dates and the seating arrangement, which were sanctioned by all parties. We agreed that Ellen would sit in front as my navigator, Olympia would have the back seat to herself. Together we chose the roads we would take and the hotels we would use *en route*, limited ourselves to one large bag and one overnight bag each, and sealed the agreement over vodka-tonics on our terrace. Lafayette, here we come!

On the morning of our departure, we arrived at Olympia's house at the agreed hour, eight o'clock, and found Jesús Maria sitting on a stack of six boxes at the kerbside, two suitcases, four gallon-sized glass jars of honey and two potted orange trees at his feet. We stopped and Jesús Maria opened our back door. We realized that this collection was our intended cargo when he started shuffling it into the rear seat. I leapt from the car to protest. 'It's what *Señora* says,' Jesús informed us, and asked for the key to the trunk.

I stamped to the cluster of goat bells at Olympia's front door and gave the central rope a powerful yank. When the racket died down, I heard her kindly voice, 'Just a minute, darling, I'm getting out of bed. Give me a moment to pee and put on my face.'

She hurried from the house but stopped short, dismayed by the space her boxes had left on the rear seat. She announced, 'Much too small. Ellen will have to sit there. I'll take the front seat and navigate.'

Ellen smiled sweetly. 'If you remove some of the extra baggage you're taking, you'll have plenty of room to sit. I'm not moving.'

Olympia gave her a hurt glance, sighed resignation and wriggled her rear between boxes like a settling broody hen. Before she would allow me to start the engine, she arranged a cardboard bar over her lap and squirmed around until she had placed on it a jug of vodka, large bottles of tonic water and a brimming ice bucket. She mixed herself a drink and waved it at me. '*A la France, Jacques!* Hneh, hneh, hneh!'

Once we started to roll, Olympia started to complain.

'You're driving too fast, darling. You're spilling my drink. You've got to slow down.' With hundreds of miles to go, I foresaw trouble, but couldn't turn back. After all, hadn't I assured everyone that I could 'handle' Olympia? In desperation, an idea flashed, and in Ronda I found a plastic cup with a cover, through which I thrust a bent straw for her to suck on. It worked. I could now drive at normal speed without sloshing the vodka from her cup. Another blessing presented itself, quite unexpectedly. We learned, with happy relief, that after two drinks Olympia took a short nap. I could then floor the gas pedal and make up for lost time.

Awake, she contradicted Ellen's directions in terms of catastrophe. 'We're lost! This is the wrong road! We should have taken that last right turn.' Ellen would point out the correct route on the road map and Olympia would fire a stock answer, 'I've been here before and I know the way, believe me!' Once, Ellen gave in and followed Olympia's instructions. We lost an hour finding our way back onto the main highway, while Olympia sucked her bent straw in silence. Unlike Trivial Pursuit, she couldn't bluff her way though the road map, so directed instead. She shrieked, 'Stop! Stop!' when a traffic light turned red a good hundred yards ahead, and imperatives like 'I need the loo, darling' came every two hours, regardless of our location. By the end of the day I was, like, totalled.

We made speed only while Olympia slept, and reached our first night's destination an hour later than planned. I parked in a garage underneath the hotel we had booked, Ellen and I took our overnight bags, registered at the front desk and headed for our room. Not Olympia. She shrilled disbelief, 'You're leaving your baggage in the car overnight? I have friends who lost everything, trusting hotel parking lots. Not me. Certainly not!'

My annoyance flared. 'You're taking six boxes, two

suitcases, four jars of honey and two orange trees to your room? Don't look at me. Get the bellhops to tackle your logistics.' Ellen and I left her standing in the lobby. The day's driving had shorted out my patience for humouring frustrated packrats.

Settled into our sparse but adequate room, Ellen commented on its cleanliness and rushed for the shower. Above the sound of splashing water, I heard a commotion in the hallway, commands that unmistakably echoed Olympia. I opened my door to find her leading four bellhops down the hallway at a brisk pace. They were lugging six boxes, two suitcases, four jars of honey and two orange trees.

She huffed, 'Imagine! This hotel tried to put me in a room with mauve wallpaper.' Near outrage, she directed her entourage, 'To the front desk! *Pronto!*'

Before I showered, a familiar tread again prompted me to inspect the hallway. Olympia was leading the same bellhops in the opposite direction. 'This hotel should be reported,' she hissed over her shoulder. 'A room facing the street. Impossible traffic noise. To the desk! *Pronto.*' Her safari made an about-face and followed without missing a step. I wanted to call cadence, 'Bot tom bom ba!' but held it.

We had agreed to meet in the bar at eight o'clock, and found Olympia already hovered over a tall vodka-tonic. She looked fresh and relaxed, hair damp and neatly brushed back, her chest, arms and fingers radiant with sunbursts of jewellery.

'You're settled at last,' I commented, avoiding sarcasm. 'You look pleased, you must have found a suitable room.'

She smiled into her drink. 'The next room they tried to put me in had yellow curtains. You know how yellow makes me look sallow? Now...'

Ellen ventured, 'You've found a room that suits you?'

'Not a room, darling, they gave me the entire top floor, at no extra cost.' A flicker of triumph brightened her eyes. 'After dinner you must come up to the penthouse for a brandy. My view of the city lights is breathtaking, hneh, hneh, hneh.'

Driving all day, we spent our second night in a modern hotel where all the rooms were identical, therefore no extras for Olympia to finagle. We left early the next morning and approached the French border at midday. A light drizzle polished the road, border guards in dark rain gear emerged from a looming customs building and signalled me to stop. Olympia tensed. 'A spot check!' she shouted 'Drive on! They're won't bother to pursue a car as ancient and impoverished as this one. Drive on!'

I ignored her and obeyed the guards. One of them approached, motioned for me to lower my window, saluted, and peered inside. His eyes zoomed to the boxes on the back seat. He started to speak, then smiled at the sweet old lady, someone's mother, head and arms resting on the boxes, sound asleep. He backed away so as not to disturb her, again saluted, and waved us on.

Out of sight of the border guards, Olympia was suddenly awake. There was a brisk rattle of bottles as she grabbed the bent straw and gulped down a full cup of vodka, no tonic. She seemed oddly shaken. I wondered why.

Olympia had promised a chateau, and we found it couched between low, unkempt hills east of Aix en Provence. I dreaded stopping my rusty car before marble steps and soaring columns, therefore was relieved to find that it didn't jar or clash, in fact, it blended like a homecoming. The vast house was more dilapidated than my limousine.

Further, it looked abandoned, except for a few goats chewing on forlorn-looking shrubbery, and scrawny chickens fluffing in dustbowls in the driveway.

The chateau had once been grand, boasting ornate iron balconies, now rusted, and stone friezes, now crumbling, its sculptural chimneys serving as pedestals for storks' nests. The building's deterioration looked ominous – the mansard roof of one wing had already collapsed. Maintenance appeared to have terminated with the First World War.

I would swear that Hollywood make-up artists and costumers had created this hackneyed set piece of titled poverty. Olympia's relatives, by a distant cousin, were ideally cast as occupants of the mouldering edifice; a tweedy old Baron, tall, ex-sensual and balding; his papery thin wife with black hair pulled back into a bun until her eyes popped, and the obligatory shy maiden daughter. All awaited us on moss dappled stone steps, pretending a show of ceremonial welcome. I honestly expected to a hear a director call, 'Don't overdo it!'

The Odeaus escorted us through a maze of derelict rooms festooned with what looked like rubber glue spider webs, and eventually we clattered into inhabited quarters towards the rear of the building. Again, cinema decorators had been at work. Old chandelier hooks in the ceilings supported naked low-wattage bulbs that saturated the remnants of grandeur with dreariness. Classicly carved furniture appeared rickety and threadbare, there were dark squares on the wallpaper that evidenced departed pictures, and the curtains sagged in petrified folds. Panelled walls featured faded hunting scenes and layers of old carpets kept the rooms chilly, even on this warm spring afternoon. In the *salon*, two hounds slept in front of a colossal stone-carved fireplace. It was boarded over, probably to prevent draught, since beside it stood a small cylindrical iron stove for heat, its flue jutting through a tin square in a stained-glass window.

A hefty woman in street clothes showed Ellen and me upstairs. She told us that her name was Marie, that she had been hired for the occasion of our visit, and assured us our room was *sanitaire*, having cleaned it herself only this morning. The canopied bed stood monumental, solid as its mattress of compressed cotton, and when disturbed, the pillows smelled ripe with fossilized feathers. The windows, starkly curtainless, highlighted two chairs of bristled horsehair. A heavy white bowl and ewer of fresh water stood atop a *bombé* chest of drawers. Marie interpreted my inquiring glance and informed us that there existed one bathroom, for all of us. However, she added, there was a *pot de chamber* underneath the bed, and that we should feel free to use it. 'And if you wish to have a bath, please tell me, and I will heat the water. Not on Friday, for that is the day *le Baron* uses the bathroom to prepare for *le weekend*.'

It was a perfect evening for sitting on the terrace, magpies scrapping in the eaves, the sun settling behind hillsides pinstriped with greening vineyards, yet drinks were served in the dank gloom of the *salon*. Two potted orange trees had recently been placed on a broken marble tabletop. The dogs remained asleep before the fireplace. Madame Odeau, wearing a loose, low-cut black silk gown and silver bracelets, reclined deep in a winged chair. Her sole movement was the twirling of the end of a string of *faux perles* draped from her neck, as Olympia tried to converse with her in French.

The Baron sat relaxed in a limp tuxedo, its silk lapels perforated by burn spots. He smoked hand-rolled cigarettes, smiling satisfaction with each deep draw, yet did not offer them to guests. Their sweet aroma reminded me of the resurrection ritual at Delores and Peter's Casa Grande back in Alciguna. The daughter was plain French yet pleasant, and wore a ruffled dress styled when she was twenty years younger. Marie served rosé wine, which tasted better than its grey colour deserved, perhaps because I had driven all day and was parched to dehydration. Olympia, distinguished in a self-styled made-in-Alciguna organdie gown, sat bibbing vodka-tonic, imported by her for her own use. Ellen toyed with her wine and drank sparingly, embarrassed by our inappropriate dress: leisure togs, sandals, no tie for me, no jewellery for her. Yet, nobody seemed to mind, we were Americans.

Further *dramatis personae* emerged from the wings: the brother of Madame Odeau, ex-Navy commander, slicked black hair, waxed moustache, a frizzy-haired blonde half his age on his arm; the son, a doctor, blue blazer sporting double rows of brass buttons, escorting a compactly built girlfriend to whom, he announced, he was engaged. Only he spoke English, and I, pretending interest, asked if he practised medicine nearby.

'Certainly not!' Claude Luc laughed as if I had made a joke. 'I live in Nice and play six months of the year. *Sans souci.*'

'Some people have all the luck...' Ellen probed.

Claude Luc continued to laugh. 'My work is seasonal. I have exclusive rights to three ski resorts in the French Alps, and have a clinic at the base of each ski jump. Thus guaranteed a lucrative flow of broken arms, legs, backs and necks when it snows, my life is *très* laid back in summer, you see.'

Try as I might, I can't remember another thought that we exchanged, other than his claim that Spain was being ruined by tourists, and my counter that France was over-socialized. Our discussion, not vital to either of us, ceased abruptly when the cook burst through a postern door. He was waving shears and clutching a handful of chives.

his shrill laughter piercing the sedate quiet of the *salon*. Oriental eyes creased his round face, and hair protruded like a horsetail from under his hat. His flowered moumou indicated a bulbous figure; he bobbed when he walked as if equipped with rubber knees, furry bunny slippers slapping his heels. One hound opened an eye to watch him shuffle towards the kitchen, giggling, 'I bring fresh *ciboulette* from the jardin. Better than from *réfigérateur*, slic, slic, because this house don't have one.'

Moving to the even darker dining room, Madame Odeau seated us around the candle-lit table. The cook reappeared with a tray to distribute bowls of vichyssoise sprinkled with the chives. He hadn't had time to wash it, and I wondered if the dogs frequented the garden.

Without warning, his exuberance bubbled out of control. He began skipping around the table, cuffing each diner's arm in passing as if playing 'tag' and chanting, 'You will like my *ragout*! My *ragout*! *Oui*?' We all paused over our soup, nobody spoke. The cook answered himself. 'You will like my *ragout*. Is fresh, I make today. Not from *supermarché*, no, I make from this farm. Hot zing-a-zing-ding, dooby-dooby-doo. Oh, you like my *ragout*!' He kicked one bunny slipper into the air and added a further 'Whoop-a-doo-doo' as he bounded into the kitchen.

Olympia dropped her spoon into her cracked Limoges soup plate, its clatter jarring the room's sudden silence. 'My God!' she screeched. 'Check the honey!'

'*Mon Dieu! Mon miel!*' gasped the Baron, and both of them dashed from overturned chairs to the kitchen.

Ellen looked heavenward when I reverted to nosey gaucherie and followed. We found the cook perched on a work counter, holding between his crossed legs one of the gallon jars of honey that Olympia had brought from Alciguna. He thrust his hand into the jar with piston frequency and licked the honey from his fingers, eyes closed in dreamy delight. The Baron snatched the half-empty jar, hugged it protectively against his chest and shouted, '*Rompez! Sortez! Sortez!*' which, I gathered, meant, 'You're fired! Get the hell out, and fast!' The cook made a grab for the jar, missed, and fled through the back door, cackling laughter as he danced through the overgrown garden.

From the kitchen door Olympia announced to the waiting diners, 'We've lost the cook. That means we'll have to ... that is ... Ellen, I believe you've written a cook book ... would you...?'

Ellen rose from the table and dropped her napkin onto her chair. 'Of course. I don't know what state dinner preparations are in, but I'll try.'

'With Marie, we should be able to make do.' Olympia again addressed the table, 'In case you're wondering about the cook, I'll explain when we return.' I noticed Madame Odeau, who hadn't offered to help, smiling behind her napkin.

After a brief wait, Ellen and Olympia returned to their places. Marie hoisted to the table a large bowl near overflowing with reddish *ragout*, its aroma mouth-watering. Madame Odeau, served first, used the kitchen ladle to lift a small amount of the stew onto her plate. Next came Olympia, who spread her hand over her plate, signalling that the vichyssoise was all the solid food she required, and reached for her vodka-tonic. Ellen also waved the bowl past, and when I glanced at her, a faint shaking of her head directed some sign at me, if I read her right, but I didn't get it. Marie held the bowl for me to help myself, Ellen tried to push my plate away. I couldn't understand her. I had driven all day, put up with Olympia's backseat driving, hadn't lost my temper once, and now Ellen was trying to starve me. I took a double helping of the stew, to prove my annoyance.

My wife is not known for inane statements, yet, tonight

she skated towards utter banality. Out of the blue she blurted, 'Recently I read that nobody knows the second verse of "Yankee Doodle Dandy". But of course I do. It goes, "Yankee Doodle came to town, riding on a PONY".' She kicked my shin under the table as she stressed the last word, convincing me that the day had been too much for her, too.

I shovelled more stew onto my plate, she threw more nonsense into the conversation, again apropos nothing. 'Picked up Shakespeare's *Richard III* the other day, and was impressed by how apt he is today. "A horse! A horse! My kingdom for a horse!"' Again she kicked my shin and glared at me each time she stressed 'horse'.

She turned her head as I began eating my *ragout*, as if the sight of my chewing distressed her. Poor thing, I thought. She's not feeling well and I must get her to bed. But first, I want to hear what Olympia knows of the cook's untimely departure. As do the other diners, except Madame Odeau, who pretends to eat, but hasn't actually taken a mouthful.

Olympia obliged when Claude Luc asked her to pause for him to translate for the others. 'Alciguna honey,' she began, eyes twinkling, 'was once famous throughout Spain. Mothers gave it to their children to perk them up, older people used it as a tonic. Until it was discovered by hippies, who descended on Alciguna like a plague of unwashed locusts. It was then that the law moved in.'

Claude Luc's translation refined the hippy reference. 'The law?' he asked Olympia.

She smiled, gratified at having provoked some response from the blonde, and intended to interest her more. 'There were fields of cannabis in the surrounding hills, and the bees made their honey from cannabis flowers.'

The blonde sat forward, blinked her eyes and admitted that she spoke English. 'Fields of cannabis? In Spain?'

'Hneh, hneh, hneh,' Olympia replied.

I dropped my cutlery. 'Is that where the honey came from that we brought through customs? Those four big jars?'

Olympia chugged her vodka-tonic. 'The Baron has an unquenchable appetite for cannabis, my dear, in whatever form.'

'You say the law moved in. Didn't they forbid the growing of marijuana in Alciguna?'

'Of course. They burnt the fields, the hippies went away, and now everything is quiet on that front. What they didn't know...'

'Not all the fields were burned?' I was beginning to sweat.

Olympia's smile turned serious. 'You mustn't repeat a word, not a word of this when we get back to Alciguna, but the law missed one of the fields. It is owned by Jesús Maria's father who continues...'

I thought of the six jars and the six boxes that we had brought to the Baron. I thought of the French customs officer who had stopped us. I saw Devil's Island rise beyond my plate and smile welcome. I felt sick.

But not so sick as I did later in bed, when Ellen told me that the *ragout* was part of a horse that had died that afternoon in the stables.

Ellen and I spent the remainder of the trip touring Nice, Cannes and Monaco, and drove to Marseille for a glorious *bouillabaisse*. On the trip home, Olympia carried no boxes of dried marijuana, instead, returned with six cases of grey rosé wine, which, of course, she unloaded and reloaded at each of our three hotel stops.

Back in Alciguna, she referred to the trip in delightful terms, calling it 'The bent straw safari'. She also let slip that I was the worst driver she had ever entrusted her life to. The response from friends was a wink and a whisper, 'We told you so.'

During the trip we had paid our own hotel bills, and shared petrol bills on the spot, but I was careless when we stopped at roadside restaurants for coffee, tea or lunch, and ice for the back seat. Sometimes Olympia paid, sometimes I paid, which came out about even, I figured. A week after we returned, Olympia arrived at our house, heavy with purpose. As we supplied her vodka-tonic, she took from her purse a wad of paper tabs. 'I've kept these bills from the stops we made,' she related, all business. 'I paid all of them. The way I see it, you owe me half.' She spread the bills on the table, proof enough of what was due her.

Ellen went to the bedroom and returned with her purse. She took from it a wad of paper tabs and placed them alongside Olympia's stack. Olympia sat back, mouth agape, treachery stricken. 'Let's see,' Ellen said, also all business. 'You say you paid bills totalling fourteen thousand, nine hundred and seventy-five pesetas. Now I have receipts showing that we paid fifteen thousand, eight hundred and seven pesetas. That means that you owe us eight hundred and thirty-two pesetas. Check these figures, to see that I'm right.'

Olympia blinked at the unexpected checkmate. She reached for her receipts and threw them into the air with both hands. 'Darling!' she gushed. 'I love you! You know, of course, that I was only joking. We agreed to evenses, so we'll stick to that, hneh, hneh, hneh.'

'Excuse me,' I said, 'but I must get back to work. A low-brow necessity, I admit, but I've got to earn a living.' I headed towards the upstairs bedroom that I now used as my studio.

Olympia called from the foot of the stairs, 'Let me

know when you can take another holiday, darling. I've got it all planned, and ready to go. Next time, Marrakech. *A la Moroc, Jacques!* Hneh, hneh, hneh.'

I dropped my paintbrush and stood from my drawing board, my day ruined.

Or it would have been, had I not recently heard about the exciting occasion ahead. Easter was approaching, and like everyone else, I was caught up in the 'Bull on a Rope' fervour, the most anxiously anticipated event on the Alciguna calendar. What we didn't know was that the bull would not be the main attraction this year. Never underestimate Henry.

30

The family pattern in most White Villages in Andalusia is the same. At the approach of adulthood, the younger generations migrate towards brighter lights and admirably enter university or find suitable employment. To stay at home means becoming a farmhand, a *peón* for a builder, a housewife. Local goatherds are paid by the government and receive a pension at retirement, but that civil position has a diminutive future. An undulating quilt of grazing sheep or goats covering a hillside is becoming a rare, treasured sight.

Large olive farms to the north of Alciguna can afford machinery for harvesting. Alciguna's small, hilly orchards must rely on young fingers for plucking, now unavailable because they belong to architects and receptionists. One of our ex-farm boys is lead model for TOSS, international up-market men's wear.

Good Friday brings home a tidal rush of affluent sons and daughters with their children, to celebrate the most family-oriented holiday of the year, Easter. Shiny cars fill Alciguna's streets, city bred grandchildren swamp the sweet shops, grandmothers sport new, bought for the occasion, black shawls. Firecrackers and rockets greet sunrise, enliven high noon and vibrate dusk, filling the sky with deranged birds, driving whimpering pets under beds and expats scurrying for aspirin. Even more abrasive, the town's brass band marches ceaselessly up and down the streets, honking and booming monotonous *pasodobles* for the edification of all. The cathedral's non-canorous bells clang without let-up – except during *desayuno* and *siesta* – for a whole week.

Palm Sunday begins with fireworks. The band assembles at dawn to lead a holy sweep of the streets, villagers wishing to have their houses blessed having hung palm fronds in front. Some owners go further and carpet the street before their doors with flowers and reeds, sometimes in leaded-window designs, biblical scenes, or simply mixed blossoms gathered along the riverbank below the town. The local priest performs the ritual by dousing the front door with holy water, altar boys troop after him, brandishing censers and tending the rites with grave dedication. A host of young girls in frilly white communion dresses bursts into joyous song. The brief ceremony completed, the procession moves to the next cottage requesting consecration. Several dozen souls dressed in sombre finery parade after the priest up the hill to the cathedral where Mass is celebrated – during which the brass band and the bells remain silenced.

Easter Sunday is different, when '*Toro de Cuerda*' or 'Bull on a Rope' sets Alciguna apart from other White Villages. This age-old event features two bulls, 'released' to charge down the streets, one in the morning, one in the afternoon. A long rope around the bull's neck is held by a group of strong young men, to restrain the beast should he become unacceptably violent. That is the theory. In fact, if the bull reverses his run and charges his minders, which he often does, they drop the rope and scale walls or climb wrought iron window grills, leaving the bull free to attack and gore at will. That's when *Toro de Cuerda* becomes entertainment for the masses.

After morning Mass, an all-pervading tension starts to build. The streets have been cleared of vehicles; bunting, bedspreads, shawls and gaudy carpets flap in the breeze on upper-floor balconies, ropes are strung across the streets, swinging stuffed dummies to provoke and enrage the bulls. Excited crowds fill the main streets, careful not to stray too far from the safety of their front doors.

The bulls, delivered by truck early on Easter morning, are stockaded on the northern edge of town, where they are joyfully jabbed with sticks and assaulted with jeers, whistles and blaring horns. Goaded into frenzy, the bulls paw and bellow, anxious to exact revenge by gutting every living creature in sight.

Since flat roofs are prone to leaks, foreigners own most of the terraced dwellings in town, and when the terrace overlooks a main street, it is the preordained site of a *Torro de Cuerda* drinks and *tapas* party. I was told that Easter in Alciguna can be cold, when wind or rain whips up the valley from the Atlantic. But this Easter, expat parties began with rooftops white with pasty arms, legs, necks and young backs exposed to the sun's underestimated treat. By the time the tubs of *sangria* were slurped dry, a lobster would feel at home among the swatches of crimson. Ellen and I were lucky to be invited to a large expanse of roof owned by the Murrys, Nancy and Martin, retired doctors who winter in Africa, teaching medicine. If not the classiest party in town it was the largest and most festive. We had a near unobstructed view of the curving thoroughfare, all the way to the distant bullpen.

Eleven o'clock arrived, the accustomed time for the morning bull to be released to confront the town's bravehearts But something was wrong. Things were expected to start happening, but weren't. Our roof party milled about with impatience, Guisante, manning his temporary bar, was swamped for refills. At last, the indomitable brass band marched into view, its blare and boom announcing that the show was about to begin. Halfway down the hill it filed into an alley, bringing its week-long *pasodobles* to blissful conclusion. Everyone rushed to the side railing for a better view. If the roof were a boat, it would have a precarious tilt towards the street. I felt squeamish, watching so many people supported by centuries old beams – but quick! More *sangria* before the bull runs!

The streets emptied, heads popped out of every jam-packed upper storey window along the bull's expected path. Faces turned towards the stockade, all ears cocked to listen. The main street now held only a few *macho chicos* who waited nervously, eyes shifting between the stockade and the nearest escape route. We were told that they would face the bull, beat their chests and taunt, '*Aja! Toro!*' And if the bull charges, bravery is measured by how fast their feet carry them from the scene.

Eleven o'clock ticked past. Eleven five. Eleven ten. We waited. There was no bull in sight. Shouts along the street called for action. The most eagerly anticipated event of the year was behind schedule. Throngs of spectators behind fences and on packed balconies, in windows and on rooftops, grew noisy and restless. Bullfights always start precisely on time, why not our bull run? Why the delay? Whistles, then chants demanded the bull's release. Protests grew louder, angry fists shook towards the bullpen Is this the way revolutions begin? I wondered.

A pinpoint of action appeared at the top of the street near the bullpen. All sound ceased, as if cut by the twist of a giant rheostat. The avenue of eyes concentrated on a lone figure bounding from a side alleyway onto the street that was expecting a bull. The figure raced pell-mell down the hill in our direction. It was hugging a medium sized box to its chest. It was Henry.

Before the spectators could grasp what was happening, another figure ran from the same side street as had Henry. It was slower, it wore a long black dress and baggy grey sweater, its arms waved with great agitation. It made an unearthly screech familiar to us all. Even at our distance we recognized Alejandra's 'Whah-h-h-h!'

I grabbed Ellen's hand. 'Is Alejandra chasing Henry?' My voice was overwhelmed by whoops of laughter. The merry uproar expanded until everyone was shouting comic advice to the fleeing Henry or cheering Alejandra; hooting, braying, applauding, blowing horns and tossing firecrackers.

Again, the crowds silenced abruptly. All eyes turned in unison towards the alleyway where the action had begun. Two men wearing dark suits charged into the bright sunlight of the main thoroughfare, paused, looked in both directions, spotted Henry and broke into rapid pursuit. The men were brandishing what looked like – I squeezed Ellen's arm – 'My God! They're guns! They're aiming at Henry! And – are my eyes deceiving me? Alejandra is trying to shield him.'

The four sprinters headed in our direction were in full flight; Henry in the lead, followed by Alejandra, followed by the two gunmen closing fast on their prey. And behind, gaining on them all – the bull.

The bull was running free, five youths trying unsuccessfully to grab the restraining rope that had obviously eluded them. Gunman number one, unaware of the danger to his rear, slowed to steady his aim at Henry. Alejandra veered, giving him clear aim. He fired. Henry staggered. In one action the bull rammed a horn into the gunman's back and heaved the body into the air, arms and legs thrashing, then slammed it onto the ground. Mindless with fury, the bull prodded the dark suit, his lethal horns mincing it into a bag of hamburger meat.

Henry slowed to a determined walk, dropped to one knee, then the other. Still clasping the box that he carried, his other hand clutched at red spreading on his shirt. The crowds, locked in horror, gave a universal groan as they watched him slowly collapse onto the cobbles. Alejandra rushed to throw her body over his, shielding it from approaching gunman number two.

Switching his attention from Henry to see what had happened to his cohort, the gunman's eyes bulged when he saw the bull's ghastly occupation. By reflex he swung his gun, pulled the trigger. The bull flinched, halted his shredding and glared at him. A second shot; the bull bellowed and headed at a fast trot for the bridge and open country, his five minders in hot pursuit, overtaking, in his van.

Windows and balconies emptied, doors opened, spectators spilled into the street. Walls and fences were scaled, the thoroughfare filled with pressing bodies. The silent mass converged from all directions on the lone gunman. He spun round, wildly aiming his gun, but seeing the hopelessness of his position, lowered it. A great wave of humanity washed over him. He thrust up his arms as if in the throes of drowning, then vanished into the depths.

31

SUR in English: The newspaper for Southern Spain.

TWO KILLED, ONE INJURED, IN INTERPOL RAID

Two men were killed in the village of Alciguna, Malaga, on Easter Sunday morning, during a raid by Interpol on a distribution centre of child pornography in the home of Señorita Alejandra del Rio. Pyotr Gusev was gored to death by a bull, Oleg Vinogradov was trampled to death by the same bull, according to witnesses.

Two more men were arrested at the scene of the raid, both admitted belonging to the Costa del Sol 'Russian Mafia', which is associated with a wider international paedophile ring. It is not thought at this time that Señorita del Rio holds rank in the Mafia.

Besides computers seized during the Interpol operation, the National Hi-Tech Crime Unit discovered over 9,000 still photos of child abuse and over 3,000 moving images, plus bundles of pornographic magazines and books. They warn that the seriousness of the crime should not be underestimated.

The raid was coordinated by Mr Henry Perry-Smith, a UK resident of Alciguna, who is well known for his crusades against various hues of illegality. While removing evidence, he was shot in the shoulder by one of the Mafia members, but the wound is not thought to be life threatening, say his doctors at Hospital Europa in Marbella.

Ellen and I found so many flowers and plants overflowing the hospital room and corridor, that our visit to see Henry was like a foray into a rainforest. Even in this early spring month, bouquets of lush summer flowers dwarfed our pot of English heather. Colourful ribbons and bows brightened wicker baskets, and there were enough potted plants, if transplanted, to fill his garden. A fat stack of get well cards on his bedside table and on floral displays all expressed one message: gratitude. Ellen and I felt downright smug. We had no reason to feel contrite, our gift was not an apology. We had stood by Henry when few villagers would speak to him.

After his spell in Alciguna's doghouse, he was enjoying a triumphant return to respectability, and beamed pleasure as he listened to gushing praise from a parade of well-wishers. He played down his shoulder wound and shrugged off his *coup*, as modest as a football champion. His smiles said, all is forgiven. Yet, only Ellen and I were asked to remain for a chat after visiting hours.

Right away, I discovered that my surmise about his wife, Serena, had been diametrically off-centre. I had pictured her as a harridan, the reason Henry spent most of his time on the streets. Instead, I found her sweet, extremely shy and vulnerable. Late forties, greying blonde hair and comely, she introduced a new insight into Henry's behaviour. Was I being overly sentimental in thinking that she might be the reason for his crusades, his larger than life interpretation of protection for hearth and home? Well, well, Henry, you've tossed me a saccharine tablet. I'll use it on my humble pie.

Henry requested tea, the nurse scurried to fetch it, Serena arranged chairs near the bed. Ellen reached and patted his good arm. 'We're awfully proud of you, Henry. What a terribly brave thing you did.'

'Right,' I added. 'You can thank your guardian angel that the bastard who shot you proved a piss-poor marksman.'

'My guardian angel was Alejandra,' Henry said, eyes lowered. 'Without her running interference, he could have taken deadly aim any number of times.'

I angled for enlightenment. 'Ah yes, Alejandra...'

The nurse brought tea and Serena served it cream first. As we drank, I thought of Lenti. But Henry was speaking.

'Ah, yes, Alejandra,' he repeated. 'You may recall hearing that her wealthy family set her up in a big house about two years ago? Her family, my foot! It was the Russian Mafia, who saw her as a front for their storage and distribution operations. She obviously promised to remain quiet so long as they supplied her favourite dish, *frijoles*. She's mad for fried beans, which were delivered once a week by the bucket-full – along with the contraband.'

'While no one suspected.' Ellen shook her head. 'Amazing.'

Henry stirred his tea, and gave a preoccupied nod. 'To go back in history: before Larry was murdered near your house at Christmas, he was obviously taking a slice of the pornography traffic to and from Alejandra's house, which the Mafia had no intention of sharing. They eliminated him, same as the murder last year on the road to the Costa del Sol. Remember that? The local police laid that one at the door of the Russian Mafia, but as usual, when facing all that money and influence, they did nothing about it.'

'How could I forget?' I grimaced. 'That alerted you to the Russian Mafia operation in Alciguna, I recall.'

Henry nodded. 'Twice, Alejandra gave pornographic pictures to children, and everyone wondered where she got them. The third time, I figured she must be close to their source, and followed her home.'

'I hope nobody noticed,' I laughed. Ellen nudged me and frowned.

'And there it was, staring me in the face, the evidence I had searched for in every house in town. Extra wiring leading into her house, rooms for storage, a concealed door to the street for loading and unloading, all windows professionally sealed and barred. After finding that ironclad evidence, I hid in a concealed doorway and waited for the big car that arrived every Saturday night.'

Henry, excited now, winced and stopped waving his injured arm. He continued the saga with quick breath. 'The Mafiosi arrived on schedule, I studied their routine. So obvious, yet nobody had questioned Alejandra's 'caring family' as they brought in boxes of food – in reality porno – to store and distribute. There were two computer operators and two mail-order handlers, who worked all night. They left at Sunday noon, delivered the shipments to several different post offices on Monday, but none to Alciguna, thereby avoiding a clue as to their origin. The shipments were destined for every corner of the globe.'

'While Alejandra enjoyed her manna from heaven,' Ellen put in.

Henry nodded. 'It was a perfect arrangement. She protected the source of her good luck, while the Mafia felt safe, believing that even if she did talk, no one would believe her. They were right, and Alejandra stuffed herself with *frijoles* once a week for two years.'

I still had questions. 'OK. But what made Alejandra turn on her providers? Why was she shielding you when you fled their attack?'

Henry made a croaking sound, reddened and glanced at Serena, who lowered her head. 'Well, you see...' Henry groped for words, which preceded a shudder. 'From the time we moved to Alciguna, Alejandra has fancied me. She used to bring me flowers, until Serena forbade it and chased her away.'

'Henry!' I laughed. 'You old Lothario. You never told us.'

'Argh-h-h-h!' he rasped, and returned to a more recent brush with fate. 'On Monday, I notified the *Guardia Nacional*, who called in Interpol, who took details and promised to conduct a raid on Sunday morning, when the Mafia goons were in Alejandra's house. But eleven o'clock came, and the *Guardia* hadn't appeared – which they claimed was due to the streets being closed for the bull run and an argument with city officials to let them pass. So I elected to do a little snooping on my own.'

I started to say, 'Oh, Henry, not you!' but held it.

Henry's second revelation expanded his embarrassment. 'Alejandra spotted me outside, and invited me in.'

Ellen gasped, 'Into the Mafia's den!'

'Into Alejandra's den!' I corrected. We strained forward in our seats like leashed hounds.

Henry twisted the leash. 'I entered her house and found a veritable supermarket of perversion. Pictures, magazines, books, shelves of tapes – everywhere, child pornography. My sudden appearance turned the place into bedlam, as you can well imagine. I saw the computer operators weren't armed, but the two other men drew guns and aimed. Alejandra ran between us. One gunman slapped Alejandra, she grappled with him while I grabbed a box of evidence and fled down the street where the bull was to run. You witnessed what happened after that. Meanwhile, Interpol arrived, arrested the computer operators, and took credit for the raid.'

What could we say after that? Ellen and I drank our tea, which we hadn't touched while Henry spoke. Serena saw us to the door and we drove home in silence. We were probably both thinking: what now? With Henry's game of Russian roulette concluded, what did Alciguna's future hold except more 'marvellous' expat dinner parties? After his diverting crusades, we saw only anticlimax.

Hold on! What about those earth tremors heralding Olympia's upcoming house-warming? A celebration of the completion of Alciguna's very own Buckingham Palace – the mother of all extravaganzas!

Even the 'Developers' looked up from their blueprints and blinked.

32

Whispers abounded, although there were no hints from Olympia, that her dream-house was receiving its final redesign before completion. Her builders stood about with nothing to do except touch up construction they had finished five years ago. She had simply run out of ideas for changes. About time, because there were comments about bags under her eyes, suggesting that the strain of creativity was taking its toll on her health.

Ah, but to declare the house completed would mean that handsome Jesús Maria was no longer required as construction manager. Rumour hinted he could be the reason the house was seven years in the building. But listening to such suspicions made me feel like a deceitful ingrate, and I promptly dismissed them. Olympia observed strict conduct rules, of her own choosing, perhaps, and she had a creative approach to the truth. But criticizing her, I felt, after all her good deeds, was a breach of confidence, an act of betrayal.

Her end of town was thrown into turmoil by wagons and carts hired to transfer household goods from her 'cave' to her 'castle' – she could no longer deny that she was moving in. OK, she admitted, but no visitors, only movers and decorators allowed beyond her front door. She informed all and sundry that she would let us know when the house was officially open, which would occur only after the grand inauguration of FAIRFIELD'S FOLLY II.

Characteristically, the much anticipated event was a

long time arriving. So many problems developed that people at dinner parties avoided subjects that might lead to a report of her thwarted progress. Oh, vexations galore, she complained, never admitting their source. The local carpenter was slow in delivering Olympia's own-design oak banquet table with sixteen three-legged chairs. In Alciguna's history, there had never been a water shortage, yet she installed a huge cistern under her house 'just in case', which now refused to release its hoarded water. Window shutters constructed of rare imported wood were rotting and had to be replaced. Since she insisted that her swimming pool be surrounded by trees, its filter choked on falling olives and the water turned Tanqueray green overnight. Her elaborate lightning-rod system limited TV reception to *Televisión Rabat*.

Unworkable innovations produced endless frustrations. Strain dulled the sparkle in Olympia's eyes, and her complexion turned pallid. Her breath grew short, each cigarette hack brought on a coughing bout. Yet, friends naive enough to suggest that she consult a doctor received a scorching lecture, along with, 'Doctors know only how to use knives. They deny proof that nature holds the only safe cures. Herbs! Organically grown fruit and veggies! No hormone tainted meat, no Frankenstein genetically modified – anything!' She pointed out, 'The Egyptians successfully treated arthritis with New Zealand green neck clam juice for thousands of years. Now who would fault that unassailable success story but a money-hungry, knife-wielding, modern doctor?'

Several of her friends, neighbours, Ellen and I, badgered her into seeing a doctor for a check-up. But not without protest. 'Not for my health, but for the sake of a bunch of do-goodnik busy-bodies,' she protested, as Grace Pennington drove her to Gibraltar for examination by an English specialist in lung and heart problems.

The joke was on us, Olympia laughed, when she returned in high spirits and announced that the doctor had given her a clean bill of health, even told her that she had the lungs of a sixteen-year-old. Grace informed us, on the quiet, that Olympia had thrown all the doctor's test results out of the car window, denouncing them as 'machine made guesses'. We had to accept Olympia's announcement as gospel that the doctor had predicted that she would live to be a hundred and ten.

Sure enough, as the house came together and celebration preparations neared completion, her cheeks glowed and the tightness of her face relaxed. She regained colour. Although her shortness of breath continued, she breezily dismissed it as over-excitement from the up-coming event, her grand house-warming.

At the post office and dinner parties we marvelled at reports of her approaching party, every day more elaborate. Nothing so corny as Coles's 'Gipsy theme'. No, this would be a banquet for all the people who had worked on the house, plus all her village friends, native and *extranjeros*, plus titled relatives who would fly in from abroad. The whole town began to quiver with expectation and nobody spoke of anything else.

The day finally arrived, perfect party weather. Extra cooks were imported from the coast, lanterns were hung and bunting strung in trees surrounding Olympia's house. Spotlights were angled to illuminate flowers and plants growing among the boulders in her hillside garden. Her swimming pool was strained clear of olives, allowing brilliant underwater lighting. An orchestra poached from a nightclub on the Costa del Sol would cater to various tastes, from foxtrot to fandango, expanded by Jesús Maria's disco speakers, the ones that had overwhelmed Peter's punk rock.

On the night, at eight o'clock the town seemed deserted,

everyone at home, donning party clothes. At nine o'clock the streets filled with high-spirited babble and the village population headed for Olympia's mansion. A few rockets went off from the church tower, suggesting a degree of divine sanction for the event. Hired attendants waved plastic light cones to direct traffic to available parking. Strollers advanced up the hill like lava in reverse.

Ellen and I heard music and laughter and jolly multilingual chatter long before we reached the house. We expected to find tables groaning with exotic food and drink – we were right. Uniformed maids stood overseeing a block-long line of end-to-end tables holding tub after tub of *sangria* and tub after tub of fried chicken wings. I smiled at Olympia's oft-repeated philosophy that a show of opulence is vulgar.

The house quickly filled with gawkers, preventing Ellen and me a glimpse of its wonders, but we knew that we would be invited later, for a better assessment of what Olympia had wrought. The pool filled with youthful swimmers, Ellen and I danced to the very good orchestra when space allowed; we ate chicken wings and drank *sangria* until two o'clock. Unable to find Olympia to express our thanks for a marvellous party, we made our way home. We later heard that the last tubs of wine and wings were delivered by truck at four o'clock, and the party reeled on until dawn. We also heard that once she got the party going, Olympia went to bed at around eleven, her usual bedtime. The whole town was being fêted, she could do no more than that.

33

Later in the week, Ellen and I were invited to see FAIRFIELD'S FOLLY II. Not a formal showing, but 'for drinks' before going on to a dinner party to which we were all invited. I could see why the house construction had taken years; every inch was custom built, its quirky designs suggesting Olympia originality rather than architect intent. The rooms were large and elegant, most with massive fireplaces and expansive windows encompassing phenomenal views. Yet, each room had a touch of Olympiana, a distinct sensibility that made it unique. Bathroom doors were camouflaged into hidden wall panels; each toilet bowl was raised on its own throne. Every wall held antique pictures, permanently covered 'for protection from light'. Woodworm had riddled several pieces of period furniture after so many years of storage in her former 'cave', but crumbling antiques still took pride of place. The handcrafted pieces designed by her, such as tables with free-form glass tops, and baroque headboards for the circular beds, were non-classifiable, a Victorian-Danish Modern-Farouk style all her own. The marble-lined entrance hall, proportioned for a grand staircase to the main floor, after her revision held a spiral staircase that one had to duck under to reach the first step.

I felt Ellen stagger when we entered the kitchen, an exact replica of the old one; the same table with its mountain of flotsam, the same jetsam-festooned ceiling. Assured that we were impressed with her creation, Olympia raised her arms, embracing accomplishment with proprietary pride. 'I strove for years to reach perfection, darlings, this house is now my monument. After all the toil and torment, I can at last sit back and relax in an atmosphere of my own design, my own invention. And wilderness is paradise enow. Hneh, hneh, hneh.'

Some people think that when they're on vacation, everyone should be pleased to forego routine and holiday with them. Such were the Marshalls, who arrived to celebrate buying a house in Alciguna; we locals to be swept away with the bliss that intoxicated them. The Marshalls: middle-aged English, well travelled, successful in business, children married, nearing retirement and could afford a second home – multiplied by a dozen other couples I constantly met in Alciguna. Faces and personalities were starting to blend together, no one couple achieving a stronger blur than the next. The Marshalls had invited us to dinner on Saturday night. Neither Olympia nor Ellen and I could think of a plausible excuse to decline, so we were on our way to yet another Alciguna dinner party. Looking back, two features of the evening dominate: one annoying, the other I recall with lashings of self-reproach.

Olympia had to rest twice on our way to the house, not typical of her when drinks are waiting. It wasn't a hot night, yet she complained, puffed and perspired like an overworked mule. She refused to sit in the dining room, claiming that it was too warm, and requested that a small table be set up for her in the entryway where there was a breeze. I can't quote the menu, only that after each course the Marshalls snatched up our plates, which we could hear being washed before the next serving. When dinner was finished, there were no dirty dishes. During the whisk-away meal Olympia sniffed derisively at her food, and turned downright scurrilous about the brand of vodka that the Marshalls served.

Now this is too much, I thought. The weather is not that hot and Olympia is deliberately attracting attention to herself, again exploiting her role of spoilt eccentric. Disapproval scudded across my mind. I had to admit that, yes, she is a magnetic personality, and yes, she is entertaining, to a point. Even so, her constant demand for special treatment does become irksome. Her elaborate palace had attracted a new band of followers, who purred and swooned and claimed to adore her endearing quirkiness. OK, let her new disciples also cater to her neurotic whims. Perhaps now was the time to distance ourselves from Olympia. I disliked the thought of losing an old friend, yet I sensed a cooling off in our relationship. Was the end of an era in the air?

After dinner we accompanied Olympia to her house. She did not invite us in for a nightcap. I wondered if, perhaps, she could be thinking of dropping us as well.

Alistair Cooke's *Letter from America* on Radio Gibraltar and bacon and eggs on the patio, had become a Sunday morning ritual since Ellen arrived. The only luxury I missed in Alciguna was the morning newspaper, especially the Sunday edition. I bought a daily paper during the week in Malaga, and saved it for our patio breakfast; we shared it and discussed the news, however stale. Then we were ready to face the ardours of a Spanish Sunday, a lazy *Domingo* of doing what we damn well pleased, usually nothing.

That's when the cordless telephone shattered *Domingo*. Ellen answered it, frowned, held it away and looked at it, bewildered.

I snatched it from her, and before it reached my ear I

heard the shrieks of a hysterical woman. I recognized the voice of Naomi Foster, and tried to calm her. 'Naomi, this is Robert. I can hear you, dear, but I can't understand what you're saying. Do you need help? Is there anything I can do for you? Is Dale with you?'

She wailed incoherently, eventually conveyed her message between sobs. 'Dale just rang me … from Malaga. Early this morning … Olympia … had a nosebleed. She got Dale to take her … to Ronda Hospital. They rushed her to the bigger hospital in Malaga … but on the way she … she … she died of a massive brain haemorrhage.'

34

My criticism of Olympia the night before transformed into guilt. She had every right to ask for a chair where she could be cooled by the breeze, she was probably feverish. It also hit me that she only complained once, about the brand of vodka served, which should have alerted us all to the fact that she was seriously ill.

Where to begin when one remembers Olympia? Without her indomitable style, will Alciguna revert to just another White Village? She alone established the town's prestige and set its tone. For certain, no one will be so presumptuous as to approach her inimitable performance as doyenne. *Sans* Olympia, *sans* Alciguna. I recalled the botched New Year ceremony that preordained catastrophe, and wondered if there could be credibility in such superstitions. Some expats nodded when Dale Foster mumbled on his return from Malaga, 'Damn those bloody grapes.' The more realistic added, 'Don't forget the vodka and the cigarettes.'

There were no facilities for embalming in Alciguna, and by local custom a body is buried on the day of death; by law, no later than the second day. Olympia's funeral was set for Monday afternoon at five o'clock. As expected, the small cathedral was full to overflowing, the whole hillside was enshrouded with mourners. Since Ellen and I were close friends of Olympia, we were allowed seats near the lectern, where the casket rested on a plain catafalque. Members of her family, most of them strangers to Alciguna, filled the first row of benches. Among them was one relative from whom I couldn't pry my eyes: Ben

Beardsley – Olympia's offspring, my nemesis. Contrary to his reputation as a seducer, I flinched at his cold, snake eyes. He was a masculinized caricature of Olympia: her face was pink and round, his a white jack-o'-lantern; her lips were full, his knife-thin; she was plump, he was a dressed hog. I wondered if the millions of pounds that he would inherit from Olympia could alter his appearance of East End sleaze.

I will say this for him, the grained oak casket he chose for Olympia was elegant, if adorned by a bit too much brass, and obviously expensive. A Catholic priest conducted the simple ceremony in Spanish. A proper Anglican memorial service would be held later in London.

With Olympia, nothing went without drama, and her burial came near to maintaining that tradition. During the sermon, Lenti, wearing wide-hipped overalls, strode to the front row pews and made a thumbs-up signal to Olympia's relatives. A wedding band flashed on her hand. The priest halted his drone and everyone watched Lenti turn on her heel, stride to the door and disappear into the street. The sermon continued.

After the short service, the Spaniards who had worked on Olympia's house, including Jesús Maria, shouldered her casket for its short trip to the cemetery. A silent host of expats and villagers trailed up the hill, then watched the casket being shoved into a vault. By the time Ellen and I reached the tree-shaded rows of layered crypts, Olympia's casket was ensconced in its ultimate address.

A disturbance was in progress, a protest by a crowd of Olympia's drinking buddies. They were already deep in alcoholic mourning, near the point of raucous bereavement. They wailed, 'The mayor promised Olympia that she could have crypt number 103, her favourite brandy!' Ready to march on the town hall, they chanted, 'He promised! He promised!' Spanish mourners looked on, mouths open.

Mayor Prudencio stepped forward, distinguished by the appropriateness of his black suit and tie. He faced Olympia's motley defenders, most in summer leisure shorts and tanktops, and addressed them calmly. 'In this new section of the cemetery, our numbers haven't reached that high yet. So I've allocated her crypt number 69.'

Cheers went up. The mayor blinked, startled by the spontaneous applause he had created, confused as to how he had so effortlessly defused a crisis.

We learned that Lenti's intrusion into the funeral service was to inform Olympia's relatives that she had found a mason. Earlier they had sent out an unsuccessful SOS for a professional who could seal the door of the crypt. Now Lenti's man, tall, with gipsy features, expertly hoisted the concrete slab over the opening and slathered it with cement to seal it permanently. With his finger he traced OLYM into its wet surface, ran out of space, and continued PIA below. He carefully wiped the cement from his new wedding band.

The Spaniards dispersed and walked slowly down the hill, probably discussing the weird customs of foreigners. Olympia's friends burst into an atonal 'I Just Called To Say I Love You', which they claimed was her favourite song. I never heard her mention it, but there were many facets of the Fairfield diamond that I hadn't known, nor been dazzled by. Word spread that there would be drinks at Olympia's house. Neither Ellen nor I felt in the mood for a wake; instead, we went home and drank commemorative vodka-tonics on our terrace. We listened late into the night to sounds emanating from Olympia's 'castle'; a boisterous celebration to sunder the gates of paradise, exactly as she would have planned it. There was no doubt who would be in charge, who would be directing her ascension into exalted realms. We toasted the driver, and hoped he was able to furnish her with a bent straw.

35

Instant betrayal, of Trojan Horse proportions, struck Alciguna. Olympia's will was settled, leaving everything to Ben Beardsley. He charged into Alciguna without delay and started buying up village houses and bestowing on them his famous Casa Potemkin facelift. He hired an offbeat architect to impose modern bric-à-brac on old façades, which clashed with neighbouring houses, but sold well to foreigners, assured by him that it was authentic *rústico*. Ben Beardsley knew his territory. I wondered how many of his buyers were drowned by rotten plumbing or electrocuted by cheap wiring.

He put Olympia's house on the market. It sold to a Swiss banker with a Cambodian boyfriend, who began adding Oriental touches at jarring odds with its Spanish design. What would be Olympia's reaction, I wondered, if she knew that her 'monument' was well under way to becoming a Buddhist temple?

As if Bacchus were a vengeful god of the underworld, the Curse of the New Year Grapes advanced inexorably. True to rumour, the first good weather brought the wrecking crews with their bulldozers, Morgan to clear land around Alciguna for new housing projects, Mike Galuzin to knock down ancient village houses and replace them with functional boxes. The townspeople split into bitterly opposing factions. Half applauded the advertisements and promotional articles being planted in London newspapers, which brought buyers by the planeload, and house prices soared. The other half saw greed ravaging their village, an endangered species facing extinction.

It was not the best of times for Alciguna. The year shambled on, piling misfortune on calamity. My friends were either dying, moving or being struck with rotten luck. Grace Pennington had a stomach problem, put her house on the market and moved to London, close to her doctor. Maggie Potter's father fell ill and she moved to Ipswich to care for him. Doreen Baker married a Peruvian cook who was usually high as a kite on one drug or another. He beat her up, she left him. In quick succession, I heard that the Bangs were returning to Denmark, where Gus had bought a stud farm near Horsens; Yahya won a contract to build a gymnasium for a girls' school in Chicago, he and Dawn had moved there. To add gravity to these unhappy events, the Nurembergs declared Alciguna as *wunderbaum*, added six rooms to their house and announced plans to remain there forever.

My most poignant loss was the death of my *Ama de llaves*, Polita, who failed to show up to clean my house one morning, and was buried the next. Another blow came when Serena developed eye problems. She felt she should move back to Kent, and Henry left to find a house there. Ilka Harvey's mother died of a heart attack. Ilka flew to the funeral in Grenoble, but an estranged sister had already scooped up La Comtesse's jewellery, and Ilka got nothing. One of Ilka's daughters had a baby, she became enamoured with it and withdrew from 'very dear friends of mine' entertaining. Viktor ran into Spanish tax problems, left for Budapest, and was uncertain about returning.

A few changes, however, were called favourable. Paul Jones-Jones found his dream mate, sold his house, and transferred bag and baggage to her farm in Norfolk. Gloria the Australian met a sea captain and sailed away on his fishing boat.

Olga Campbell went near apoplectic when developers started their 'Operation Money Storm', she called it, swore never to step foot in Alciguna again, and demanded that it be saturation bombed. She refused to speak to anyone who remained there, saying that by condoning developers, they were all traitors. She switched her activities to the coast, including her post office box.

With Olympia no longer on hand to force her to bathe, Alejandra wandered the streets, shabbier and smellier. Denied the weekly bucket of *frijoles*, she refused to eat what townspeople donated and became gaunt and stooped, even threw away the new clothes and wristwatch that Henry and Serena bought for her. She continued to stand in the street and direct traffic on a whim, but now, due to early stages of Parkinson's disease, did it with a shaky hand. Her 'Whah-h-h-h!' lost its music. It no longer terrorized children nor cleared the streets of dogs and tourists.

My Alciguna was falling apart around me, while the Morgan, Mike Galuzin and Ben Beardsley stars were ascendant. More foreigners were buying houses, moving in, falling in love with Alciguna and declaring it Paradise Found, as I once had.

I was not spared the Curse of the Grape. Ellen was over the moon with joy when New York offered her old job back. Of course she had no choice but to return, a chance of a lifetime to reclaim prestige as a television presenter of microwave cuisine, plus a salary cheque that mocked mine to shame.

The fortunes of others fluctuated and my workload tapered off, leaving me time to brood over the changes in Alciguna. Dinners were out, drinks parties were in. My reliance on the diminishing round of gourmet meals became critical; during Ellen's stay, I hadn't bothered to learn from her cooking expertise and now, unless invited out, I was back to opening cans and microwaving frozen potluck.

Among the new arrivals was a London publisher, who moved into one of the bigger houses, set up an office filled with electronic equipment, and switched his business operations from the City to Alciguna. His wife, a decorator, showed how a village house interior could be made tasteful without *rústico* clichés, but found few followers. These new expats adored the town, raved about it, and failed utterly to understand how I could claim that it had gone flat.

Professional artists and sculptors replaced local dilettantes. The little restaurant with six tables, Red de Seguridad, closed its doors and reopened in a modern building with twenty-four tables, its prices quadrupled. I avoided, 'You should have been here when –' or 'This town ain't what it used to be', and never once mentioned 'good ol' days'. Most new settlers looked forward to a profitable future, to hell with the past. Everywhere phoney *rústico* was replacing original quaintness. The cobbled streets were resurfaced with imitation stone, goats no longer fertilized them with their pellets. Two friendly donkeys that lived across the street moved away, their shed replaced by a fancy garage, home to two Jaguars. Bucolic Alciguna was rapidly becoming 'up-market', its transformation no longer a dreaded prediction.

Thanksgiving in Europe is just another Thursday, except this one, the day my company confirmed the inevitable. Since American hype had become commonplace, Spain could now produce its own and our talents were redundant. Our Malaga office was obliged to return to Boston. That included me. I was directed to complete the company's current commitments, and given three further weeks, on salary, to settle my personal affairs. Then I was to return to the States. Happy Thanksgiving.

Finishing off the niggling artwork backlog allowed ample time for me to prepare Casa Potemkin for the market and to get its legal papers in order. I had spent 'a bundle' converting Ben Beardsley's theatre set into a habitable house, and although property prices had soared, I couldn't expect to break even. So what? I could never resent the loss of mere money on the most rewarding two years of my life.

And us, my dear? Oh, we had our hi-ho's, didn't we! Now you're back in New York, New York, lapping up the limelight, I return soon to busy Boston to take up where I left off in the all-embracing advertising business. Everything the same as before Alciguna. It was Alciguna that gave our relationship wallop, don't you think? Could we ever recreate the intimacy that we shared in this small village? I doubt it. I believe that during that time we came perilously close to – for the lack of a more pertinent word – love. Hey, that was love, wasn't it?

Alciguna Christmas parties filled the calendar, yet when I went to one I felt like a stranger; old faces – gone. The capricious characters who might swear by a fanatical view on some inane subject, then next week defend its opposite to grim death – gone. Not long ago any lapse of morals or judgement was fair game, amusement for all. Now, party conversations revolve around money, how much a certain house sold for, what was offered for another, which house was going onto the market at what price. The new owners were indifferent to conservation or history, unless it affected price.

Ilka Harvey invited me to Christmas dinner, probably out of respect for Ellen's abandoning me to my own culinary devices. The meal was a facklustre event, with no 'very dear friends of mine' from society, politics or theatre to brighten the pauses between courses. Children scampered and squealed around the table, providing the party's only live action.

Ah, but New Year's Eve proved eventful, even pivotal. Invited to several parties, I chose the one closest to my house, simply for convenience. Its celebration swirled with new personalities, there were no ceremonies to suggest Spain, no Spanish rituals planned that could match the grape debacle of a year ago. There was, however, a disaster. A major one. I came face to face with Ben Beardsley, who celebrated New Year's Eve by presenting me with a catchpenny booby-trap.

Of all the casually dressed guests of this typical Alciguna party, two people ranked top hat, a young man wearing a tuxedo, and his wife, sheathed in a fashionable Paris evening gown. Upon arrival, the wife engaged in seasonal chat with other women, the man, tall, clean-cut, neat French hairstyle, drifted among the crowd. We met and fell into conversation, exchanging the usual party pleasantries. He quickly established that he was French, and in Alciguna to look for a house to buy. I as quickly advised him that I had one to sell, he slapped his hands together and we were at once discussing price and details.

Without apology, a man forcibly shoved his dumpy body between us. His ice blue eyes were chilling, his high-pitched words sloshed, each vowel umlauted. 'I'm Ben Beardsley. You bought your house from me, now I hear you're trying to sell it.'

I almost crushed the glass of *sangria* in my hand as I bared my teeth. All I could say civilly was, 'Yes, I've heard of you.'

'May I introduce Bernard Allard? Bernard Allard, this is Robert Brooks.' Uninvited, yet officiating, a strange expression of triumph twisted Ben Beardsley's face. Why? I wondered. I was to find out soon enough.

'Bernard and his wife are from Lille and are looking for a holiday house to buy,' he stated, as if I didn't already know. 'Tomorrow I will bring them to look over your property. What time is convenient?'

Bernard and I looked at each other, eyebrows raised in mutual surprise. 'Tomorrow is New Year's Day,' I informed the intruder. 'A holiday.'

'Rubbish,' Ben Beardsley countered. 'Tomorrow at ten o'clock sharp. We'll be there.' As I tried to bring my quick boil under control, he waddled off to interrupt another conversation.

Bernard looked embarrassed before smiling. 'Looks like it's established, then, that we'll meet tomorrow.' We shook hands, I ranged through the party, exchanged holiday wishes with a few people, and went home.

On television, Vienna was celebrating its Straussy New Year an hour ahead of ours. I uncorked a bottle of *cava* and toasted their old world schmaltz. At midnight, I went up to my cold, windy terrace and watched the fireworks of five towns and villages sparkling in the black mountains and fizzing brightly along the coast. I could see them but couldn't hear them – 'Tomorrow at ten o'clock sharp' kept banging in my head, noise enough.

At ten o'clock on New Year's Day, the doorbell rang. I opened the door and Ben Beardsley barged past, leaving me to invite Bernard and Jayne Allard inside. Olympia's son charged through the house looking high and low, left and right, assaying everything in sight. 'This house is a jewel,' he announced. 'I sold it to you much too cheaply. I hope you appreciate that.'

I held onto the door. The porous roof, the crumbling

floors and weeping walls, the rotten plumbing and exposed wiring, the drainless patio, the blocked chimneys, woodworm and dry rot, all came roaring at me like a freight train out of hell. I have never lambasted a man in anger; I rammed my fists into my pockets to keep from breaking a precedent.

I showed the Allards through the house at a leisurely pace and afterwards served a New Year's *cava*, while Ben Beardsley continued his inspection tour. As they were leaving, the Allards said they liked the house and would telephone me tomorrow. Ben Beardsley, ignoring their statement, added, 'I'll contact you tomorrow.' At last, I began to suspect something nasty.

Next day the Allards rang. They wanted to look at the house once more, but in principle, agreed to meet my asking price. Ben Beardsley came with them, interceded, and agreed to the terms. I had intended to call in Doreen Baker, but since Bernard and I had no need for an estate agent, we brought in our solicitors.

They exchanged our contracts within a week, no complications. The operation went smoothly, so promptly that I felt desolate and disorganized. I have sold Casa Potemkin, I tried to convince myself. In two weeks I will leave Casa Potemkin! In two weeks I will leave Alciguna!

Then came the shocker. I didn't have my wits about me, or I would have seen it coming. Ben Beardsley sent his bill. It was charges for introducing a buyer, Bernard Allard, to me, and for arranging the sale. The 'normal' fee paid for such a service, he informed me in a business letter, was the equivalent of eight thousand dollars.

That floored me. A person who had recently inherited a fortune, attempting to fleece a peasant of my standing? He not only looked like East End sleaze, his morals confirmed it. At the time, I was depressed about giving up my house, and suffered mixed emotions about leaving Spain and returning to the States. Still, that's no excuse for allowing emotions to rule, which nonetheless happened. I should have trashed Ben Beardsley's bill, saying that he had taken me for a sucker once, I would simply ignore his second attempt. Instead, I sat down and wrote to him. I corrected him about my chance meeting with Bernard Allard and listed the extensive faults of Casa Potemkin, pointing out that he had misrepresented its condition to me, and since very expensive repairs had been required to make the house fit for habitation, I certainly didn't owe him any more money. Besides that, he had no licence to sell real estate, and had appointed himself as 'finder' without my knowledge or consent.

His response was hand delivered, probably to prevent squandering the cost of a postage stamp.

Dear Mr Brooks,

In response to your extraordinarily unpleasant and inaccurate letter, it is you that is being untruthful. Or, could you have forgotten the true sequence of events, albeit in such a short time? Being generous minded I prefer to think the latter, and am so sorry you are having problems with your memory. Perhaps you should see somebody about it.

I'm happy to say that Bernard and I have excellent memories. He confirms that I made the introduction to you and your house. Also that I arranged an appointment for him to view it on the morning of 1 January (this was hardly a social call) and that it was only because of my intervention that he approached you to buy it. Furthermore, he stated that in no way would he have bought the house through your agent, Doreen Baker. So, my dear Mr Brooks, it is clear to everybody but you, that you would not have sold the house to him but for my involvement.

Incidentally your long-term memory seems even worse than your short-term. Why did you buy my house if you considered it such a bad deal? You seemed delighted with it at the time. I sold it to you in good faith, and I did not, repeat, not, take the light-bulbs, nor did I charge you more than they were worth for their return.

Good luck with your move to the States, the way of life there should suit you well.

Benedict Beardsley

After living in Andalusia for two years, I found Ben Beardsley's letter a proper send off. Should I ever feel homesick for Alciguna, all I need do is read it.

No, I couldn't mean that. I would remember Casa Potemkin fondly, a rewarding, if sometimes exasperating, experience. Heavy on problems and frustrations, perhaps, but that was its unique personality. And Ben Beardsley? Piffle. A non-person.

On my last evening in Alciguna, I waited for the van that would transport my personal gear to Malaga for shipment to Boston. I sat with a glass of wine by a picture window view of the south side of the village, in Jesús Maria's flashy new bar. He had built it soon after Olympia's death, giving rise to all sorts of scurrilous hints as to how he financed it. I felt suddenly bereft. From now on, the fundamental components of life in Alciguna, rumour, gossip and intrigue, would be irrelevant; wiped out like pesetas vanquished by new euros. I gazed at the jumble of white houses with pink roofs that ranged up and over the hilltop. They were growing dark, their lights coming on, swallows careening to nests in the eaves. A thin wafer of a moon hung above the tenth-century castle ruins. The tower, now floodlit since being declared a national treasure by the government, was spectacular, but no longer the symbol of an unspoilt Alciguna.

Of course memories came flooding back, but I didn't dwell on them. Except the oldest of all, that morning when the collapsed bridge stranded me in Alciguna. My only fear then was *bandidos*. I have laughed many times at my outmoded concept of Andalusia.

I'm not laughing now. The developers, Morgan and Mike Galuzin and What's-His-Name, are making out like real bandits. It's the Alciguna I first saw, glowing at sunrise, that no longer exists. I recall two Australian backpackers who told Olympia and me, 'Yeu're living in a fantasy world. This 'ere Camelot, it cawn't last.' We laughed and said they were drunk, what did they know? Yet, in wine there is truth, even when the wine comes free with dinner. Meanwhile, nobody can say that Alciguna has become a dull place. Certainly not. This morning I walked to the parking lot up by the convent. Tour buses were parking for the day and guides were forming enthusiastic sightseers into groups. Children queued before a man who was prodding a number of donkeys into a nose-to-tail line. 'Donkey rides!' he shouted to his happy customers. 'Who's ready for a donkey ride?'